A HERO'S WELCOME FOR
14 PECK SLIP

❖

"A terrific debut. . . . Filled with plenty of interesting sidelights and enough cop angst to satisfy any stickler for realism . . . Dee manipulates the entangled plots of this police procedural with a surprisingly sure hand."   —*Kirkus Reviews*

❖

"This novel reeks of NYPD . . . Dee seems to me by far the best writer of all the ex-cops I've read."

—Robert Daley, author of
Prince of the City

❖

"The real thing . . . an authentic and powerful voice."   —*Publishers Weekly*

❖

"Full of authenticity and written by someone who knows how to tell a good story."

—*Arizona Republic*

more . . .

❖

"This is good, gritty fiction, and a baffling mystery to boot . . . Dee's police experience shines through clearly in his cop slang and in his manifest knowledge of life in blue on the mean streets of New York City. An outstanding debut performance . . . Remarkably timely."

—*Houston Public News*

❖

"This debut by a twenty-year veteran of the New York City Police Organized Crime Unit sneaks up on you like a pickpocket and steals away with your admiration."

—*Charlotte Observer*

❖

"Fast paced, taut and very human . . . this has an authenticity that's impossible not to believe."

—*West Coast Review of Books*

❖

"Mr. Dee makes a strong impression with his initial fiction, and his voice—understated, authentic, even quietly lyrical—is entirely his own."

—*Wall Street Journal*

❖

14 PECK SLIP

ED DEE

WARNER BOOKS

A Time Warner Company

WARNER BOOKS EDITION

Copyright © 1994 by Ed Dee
All rights reserved.

Cover design by Daniel Bond
Cover illustraion by Joe and Kathy Heiner

Warner Books, Inc.
1271 Avenue of the Americas
New York, NY 10020

W A Time Warner Company

Printed in the United States of America

Originally published in hardcover by Warner Books.
First Printed in Paperback: August, 1995

10 9 8 7 6 5 4 3 2 1

For Bailey

Acknowledgments

My thanks to all the men and women of the NYPD, and their parents, spouses and children. Their stories are the inspiration for this book.

To all the people at the Arizona State University Creative Writing program: my buddies Penelope Corcoran, Diana Greene, Barbara Nelson and Diane Nelson, for their loyalty, warmth, and love; for the advice of mentors such as Paul Cook and William Kittredge; Mark Harris for his patience and wisdom; and I am particularly grateful to Ron Carlson, and extraordinary teacher and friend.

To Gail B. Hochman, more than just a great literary agent, but also and ever-present source of encouragement and counsel. And to Heather Cristol and Mary Ann Merola for their faith and optimism.

To Maureen Egen and Rick Horgan for believing in me; and Anne Hamilton for smoothing out the editorial process; Sona Vogel, truly a magician with a red pencil; and Joe Heiner, Kathy Heiner, and Dan Bond for the wonderful cover.

To my family and friends for all the years of love and undrstanding. Maybe I've finally figured out what I want to do.

Most of all, to my wife Nancy, for a million reasons.

1

AT ONE A.M. we stepped out of the warm Buick to stretch and brush off the crumbs and ashes of a night of surveillance. It was the tenth of December and fine wet flakes floated through the lights of the New York waterfront and fell softly into the East River. My partner, Detective Joe Gregory, walked toward the edge of the river, peering out toward Brooklyn, squinting as if to see his forefathers in the fog off an Irish shore.

"Check this out, Ryan," he said, pointing. "Is this wrong or what?"

Fifty yards across the water, a forklift rumbled over the rotting planks of Pier 18. The hazy silhouettes of three men could be seen as they moved in the glare of overhead lamps. Through binoculars I saw a big man driving the forklift, his bulk spilling over the seat as if he were on a child's tricycle. He was wearing a suit. Two other men, in windbreakers, walked alongside, steadying a white fifty-five-gallon barrel, which trembled on the blades.

Joe Gregory said, "I'll give you odds there's somebody in that barrel."

"Right," I said. "It's a new cruise line. Cabins are cramped, but the price is right."

Gregory flipped a bag of empty coffee cups down into the icy black river. I handed him the binoculars and blew on my hands.

"My money says they're dumping a body," he said. "Two to one that barrel's a coffin and the guys walking are pallbearers."

"Please," I said.

The procession moved to the end of the dock, then turned to the north side. They stopped at the edge, facing the Gothic altar of the Brooklyn Bridge. It took all three of them to slide the barrel down the blades, and it thumped off the end of the old timber, slammed into the river like a ton of cement, bobbed once, then sank. Water slapped against the pilings.

"Maybe your X-ray eyes can identify the victim," I said.

We were standing in the darkness, on the lumpy black-top under the FDR Drive. We were on the uptown side of the six-block enclave called the Fulton Fish Market, more than a hundred yards from the main action: sixty wholesale fish companies, with two thousand workers who shouted and cursed under the glare of bare bulbs hanging from tin canopies. Doing business in the raw night air as if it were hand-to-hand combat.

"Answer me this," Joe Gregory said. "Three guys to dump one barrel? Give me one reason."

"Laziness, weight, union rules," I said.

"You're stroking yourself, Ryan. These guys don't do grunt work. That's why they grease all those palms in Sanitation."

Water beat more insistently in the wake of the barrel.

"Maybe it's toxic waste," I said. "Diseased eels, something. . . ."

"What the hell do you need?" he said. "A guy with a bugle, playing taps? This is a funeral, guaranteed."

Gregory let the binoculars hang down on his chest. He hooked his index finger over the top of his cigarette and blew smoke rings that faded in the mist.

"You have some imagination," I said. "We haven't lived down your last vision yet."

"Vision, shit," he said. "These are wise guys. That big bastard's wearing a suit. Dumping garbage? Give me a freaking break."

The forklift sputtered and backed up, then turned toward solid ground. The driver had a huge head, sliced off in the back, like the cliffs of the Palisades. We could hear the men talking and laughing.

"Being a little noisy, aren't they?" I said.

"You telling me you never laughed over a dead body? They're like morticians, having some giggles in the hearse, after the ceremony."

A foghorn sounded in the harbor as we watched the forklift disappear behind the Tin Building. Gregory flicked his cigarette into the river. I knew what was coming.

"I'm tailing them," he said. "I feel this one." He threw the binoculars into the car and smoothed down his hair.

"Let's go get a drink," I said. "We're wasting our time, and it's freezing out here."

For two nights we'd been trying to locate Bobo Rizzo, the hood who had run the Fulton Fish Market since the fifties. The city was negotiating for a multimillion-dollar seaport mall on Fulton Street. Construction was slated to begin late in 1983, less than a year away. The police commissioner wanted to know what kind of grief he could expect from the fish market mob. Mob grief was our specialty.

"For once in your life, Ryan," he said, "do something bold."

Gregory snapped up his raincoat collar, walked twenty feet, and waited behind a highway support pillar until the forklift emerged from between the Tin Building and the New Market. I shoved my hands into my pockets and positioned myself wide to his right. Backing him up, as I had for the last fourteen years.

The forklift veered right, going toward Peck Slip. I stepped into the hollow of a steel girder. Behind me was a parking area, then the stone supports for the century-old Brooklyn Bridge. I could feel the velocity of the cars on the highway above and smell the stench of urine. Gregory walked into my peripheral vision a long flickering shadow. For a second I thought he'd decided to forget about it, but he was swinging a wider circle, a tailman's arc. A good tailman changes the angle, doesn't get too close.

Gregory sprinted across South Street in front of a slow-moving Con Ed truck. He followed the forklift, heeding his instinct.

It's not instinct, my wife says, it's cop paranoia. She says that people who trust no one are bound to be right often enough to believe they can see through any lie. I tell her that cops deal exclusively with deceit and learn to read the signs. The signs flashed in neon to Joe Gregory.

Icy snow pelted down as I left the cover of the highway and hustled across to a row of parked cars on Peck Slip. Peck Slip was a wide, deserted street, named a century ago when fish arrived by boat. The wind off the river pinned my raincoat to my back as I crouched and felt my way along the wet, cold cars. I could see Gregory within spitting distance of the forklift. At forty-seven, five years older than me, he was doing a Chuck Berry duckwalk, behind the bones of a stripped Camaro.

The forklift stopped in front of an open garage door at 14 Peck Slip, a grimy brick warehouse on a street of sooty brick buildings. The big guy in the suit climbed down from the forklift and lumbered over to a dark Plymouth, parked in front of the warehouse, just beyond where an angle of yellow light cut across the wet pavement. My ears and nose burned from the cold as the big man slapped a forearm on the car's roof and leaned in. The car had an antenna on the trunk, like one of ours.

In the quiet I could hear traffic humming on the FDR and the roar of commerce from the market. I touched the .38 against my hip, ran my fingers along the cylinder to feel the shell casings. I've been known to forget to reload for weeks after leaving the firing range. Not a good habit for a detective with a partner like the Great Gregory. But Joe was being patient.

The fat pallbearer with the Mets hat drove the forklift up a ramp into the warehouse. We'd seen "Mets Hat" all over the fish market, bullshitting everyone like a politician, always wearing that greasy blue hat. He disappeared behind a wall of crates and boxes. Crates were everywhere inside the warehouse, in random stacks, water running all over the floor.

Finally the big guy stood up and banged the top of the Plymouth in a gesture of dismissal. He walked heavily up the ramp as the car pulled away, its tires hissing on the wet stones like the steam radiators in my old apartment. The overhead door at 14 Peck Slip clanked down, returning us to darkness.

Joe Gregory walked backward for a few steps, staring at the warehouse, at a light on the second floor. The rooms above the warehouse were known as the Box Hook Club, a long-time meeting place for mobsters and the union reps they owned. Gregory turned and broke into his rolling walk, head down, shoulders hunched, arms swinging, the backs of his meaty hands facing forward.

"Were those guys cops?" I said.

"Which guys?"

"In the Plymouth?" I said.

"Chrysler. It was a Chrysler."

"Were they cops?" I said.

He stopped and patted his pockets for his cigarettes. "I don't think so," he said. "But we better get the scuba divers."

"Are you serious? For the body in the white barrel?"

He nodded and flipped up the lid of his chrome Zippo lighter, embossed with a blue anchor over the words USS *Francis Marion*. In the light of the flame I saw that his face was set. The Great Gregory was on the case. Nothing I could do.

"Let's call the divers from Brady's," I said. "Get our feet warm, get a drink."

The wind off the river blew wet snow in our faces. But it wouldn't amount to enough to slow down the early morning commuters. We walked back to the Buick with short measured steps, through slippery streets, on cobblestones coated with grease from a century of fish.

2

Six hours later we were back, parked in the same spot facing the river. Emergency Services had classified our request for divers as a nonemergency and made us wait until the day tour. The sun was shining over the Brooklyn skyline, and the Buick smelled of coffee and fried-egg sandwiches.

The streets of the fish market, teeming a few hours ago, were empty except for a few men sweeping and hosing away the night's debris. Morning traffic splashed through potholes and bounced over the undulating roadway of South Street. Drivers weaved around cardboard boxes, crates, cups, and cans. It looked like the day after Woodstock.

Two young police scuba divers fidgeted on the end of the dock, looking cold and frail in black wet suits. Above their heads the sky was a clear blue. At their feet was a fresh gash that had been cut in the pier by the falling barrel. It pointed downward, like a trailblazer's arrow.

"We don't bounce back like we used to," Gregory said.

"I feel great, myself," I said, wondering if my stomach was strong enough for aspirin.

Gregory had been quiet since we parked. He'd pulled in too quickly; the front tires slammed into the rotted railroad ties that bordered the river's edge. As the car rocked he gave me a look that said "Don't even mention it," his blue eyes drowning in red. His eyes looked the way they did on those mornings a few years ago when we were drinking heavy, when over coffee we tried to assess the night's damage. Like many, many mornings in the mid-seventies. Probably every morning in 1977. The year we went out for a drink.

"You watch," he said. "We'll score big here. My old man worked on these guys. Says the fish market crew is scum even for mob guys."

He pointed to the glove compartment. I opened it and pulled out a handful of ketchup packets. "Enough?" I asked, dumping them on the seat.

I set my coffee on the dashboard, adding another wet ring to a pattern of linking circles of stain. I left the lid where I could reach it, just in case an emergency run came over the radio. The divers were pulling tanks and hoses out of the back of their van.

"My old man, there's an example for you," he said. He ripped open a ketchup packet with his teeth. "Aged fifty years since he put his papers in."

"Let's not start this again," I said.

Gregory's father, Liam, was a legendary first-grade detective who was forced to leave the Manhattan DA's Office because of age, after forty years as a cop. Liam was a widower who spent half his time in Ireland, the rest in his backyard in Brooklyn, building picnic tables and telling war stories to whoever would listen.

I was four months away from the end of my twentieth year and the option to retire with half pay. I had made the mistake of telling Gregory, who has twenty-four years' service, that I was thinking about retiring. To him it's like quitting the priesthood.

"Whatever you do," Gregory said, "don't ever mention retirement to your old lady. You do, and it's out of your hands. Next thing you know you're a civilian, staggering around some mall, arms full of packages, wondering where your balls went."

Retirement didn't frighten me as much as it did Joe Gregory. Unlike him, I didn't grow up among cops telling stories, reinforcing the sanctity of the job. My father drove the Broadway bus to Dyckman Street until he took his city pension and barmaid girlfriend to West Palm Beach. My mother, the only child of Italian-speaking parents, was a high school English teacher who died never understanding the Irish or why I became a cop. I went to high school having read Hemingway and Fitzgerald; earned an MA in American lit in night school, pushed by her firm, warm hand. But I was also the son of my father. I'd kept a pint of Jameson and a yellowed copy of Spillane's *I, the Jury* behind the water heater in the basement.

Out on the dock Sergeant Vince Salvatore checked the tanks and shook his finger at the divers. Gregory pointed at them with the red-stained ketchup package. "We come up with a high-profile body here, maybe some underboss, some *consiglieri*, we'll get ourselves assigned to the case. Any freaking luck at all we make first-grade detective, guaranteed."

"Not with our luck," I said. "We'll come up with another dog."

He laughed as though it couldn't happen again. Five years ago the Great Gregory came up with information about the body of Jimmy Hoffa. We pushed the brass to approve an expensive excavation of the basement of a brownstone two blocks west of the old Madison Square Garden on Forty-ninth Street. All we dug up were the bones of an Irish setter.

"Nobody gets promoted writing intelligence reports on the mob," Gregory said. "Streets are named after this assignment: dead end. We need a big case. We need our names on the PC's desk."

We'd been transferred from Bronx Homicide to the then newly formed Organized Crime Control Bureau's Intelligence Unit nearly eight years ago. Working organized crime meant working mostly nights, but we didn't have a caseload or a clearance rate to worry about. Sometimes we had too much time on our hands, but there was no schlepping to court, no dealing with pompous DAs. We worked like feds, and that's what Gregory hated.

Gregory sipped his tea. He was a tea drinker who never removed the teabag. The blue paper tab, from the teabag, hung down like a price tag and fluttered in the heater's draft. Steam rising from the cups clouded the windshield with a damp film, but I could see the divers pulling on their masks.

"We should be out there with them," I said.

He wiped the ketchup from his mouth with a piece of paper bag, then said, "Dress warm."

After leaving the market last night, we drank until last call at Brady's Bar, 119 steps from the back door of headquarters. We left after Shanahan from Missing Persons sang "Danny Boy," and we grabbed a couple hours' sleep on our desks. At dawn, with Gregory snoring and the cleaning crew banging trash cans, I signed us into the day tour. Joe could sleep on broken glass as long as a police radio was crackling in the background.

"Tell Salvatore we owe him one," he said, and rolled his raincoat into a pillow.

My raincoat flapped in the wind as I walked out to the dock. Both divers were ready. Carefully they lifted flippered feet onto the long piling. Sergeant Vince Salvatore ticked off the instructions on his fingers. "Three rules to live by," he shouted. "Stay together, stay together, stay together."

They jumped. And in that silent, freeze-frame, airborne moment, I felt the blood drain from my face. I've seen people in the slow motion of final flight. But this splash was harmless and soft. Bodies disappearing in water.

"I hate this fucking river," Salvatore said, pointing his finger at me as if the river were my fault. "The current is fast and it's black like shit down there. You got to feel your way. Cars, and fucking trucks, glass, sheet metal. A fucking underwater junk yard—

"What?" Salvatore yelled.

I hadn't said anything. But I had one of those dull hangover headaches, so I couldn't be sure.

"Insurance jobs," he said. "Assholes take their car for a half gainer, then report it stolen."

I buttoned the top button on my raincoat as wind blew through it as if it were Irish lace. "What are our chances here, Vince?" I said. "Finding this thing?"

"No chances, is what. 'Jack' fucking Cousteau couldn't find anything down there. I'm giving this two hours for show, then I'm out of here."

Out in the river an outbound oil tanker, riding high above the waterline, passed a small sailboat. My wife, brought up near the sea, says the water that surrounds and runs through this city almost redeems it.

"Anthony fucking Ryan," Salvatore said. "You consider yourself a mick or a guinea? How the fuck you stay so thin, anyway? Only guys I knew ever stayed thin on this job died of fucking cancer."

"I keep in shape," I said defensively. "I work out."

"Yeah, right," he said, lifting an imaginary glass to his lips. "Bench-press twelve ounces, right?"

The pier creaked in the powerful tug of the river as I began a stroll to get my blood moving. The four huge masts of the steel bark *Peking*, one of the ships berthed in the South Street Seaport Museum, towered above the pier, above the traffic on the elevated FDR Drive. In a city of contrasts, the masts stood framed against the high rises of Wall Street.

The city fascinated me. I'd been criticized for padding intelligence reports with historical background, writing beyond the two-page max. Irrelevant bullshit, my boss says. But I keep thinking they'll want to learn from the past. In the wake of the oil tanker the hulls of the old ships groaned against their ropes and beat even louder against the shore.

Vince Salvatore watched the dark water for a ripple of his young cops. His weathered face jutted out like the hood ornament on a '57 Pontiac.

Gregory, his balled-up raincoat against the car window, was surely snoring by now, a trace of saliva staining his London Fog. Joe loved the tailing part of intelligence work, the movement and action of it. But the down time, the waiting and the writing, bored him.

For the last six months we'd worked in the garment

district, analyzing how the mob controlled the garment industry, because they controlled all trucking. It took me almost two weeks to finish the final report. All the while Gregory was edgy, wanting to get back out in the night streets, back on the hunt.

My coffee was cold, but I caught myself before I threw it into the river. I set it down against the back wheel of the van, then found a spot out of the wind. I pulled my cash from my pocket and counted it, hoping I'd only bought a couple of rounds last night. The money smelled of smoke and stale beer.

Then Salvatore was yelling something, pointing. A diver had broken the river's surface. His mask off, he flashed the thumbs-up sign with dark rubber gloves. In the swirling blackness his face looked small and pale.

"Bad shape," the diver yelled, sounding far away. "Need to wrap it."

I pocketed what was left of my money and tried to remember what procedural step was next, what notifications, what paperwork. Most of the searches I had been on were long days, and all you went away with was coffee stomach. Salvatore flung open the back door of the van and began throwing ropes out onto the dock.

"Help me with this shit, Ryan," he yelled.

Coiled in the rear of the van under chains, blankets, and harnesses was canvass strapping about half as wide as a flattened fire hose. I grabbed the strapping and began pulling. Salvatore went to the edge of the dock, squatted, and fed it down to his diver.

"Got to wrap it," he said. "So it don't break apart in the fucking pressure. And Ryan, you got to get a tow truck to pull it up."

"Why didn't you tell me before?"

"Who fucking knew?" he said. "I was betting, I wouldn'ta laid a dime on this."

I ran back to the Buick thinking that some interagency policy requiring endless endorsements and signatures would stop us cold. But I knew Joe Gregory would find a short cut, a back door. He'd know a secretary in some perfumed office who'd hand him the keys to everything. First thing he said was, "Piece a' cake, pally."

We'd pulled enough canvas hose to reach Brooklyn when Gregory, his hair slicked back, banged onto the dock in a traffic department tow truck, driven by a middle-aged black woman. The dock swayed, startled by the weight.

"He understand gravity?" Vince Salvatore said. "This ain't a fucking trampoline."

Gregory jumped out and began waving the tow truck back. He was trying to get her back far enough so the cable would hang straight down. But the woman wouldn't buy Joe's act. She got out and marched to the edge to check the position of her back wheels. She was a big woman, who wore only a brown cardigan sweater over the brown traffic department uniform. When she went back to the truck she gave Gregory a gladiator's glare, beads of sweat glistening like fine oil on her nose. Then she backed the truck to within a foot of the edge.

I made notes of times and names of those involved as the tow cable moved downward toward the diver's outstretched hand. He grabbed the hook and disappeared. The winch motor started to whine. I stepped off the distance from the cable to the fresh gouge the falling barrel had torn in the pier. The current had moved the barrel almost ten yards from where it had slammed off the edge of the dock.

"Slowly," Salvatore yelled to the woman, moving his hands like a symphony director.

Dry tow cable moved back over the pulley and down the boom. Wet cable followed. Nothing happened at the water's surface. We all stood looking down as the noise of the grinding motor drowned out the traffic and the seagulls.

Then suddenly the canvas wrapping was visible. Muddy, rusty water rushed off the barrel as it broke the surface. It came up quickly, water *whoosh*ing, then began to sway in the air. Gregory and I dropped to our knees like storefront preachers. We held out our hands to keep it from smashing into the bulkhead. We stood as it rose above our heads. Water, mud, bits of concrete, and rusted metal rained down.

"Wrong one, godammit," Gregory said. "It's an old freaking garbage can."

As it twisted in the sunlight I could see it wasn't our white barrel. It was an old metal trash can, rusted through, water spilling from holes. But near the bottom, near the largest hole, a crab clung to the bones of a hand.

"It's not our barrel," I said. "Definitely not."

The can smashed down onto the dock. Chunks of concrete tumbled across the wood like crooked dice. And then I saw the shredded sleeve just above the skeletal fingers. I knew it was blue wool. I knew the four rusted metal buttons held the seal of the city of New York.

"It's ours now, pally," Joe Gregory said.

3

SEAGULLS SCREECHED and strafed the dock as we stared at the shreds of blue wool and bones. Water ran from the old can, soaking my shoes. Joe Gregory chipped concrete with a tire iron, exposing a piece of metal extending from the skull.

Jammed into the teeth of the skeleton was an NYPD detective's shield, the number intact. It wasn't necessary to call Personnel; we knew this number by heart. Detective John "Jinx" Mulgrew, a cop missing for ten years. The notorious Jinx Mulgrew, the king of the bagmen.

Gregory drove to One Police Plaza to make official notifications according to the patrol guide and to whisper into the right ears. This kind of information had career investment value we never squandered. Vince Salvatore combed his hair in the side-view mirror of the van while his divers changed clothes inside. Joe had tossed the crab into the tow truck, where it clattered across the truck bed like a tap dancer on ice. I waited with the remains of the man the *Daily News* once called "the major link in police corruption in Manhattan."

Ten years ago, in the spring of 1972, Jinx Mulgrew and his partner, Sidney Kaye, had been arrested shaking down a pimp who was wired by Internal Affairs. It was rumored that Jinx then agreed to a deal to appear before the Knapp Commission investigating police corruption. He was expected to tell his life story before a rapt TV audience, mostly dressed in blue. But a week before his performance he disappeared. The word was he'd fled to hide with the leprechauns.

The story in Brady's Bar was that Jinx picked up more currency every month than an armored car in Vegas. He'd spent almost all of his career in lower Manhattan, sipping cappuccino with mafia dons who dropped brown paper bags filled with cash into his lap. When he disappeared he also left behind a relieved clique of NYPD brass who'd protected him out of gratitude for their thick monthly envelopes.

Gregory was back within a half hour, but the dock was already crawling with civil servants. A 1st Precinct radio car blocked off the dock to isolate the crime scene while the system converged. Gregory had called an ambulance to pronounce death; the medical examiner to call it murder; the Crime Scene Unit to collect and preserve physical evidence; and the 1st Precinct detective squad to commence the investigation. Since the body was found in waters contiguous to the 1st Precinct, it was officially their case. All in all, the New York waterfront hadn't seen so many uniforms since the bicentennial.

Even our boss, Lieutenant Eddie "the Flash" Shick, made it. Shick, a man rarely seen outside of headquarters without a martini in his hand, strutted out onto the dock wearing a green felt fedora straight out of a Bogart movie.

"What's this bullshit I hear?" he said, snapping his

fingers while slapping his fist into his palm. Shick was balding, beer-bellied, and had a nervous system strung tighter than the springs in an army jeep.

"We're going to ruin your Christmas, boss," Gregory said.

"Let me tell you, boyo," Shick said, "I ain't had a good Christmas since Santa Claus died. You sure it's Mulgrew?"

Gregory put his arm around Shick and led him back to the tow truck. I walked to the opposite end of the dock. I was beginning to realize what was happening, and I wanted to appreciate the moment. Cops were going to tell this war story in gin mills for years, swearing they were here. Front-page tragedies were what we talked about at cocktail parties, like nuns talk about seeing the pope or Republicans about meeting the Gipper.

Joe Gregory says that being a cop in this city is like having a front-row seat to the greatest show on earth. At times like this I wondered if I could really give up my seat.

Media crews lugged equipment to the edge of the yellow tape. Joe Gregory pointed with his tire iron at a metal eye hook cemented into the top of the can as a *Daily News* photographer snapped the first pictures. Gregory had called his friend on the *News*, no doubt in my mind. He stockpiled favors, and now they owed him a big one.

More seagulls came screeching, excited by the strange crowd, as Shick and Gregory walked back to me. Shick flipped open his spiral notebook. Gregory winked.

"We're going under the assumption it's Mulgrew," Shick said. "Pending positive ID. The PC wants to call a press conference forthwith. Nip any criticism in the bud."

"Wise move," Gregory said.

"You two," Shick said. "Get your asses back to the office soon as you finish here. I'll chase these First Squad bastards for you."

"Why chase them?" I said.

"Don't give me that altar boy face, Ryan," Shick said. "Go get your hands dirty. Our case, it's our crime scene from the get-go."

"We're Intelligence, Lieu," I said. "Intelligence does not handle homicide."

"Hey, prima donna, I don't care how many cases you solved way back. Nobody rests on their laurels in my squad."

"This is the bureau's case," I said.

"Use your head, Ryan. Jinx Mulgrew worked with half the bosses in the Detective Bureau. If the PC gave this case to the bureau, the press would crucify him. It's all settled; we got it. Say no more."

"Internal Affairs," I said. "It should be IAD, then."

"Very wrong," Shick said, waving his pen in my face. "You're assuming cops are involved. Don't assume. You know what that makes you and me."

"We can handle it," Gregory said, winking at me again. "No problem."

"Of course," Shick said. "Who the hell else they going to give it to, Scotland Yard? You found the body. You got the stool."

"No stool," I said. "We don't have a stool."

"Don't bullshit me, Ryan," Shick said. "How did you know he was here? Crystal ball? Give me a name, Gregory. I ain't got all fucking day."

We both looked at Joe Gregory, but I knew what was going on. The Great Gregory was slipping and sliding, manipulating the NYPD. Eddie Shick waited, drumming a tattoo with his pen on the notebook. He held the notebook at the X where his tie crossed. Shick never knotted a tie, merely crisscrossed it, securing it at the apex of his belly with a tie tack with the seal of the Honor Legion.

Finally Gregory said, "He's a brand-new informant, boss. Ain't registered yet. You know how Ryan is. The perfectionist can't stand loose ends."

Shick flipped the notebook closed and slipped it into his jacket pocket. With his pen he scratched at a piece of flaky red skin near his nose. "This ain't a freelance job, Ryan," he said. "We got a big rule book you ought to read sometime."

"We'll have the paperwork in forthwith," Gregory said.

"Next time you see me," Shick said, smirking. "We best be copacetic on this." He took his car keys out of his pocket and pointed them. "One more thing, both of you. Ease up in the bars. Need I say more?"

The lingering chemical smell of Lieutenant Eddie Shick's cologne, overpowering despite the fish and the river, made me realize how tired I was. The adrenaline had worn off, and I was beginning to feel that anemic weakness, the second stage of a hangover. Shick backed his Crown Victoria out into the traffic of South Street, hustling back to One Police Plaza to play power games in the hallway, armed with new importance.

Joe Gregory smiled as if he'd won the Irish sweep-stakes.

"I can't wait to hear this," I said.

"You know me. Always thinking."

He flicked the striker wheel on his Zippo until flame rose. I could smell the lighter fluid; odors seemed sharper near the water. Gregory stood blowing smoke and flipping the lighter lid, enjoying the squeak of the metal.

"We got an informant," he said, nodding confidently. "That old guy, cleans up. You always ask him 'How's business?'"

"You mean Zipper," I said. Seagulls flew above us, blotting out the sun. Gulls as big as eagles from generations of easy meals in the gutters of South Street. "Zipper's retarded, Joe."

"That's the beauty of it," he said. "Zipper won't know if he told us or not. His word against ours."

"I'd believe him."

A siren wailed off in the distance. I'd been out on the dock so long, I thought it was a call from the sea.

"The important thing, we got the biggest case in the city. And we got first-grade detective in the bag," Gregory said.

I almost reminded him that was what he'd said when we dug for Hoffa. But I said, "What about the white barrel? Still down there."

Gregory looked down at the water. I knew he had forgotten about it. He sent a perfect smoke ring wafting toward Brooklyn.

"We save it for a rainy day," he said.

4

IT WAS late afternoon before we finished on the dock and pulled into the parking area behind One Police Plaza. Our connection in the headquarters garage worked only nights, so during the day we parked in the dirt lot. The lot, under the approach to the Brooklyn Bridge, was a maze of contoured dirt hills that seemed to grow like the burial mounds of a shrinking tribe.

Gregory yanked the emergency brake to the last click and sat back. "This case is risky," he said. "I admit that. I need to know, you in or out? Just say the word, we back out."

We were parked on an angle looking up into the gray stone of the bridge. It occurred to me that Gregory had never asked me this question before. He knew what I'd say.

"Risky?" I said. "More than risky. I haven't any idea where to begin."

"The ball's in my court," he said. "I got some ideas. We'll be okay here."

"Next time, clear any brainstorms with me."

"Swear to God."

I stepped out of the car stiff legged, feeling as though

I'd been up for days. I asked Gregory if he wanted anything from the coffee truck.

"Get me a bow tie," he said. "And a large tea."

I waited on the coffee line while Joe hustled into the building. One Police Plaza is a redbrick fourteen-story cube between the Brooklyn Bridge and the courthouses of Foley Square. It has been NYPD headquarters since 1972. But headquarters is no longer a social club for aging Irish and Italian street kids. The first thing an old-timer notices on a visit to the new building is the number of civilians, especially women. Joe Gregory says it's like the phone company now, a ladies' room on every floor.

The cop at the door didn't even pretend to check my ID. Joe Gregory was waiting in the lobby, glaring at the civilians packing into the elevator. My wife says only cops and psychos stare shamelessly at people.

"They were out of bow ties," I said. "You have prune Danish."

"I was just upstairs," he said. "Neddy Flanagan's in with Shick now. Carried in all kinds of old records and shit. I got to talk to you, though. We got a little problem."

Gregory pushed me into a crowded elevator, which was toxic with cheap cologne. "Floors?" he said. He reached over heads and hit the numbers they called out, then he banged the "close door" button at every stop to encourage the dawdlers. We got off at twelve.

"Let's hit the head," Gregory said.

I splashed some water on my face as Joe stood at the urinal, checking back over his shoulder, checking the stalls behind us. Checking for shoes, because shoes mean ears. Gregory had something hush-hush to say, but a pair of wing-tip brogues straddling a pile of cigarette ashes in the handicapped stall stopped him.

"NYPD men's room, pally," Gregory said loudly, gesturing at the wing-tips. "This is where all the big dicks hang out."

We never talk in elevators, rarely in men's rooms. You never know who's listening. Just because you're paranoid, Gregory says, it doesn't mean they're not following you.

Outside, he put his arm around me and whispered, "We got first-grade locked up if we keep it exclusive. Just you and me."

I could smell Old Spice and a hint of last night's gin. "What's the problem, then?" I said.

"Your little apprentice is trying to horn in," he said.

"Murray could help us," I said.

Detective Murray Daniels was a rookie assigned to our technical team. Gregory called him my "little apprentice" because he hung around me, constantly asking questions about cases and investigative strategy.

"The more people we let in," Gregory said, "the more we dilute the credit. They'll promote two guys, but not three."

"Bullshit," I said.

Gregory handed me a Motor Vehicle Bureau printout of the dark Chrysler in the market. "Was I right on this?" he said. "Am I ever wrong?"

The Chrysler we'd seen in front of 14 Peck Slip was not a city vehicle. It was registered to Fulton Protective Services, 14 Peck Slip, NY, NY.

"Private security," Gregory said. "Mob scam, guaranteed. Extorting money out of the legitimate fish whole-salers. Buy protection or buy a burglary."

I threw my coat across my desk and took the lid off my coffee. Murray Daniels was trying to make eye contact with me from his desk in the front. I concentrated on the coffee. Footsteps were coming down the hall.

"Just me and you," Gregory whispered. "We don't need nobody else."

Inspector Neddy Flanagan personified the word *somber*. He was slender, gray-haired, and never wore anything but black suits and ties, white shirts. He'd been the police commissioner's personal driver since he was a patrol sergeant on the Bronx Zoo detail. Now he was keeper of the secrets of the crown. Two young cops preceded the black-cloaked Flanagan. They whisked by like a papal motorcade.

"Morning, Father," Gregory whispered as Neddy's contingent swept out the door. Gregory genuflected and made the sign of the cross as Lieutenant Eddie Shick hustled in.

"Got no time for coffee, Ryan," Shick said, shrugging a plaid sports jacket off his shoulders. "I got a ten hundred with the chief, then a eleven hundred meet with the PC. The two of you"—he pointed down the hall—"office, now."

Eddie Shick's office was evidence of how far he'd come from a traffic post in Rockaway. He was proud of the northwest corner, looking up Park Row toward Chinatown, a direct sight line to the statue of Confucius. Shick plopped on a high-backed leather chair.

"You going to get me an informant number, Ryan?" Shick said. "Ain't that right? All the proper forms, i's dotted, t's crossed? I don't need to get into a pissing contest with Inspector Flanagan over this."

"The market is closed," I said. "We'll find him as soon as it reopens. You'll have it by Tuesday."

"This ain't no time to be yanking my chain," Shick said. "This case is serious business. It behooves us to do this by the numbers. You catch my drift? We play our cards right, no telling what can come out of this."

"Biggest case in the city, boss," Gregory said, still standing by the window.

"Let's make sure we understand each other," Shick said. "What we got here is a unique chain of command situation. You two work on nothing else but this. I'll farm out whatever else you got going now. I got the analysts pulling everything on Bobo Rizzo and the Fulton Fish Market crew. Pictures, yellow sheets, whatever. You talk about this to no one but me. *Comprende?* Sit the fuck down, Gregory."

"We're going to need some time, Lieu," I said. "We haven't handled a homicide since . . ."

"1976," Gregory said. "Rafael Quintana, the Soho Strangler. No problem. Like riding a bike."

Shick's office was filled with gym equipment: dumbbells, hand grippers, chest expanders. Gregory walked around, lifting and squeezing.

Shick said, "Time is fine, Anthony. We ain't got a lifetime, but ninety days is plenty. So there's no big rush. Thing they don't want is a witch-hunt. Some hard charger, thinks he's the new Serpico, stirring up old shit."

On the wall behind Shick's desk were pictures of the president, the mayor, the police commissioner, and Cardinal O'Connor.

"Have I misunderstood, Lieu?" I said. "Is this case about corruption?"

"Don't start, Ryan," Shick said. "Did I say anything about corruption?"

"But now that it's been mentioned, the thought crossed my mind that Jinx Mulgrew had a lot of friends."

Shick nodded. "One hundred and twelve active detectives and bosses worked with him at one time or another. So what?" He scraped at the flaky skin in his eyebrows.

"Ninety days isn't that much time," I said. "I can see a lot of animosity coming from within the job. Problems getting personnel records, IAD files, the interrogations of Jinx by the special prosecutor."

"You don't need those files," Shick said.

Gregory sat down, knocking a silver ashtray to the floor. The ashtray had a vertical stainless plate that contained miniature replicas of Shick's shields: patrolman, detective, sergeant, and lieutenant. There was room for more.

"He means like the Q and A, after Jinx flipped, so we can see what mob guys Jinx mentioned," Gregory said, his face thermometer red from picking up the ashtray.

"Jinx never flipped," Shick said. "He bullshitted everybody, plain and simple. Told IAD and the special prosecutor he'd cooperate. Asked them to wait until he presented the Honor Legion medal. Said after that he'd tell them every damn thing he knew. The schmucks believed him. Mulgrew was just jerking them off, buying time."

"I always heard he spilled his guts," Gregory said.

"You heard wrong," Shick said. "That was the idea. The special prosecutor leaked a phony story that Jinx had already given information. They wanted to isolate him, cut him from his friends. So he couldn't change his mind."

"Did everybody know that was a phony story?" I said.

"It wasn't no state secret," Shick said.

Gregory pointed to the stack of boxes. "This is what, then?" he said.

"Original case files on the disappearance," Shick said, reading off a receipt. "Locker contents, Mulgrew's personnel files."

The boxes were taped shut, signatures across the seals. I could smell musty wool.

"Don't get me wrong," Shick said. "I ain't saying shitcan corruption information. You know me, I'm death on corruption. Thing is, we don't want to make it look like we're going out of our way to dig back into 'clothes.' We let IAD handle that shit."

"Clothes" is shorthand for plainclothes, an assignment to a unit responsible for gambling investigations. Before Knapp, when the money was flowing, "clothes" was anything but plain.

"What about Mulgrew's partner, Sidney Kaye?" I said.

"Kaye made a deal," Shick said. "Told what he knew to get probation. His testimony's available. Wasn't much. Mulgrew kept the money men to himself."

The church bells from St. Andrews rang at ten. Shick reached for his jacket; the meeting was over.

"We copacetic now?" Shick said. "Any questions, Ryan? You always got questions."

"If we need technical help, can we use Murray Daniels?"

Gregory stood up, sighing, and walked to the chinning bar.

"Can't spare him full time," Shick said. "I got a shit-load of wiretap work coming in. A day here, a night there, okay."

"Where are you going to store the boxes Flanagan delivered?" I said.

"I signed for that shit," Shick said. "You safeguard it with your life. I don't want it walking out of here."

Joe Gregory hung from the chinning bar. Not chinning, just hanging there, his nose barely over the bar.

"I'm going home," I said. "I need some sleep."

"First give me some paper, for the PC," Eddie Shick said. "So's I got all the facts. One page, short and sweet, no ancient history, no flowery shit. None of your bullshit. Then get some sleep. But not too much. You got ninety days, and the clock is running."

Murray Daniels kept thanking me as he helped us carry the boxes back to my desk. Gregory ignored the young cop. Joe's face was still bright red from the chinning bar as he walked through the office as if he owned it all. He walked through the records section, a maze of brown metal filing cabinets, past cops and clerks reading quietly in cardigan sweaters, and past the analysts. Reports from the field spilled over their desks as they underlined and redlined, looking for a trend. The snip of scissors was the only audible sound.

Our own section was almost empty and smelled of beer spilled in a desk drawer. The wiretap team was preparing to go out on an installation; Narcotics Intelligence was due in at noon. There were guys in this unit I'd never met. Murray Daniels went back to the records section to start pulling old files.

"Don't be so generous from now on," Gregory said. "Hear what Shick said? This behooves us, career-wise."

"Ninety days," I said. "We'll need all the help we can get."

I cleared a space between the boxes we'd put on my desk. Our desks were in the back corner of the investigator's section, a room containing eighteen metal desks in three lines of six. Gregory hung my coat in the locker and followed me into the coffee room.

I said, "We should have admitted we lucked into finding Jinx."

He picked up a dirty coffee cup, swished some fresh coffee around to clean it, then poured the coffee in the trash. I handed him a teabag.

"First-grade detectives make their own luck," he said.

5

From the window of the second-floor room we had converted into a den, I watched my wife leaning out the back door, shaking a dust mop into the wind. Leigh's short flannel nightgown rode up her thighs and hugged her hips. Her brown hair was losing the battle to gray; the new gray, wiry and strong, reflected light as it blew in the breeze. Sheets and towels flapped on the clothesline.

Housecleaning had become Leigh's Saturday morning ritual since the kids moved away. She worked all week as a secretary at Sacred Heart High School, three blocks away. Saturday she cleaned. Sundays we tried to find something to do. Leigh continued to clean the kids' rooms downstairs, but I knew they wouldn't return. Children of cops often flee at the first chance, tired of being under suspicion.

I was on the phone listening to Joe Gregory read from *Newsday*. In the background I could hear Sinatra singing "A Cottage for Sale." When Joe's wife threw him out for the final time, he took only his clothes and records. He lived alone now, in his father's house in Brooklyn, and seemed more content.

"Listen to this line," he said. "The whitewashed bones

of the alleged bagman were discovered by members of the elite Intelligence Section of the Organized Crime Control Bureau."

"Do they mention the dog this elite unit once dug up?"

"Not for nothing, but you got to learn to forget about that case. Look at all the good cases we worked on: Son of Sam team, the Figueroa case, the Big Paulie hit, the Galante hit, and on and on. All good stuff."

"Remind me of how good we are when guys we know start surfacing in this case."

"What's with you, Ryan? You heard what Shick said. What makes you think cops killed this guy, anyway? This reeks of mob."

"I didn't say cops killed him. What I'm saying is people we know are going to surface, as members of the pad, as something, involved somewhere. I know guys who worked in that division. So do you."

"Time out," he said. "You know me. I will not work on cops. May God strike me down dead. But we got no problem here. I'll guarantee you Jinx was killed by the crew from Fourteen Peck Slip. That joint's been a den of iniquity since Teddy Roosevelt was the PC."

"Give me motive."

"Mob guys got sources, right? They hear Jinx is talking; they don't need that shit. They lure him down there, maybe a money lure. Look at where they found his car, around the corner. Am I right?"

"Got it all figured out."

"Listen to me. If the job is direct traffic, you direct traffic. If the job is homicide, you do homicide. We let

IAD worry about the pad, it's not our business. End of argument. Let me finish this article."

I took my feet off the desk and stretched. The sun, shining through pale blue curtains, warmed my back. We'd bought this house when I made detective. It's a fifty-year-old red-shingled Cape Cod, on a hill in Yonkers, New York, ten miles from Times Square, in a city of hills, where nothing is on the level.

After the kids left, Leigh and I moved upstairs: two rooms with slanted ceilings and a bath. Our bedroom is across the hall; this room is a den and contains a convertible sofa, TV, rocker, and a personal computer setup. The floor is covered by a red woolen rug we bought in Mexico on the only vacation we took outside of visiting family. The walls are covered with pictures of kids.

The empty rooms downstairs bother me, but I will not move back down. I've seen too many couples splayed across bloody sheets, and I am no longer comfortable sleeping in a room that is on ground level. I like the safety of these rooms, as well as the slanted ceilings, morning light. Far above the street.

"What does 'exacerbate' mean?" Gregory said.

"Look it up," I said.

Leigh and I have two children. Anthony Jr., a drama major at USC, says he's a West Coast kind of guy. Our daughter, Margaret, is twenty-two years old and a single parent. Margaret works for the South Carolina Highway Department and lives with our granddaughter, Katie, and Leigh's mother in the house Leigh was born in. A damp colonial, two blocks from the Atlantic in Myrtle Beach.

"My old man's coming home Tuesday, for the

funeral," Gregory said. "There'll be a ton of old-timers at this funeral—their age, funerals are the only reunions."

"A lot of them will be there to make sure he's dead," I said. "How did your father find out?"

"He's got a number in Dublin, a service. I figured he'd want to know. They were old friends until Jinx got in bed with the guineas. Sorry, pally, always forget you're half guinea."

"That's the problem. All of those old guys know each other, and a lot of them were in bed with the mob."

"Look at the bright side. Maybe one of those old guys knows something that can help us."

"No one is going to talk to us, Joe."

I'd started listing names and all the facts of the case on the IBM PC we'd bought for Margaret, hoping she and the baby would stay. As Gregory read from the paper I entered the names on the roster of Jinx's last squad, as well as the names of all known habitués of 14 Peck Slip.

"You ever work with Jinx?" I said.

"During the riots at Columbia," he said. "Classic hairbag. A legend below Fourteenth Street, but a freaking bull in a china shop when they sent him uptown."

"What kind of guy?" I said.

"Cocky little bastard, couldn't have been five eight. Must've stood on a twenty-dollar bill to get the job. Liked the broads, though. Listen to him, you think you're hearing Errol Flynn."

"What kind of cop?"

"Good cop, stand-up cop. But you knew he'd take a hot stove, guaranteed."

Piled on my desk were spotty Xerox copies of old reports. A UF 49 from the 1st Precinct, dated October

9, 1972, documented the discovery of Mulgrew's tan Impala parked at a meter on Water Street, around the corner from 14 Peck Slip. There were some yellowing newspaper clippings and a stack of interviews, including ones from Mulgrew's wife and the Spinellis. Detective Charles Spinelli and his wife, Donna Rose, lunched with Jinx after a medal ceremony at the Police Academy the afternoon of his disappearance, October 6, 1972. Apparently no one saw him after that.

I watched Leigh step barefoot out onto the stone step as gray balls of dust blew across patches of snow and grass. Church bells from Sacred Heart were ringing.

Gregory said, "Your kids coming home for Christmas?"

"Margaret is. And the baby."

I heard Leigh close the door and start coming up the stairs.

"Let's get this informant thing over with pronto," Gregory said. "Before Shick gets a bug up his ass."

"Zipper's easy to find," I said. "He's either cleaning the streets or with his pigeons."

"Pigeons?"

"He keeps homing pigeons. Has a coop on one of the roofs in the market."

Leigh came into the room with the dust mop and the *Daily News* in her hands. I told Gregory I'd meet him in Brady's, about one A.M. on Monday, then hung up. She dropped the paper on my desk and shoved the dust mop in my hands.

"Upstairs is your responsibility," she said. "Look, you made the front page."

She sat on a slat rocker near a window that overlooked Kelly's backyard. Kelly's twins were playing in the sandbox. It was on that chair that Leigh had rocked Margaret and Margaret had rocked Katie.

"How come you're still hanging clothes on the line?" I said.

"Weather's good, why not?"

"Ever use the new dryer at all?"

"Rainy days. Nights when you're working. I hear you say you're working tomorrow night?"

"We have to find an informant."

"An informant told you about this?"

"That's confidential," I said.

"Excuse me," she said. "I forget my place."

She got up and reached over my shoulder, pointing at the paper. "This is you here, isn't it?" she said. "Or some other secret agent."

I pulled her onto my lap. Her skin was cool and damp. Under the headline MISSING COP FOUND was a picture of Gregory with his arm around the rusted can, which still hung from the tow cable. He looked like a sportfisherman who'd just landed a prize marlin off Key West. I was a shadowy figure in the background looking off toward Ellis Island.

"How did they get him in that little can?" Leigh said. "Doesn't rigor mortis stiffen the body?"

"It depends on when he was put in. Lot of variables: heat, weight, time. Rigor usually starts one to six hours after death, but it goes away in twelve to forty-eight. Joe says Jinx was skinny. They usually get it fast. Some fat people never get it."

"I'm glad to hear that," she said.

I ran my hands over her back, the thickening curve of her waist and hips. Her body had a fullness now I wouldn't have predicted when I first saw her on Myrtle Beach when we were both eighteen. Lately she's decided she's getting fat, but the weight looks good. Sexy.

"Nights again," she said. "More and more nights."

"Wise guys work nights," I said. "We work nights."

"At least bring home some bagels. From that place on Broadway across from Zabar's."

"Four plain, four poppy, four pumpernickel."

"You memorize well, but you forget about me as soon as you step out the door."

Leigh and I met on my first weekend pass from Fort Bragg, and I fell in love with her smile, her body, and the way she talked. After I met Leigh, New York girls sounded like the Bowery Boys. Twenty-five years later I can still hear traces of that slow drawl and the waves slapping on the shore.

"How long will this case take?" she said.

"Ninety days, not a second more. They don't want it to drag on."

"Think you can solve it?"

"A mob hit, after ten years? Forget it. The boss just wants it handled cleanly."

She stood and hiked her nightgown up over her hips, so I could get my hands underneath. I scratched her back in the slow circles she loved, then I reached around and caressed her nipples until they were hard. She was reading text from the computer screen, but I knew she wasn't ignoring me.

These Saturday mornings have become a slow-motion replay of the sweet, long, sexy mornings when the kids were still in school. I would come home after working all night and wrap myself in her sleepiness and the soft

warmth of her body. Later I would fall asleep alone to
the roar of lawn mowers and the squeal of kids and
clotheslines.

She turned around facing me, straddling my leg. "I'll
bet the Great Gregory doesn't say it's impossible," she
said.

"He thinks we can make first-grade detective out of
it."

"Just like his daddy," she said. "You didn't tell him,
did you?"

"He knows I'm thinking about it. There's time."

"Not much. Your twenty is up in April."

"After Christmas I'll tell him."

I pulled her toward me and kissed the familiar dampness of her neck, inhaled her nighttime smell.

"Murray Daniels called twice this morning," she said.
"I could hear his kids yelling in the background. He
sounds so young."

"A little young," I said. "But his heart's in the right
place. Not like some of the young turks coming into the
job."

"I hope you understand that I wouldn't mind the job
as much if you didn't work so many nights. You won't
admit it, but night work isn't good for you, either. Your
stomach and all."

She said my health, the bad hours, but the message
was about drinking. We spent most nights in bars because
of the nature of the job. It was where the people we
worked on spent their nights. She kissed me hard, then
got up, tugging her nightgown down over her hips. I
looked toward the doorway.

"Don't worry, don't worry," she said. "I'll make sure
the door is locked."

Her feet padded on the oak steps as the church bells started again. I have lived almost my entire life within the sound of those bells. I could remember when I was a kid walking home from playing ball in the park, feeling complete happiness when I heard them. As if I were part of something powerful, loving, and benevolent. Now I wondered why they were ringing so much on a Saturday.

6

MONDAY, ONE A.M., Brady's Bar was as quiet as a chapel.

"It's what I heard," Patti O'Brien said as she wiped the scarred mahogany bar. "Maybe just the booze talking. What can I tell you?"

Patti O had been a barmaid in Brady's for only five years. But she knew more about current cases than the chief of detectives.

"Who said it?" Gregory said.

Patti gave him a look as hard as her forty-year-old body and walked toward the end of the bar. She had told us that some guys were saying that we were looking into the old plainclothes divisions. She was too smart to mention names. I knew it was only a matter of time before some cop accused us of working with Internal Affairs.

"It ain't true, Patti," Gregory said. "All's we're working on is the homicide."

We downed a shot of Jameson and left the bar, drove only a mile to the Fulton Fish Market to find Zipper. One of the bonuses of working the market was its proximity to One Police Plaza. In three minutes we were on cobblestone. We parked behind the Peck Slip Post Office. Nobody expected headquarters cops to walk anywhere.

"Streets are safe tonight," Gregory said as he turned up his collar. "Jack Frost, the best cop in town, is walking the beat."

The wind off the river blew stiff in our faces as we turned off Pearl Street into Peck Slip. Gregory shifted the brown bag with coffee for Zipper to his right hand, away from the wind. He was wearing his navy pea coat and black watch cap, pulled down to his eyebrows. He liked to dress the part; only cops in bad movies read the newspaper to look inconspicuous.

We had only been in the market for a few days, but I was sure we'd been noticed. It's expected in places like the market. Despite that, Gregory dressed like a longshoreman, part of the scenery—except for his red argyle socks. These were from his lifetime supply of argyles, which he swears fell off a truck in the garment district.

"You see the problem with this case," I said. "A lot of guys have closets overflowing with skeletons. They're afraid we're going to open the wrong door and something bad will fall out."

"So we don't open any wrong doors," Gregory said. "I'm the one saying no problem. You're saying cops are involved."

"I didn't say cops were directly involved. Peripherally involved, is what I said."

"Let me ask you this," he said. "Why was the eye hook cemented into the top of the can?"

"Because they intended to tow it out to sea. Probably couldn't find it later."

"Right," he said. "That MO's not cops, though. Too

much exposure. Too risky. Too close to home. Cops do some crazy shit, but not that crazy."

"Maybe it was a joint effort," I said, nodding at 14 Peck Slip. The garage door was raised, and we could see Mets Hat loading empty crates on a handcart.

"We ain't never been that cozy with the bent noses," Gregory said. "It's like when we were kids in the neighborhood. They got their gang, we got ours."

The warehouse was only half as full as the other night. Voices echoed inside as Mets Hat rattled down the ramp, steadying the empty crates on the cart with his free hand. He made a right turn toward South Street. As usual, lights were on in the Box Hook Club on the second floor. The rooms above the warehouse had provided a safe gathering place for decades of fish market thugs. An arrest record was the only entrance requirement.

I said, "You think someone in that place is just going to tell us who killed Jinx?"

"Not voluntarily, we got to squeeze. We just need leverage."

"Leverage," I said.

"See that fat bastard with the Mets hat? He ain't working, he's scamming. That's our first target, right there. That fat bastard."

"Later," I said. "Coffee's getting cold."

Mets Hat disappeared around the corner, into the bright lights of South Street. We walked down deserted Water Street, walking close together, bumping shoulders as we talked. My wife says two guys from New York will keep bumping into each other even if they're walking across an empty football field.

"He's been here," Gregory said. "It's clean."

Zipper worked as a street cleaner for the Fulton

Wholesalers Association. He picked up trash by precise schedule. He began on Water Street, then worked his way to South Street and the river.

Water Street was once the original waterline for Manhattan, until early New Yorkers dumped tons of garbage, adding two full blocks. More than half of Manhattan below Chambers Street is landfill. We turned down Beekman Street, looking for Zipper's trash line.

"Maybe he's up with the pigeons," Gregory said.

"Not at night. He's cleaning somewhere."

The market was beginning to show signs of the upcoming construction. Buildings boarded up, Dumpsters dropped in the street. An aluminum construction trailer sat at the curb in front of a building where Duncan Phyfe once crafted mahogany tables.

I said, "Which one of us gets to say 'Greetings, you're a registered informant'?"

"He don't have to know nothing," Gregory said. "It's only paperwork. We get the minimum: name, address. Cover our ass, that's all."

Front Street was a dark row of five-story warehouses with black fire escapes strung down the front like columns of linking spiders. The old brick was so eerily dank and stained, you almost expected to find the front gate of a Dickens orphanage. Puddles of water shone in cracks of broken cobblestone. Halfway down the block, standing in a cloud of sewer gas, a small bent-over figure speared trash with a spiked stick.

"How's business?" I said.

"Picking up," Zipper said, grinning. An elf with two days' growth of beard.

Gregory looked back down the empty street, then put the brown bag on the hood of an abandoned pickup truck. He lined up the containers on the hood but kept checking the street. Zipper peered through the slits of his hooded eyes and grinned as I handed him the coffee. He wore a light denim jacket, an orange hunting cap with hanging flaps, and black cloth gloves with the fingertips cut out.

"Your truck, Zipper?" I asked.

"It got no wheels," he said, shaking his head.

"How do you get to work?" I said.

Zipper lifted his foot and pointed to the sole of his shoe. He smelled sour, like the sewer gas he warmed himself in.

"You walk," I said. "From where?"

Zipper pointed west. I heard a sound, like the crackle of static from a walkie-talkie or a two-way radio. Gregory put his tea on the hood of the truck and bent the side-view mirror back so we could see behind us.

"You walk from New Jersey?" I said.

"Duane Street," Zipper said. "Under the Greenwich Bar. I'm the super."

In the truck mirror we saw a red glow of lights from an alley down the block. With his index finger Joe Gregory pulled down the skin under his eye, a gesture that meant the "eye" of IAD was watching us. Cops worry more about Internal Affairs than any threat from the street.

"Your name really Zipper?" I said.

"Casimir. I'm a Polack."

"Cas," I said. "We'll call you Cas. I bet your last name ends in ski?"

"Poniatowski," he said.

"Hey, Cas," Gregory said, "what do you call a Polack in a five-hundred-dollar hat?"

Zipper looked at me and shrugged, his decayed upper teeth poised on his bottom lip.

"The pope," Gregory said as the car pulled out of the alley.

Only Zipper turned to look. Joe and I watched in the truck mirror. It looked like the dark Chrysler we'd seen in front of 14 Peck, the private security car. The trunk antenna was visible in the streetlight, but it was too dark to see in the windows. The driver paused, then drove away quickly, toward Pearl Street. Zipper looked at us, then back at the car.

"My aunt was a Polack," Gregory said. "Family secret."

"Maybe we're cousins," Zipper said.

"Let's get out of here," I said. "Before they come back."

We had enough to register him as an informant, and I wanted to get away from Zipper. I didn't want to be seen meeting with an informant so openly, no matter how useless he was.

Gregory said, "Who's the fat bastard, Zip, always wears the Mets hat? Always pushing a handcart around."

"Salvy," Zipper said. "He taps fish for the club."

"What's that mean?" Gregory said. "He taps them like this." Gregory tapped the truck with his index finger, in his typing motion.

Zipper shrugged, looked at me.

"The club upstairs at Fourteen Peck, right?" Gregory said. "What's the deal there? Who stays there?"

"Koch," Zipper said. "But he's sick at the doctor."

"Koch?" I said.

"He shits in the club," Zipper said. "I walk him, but he still shits."

"Koch is a dog?" I said.

"Doberman," Zipper said. "I got a mutt home, never shits."

I dumped my coffee and told Zipper we had to go. Gregory tried to shove something into Zipper's jacket pocket, something he had balled up in his fist. Zipper pulled it out and looked at me. It was a rolled-up twenty.

"Coffee money," Gregory said. "Listen around, okay? See if you hear anything about the cop we fished out of the river."

"He's dead," Zipper said.

"Only if you hear something," I said, pointing to my ears. "Just listen, don't ask."

Zipper was thinking hard. He had survived here for decades because he understood the simple street wisdom of minding your own business.

"It's the American, patriotic thing to do," Gregory said. "What any good Polack would do. Help his country."

Zipper looked at me and nodded.

"Just listen," I said again. "Don't ask any questions, understand?"

Zipper took the empty containers and put them in the canvas sack that hung from his belt. I patted him on the shoulder, told him to be careful. As we walked to the corner I heard Zipper's wrench clank as he opened the fire hydrant; he flushed the gutters using water from the hydrant.

"That was painless," Gregory said. "We're covered. No one got hurt. Let's get it on paper."

"I hope some DA doesn't want to interview our big informant," I said. "This could easily come back to haunt us."

"This whole place could haunt you," he said.

As we walked down Front Street water rushed past us, sending fish scales and entrails, crab claws and shells, floating down into the sewers beneath the Fulton Fish Market. Every day in the Fulton Fish Market massive amounts of fish waste were flushed down those sewers and through gurry holes, the large garbage chutes in the warehouses. Waiting below were rats the size of dogs, sewer pythons, rabid gerbils, alligators, and the toughest of the exotic pets flushed down the toilets of New York.

"Tapping fish," Gregory said. "What bullshit. What it means is stealing fish, guaranteed."

When we walked into the parking lot behind the post office, our Buick was bathed in the glare of security lights, so we easily found our first load of stolen fish. The Buick was covered. Slimy, shiny fish lay across every inch of the General Motors paint job. Dozens of dead walleyes stared. An eel was wrapped around the wipers like garland.

"See if there's any loaves laying around," Gregory said. "This could have been a miracle."

He picked up a flattened beer can and began scraping. Fish smacked onto the street. I looked back down the dark street, toward 14 Peck Slip. We were less than fifty yards from the spot where Jinx Mulgrew's tan Impala had been found.

"Maybe not a miracle," I said. "But definitely a sign."

7

TUESDAY MORNING we worked a day tour. Joe had to meet the Aer Lingus flight carrying his father back from his third pilgrimage to the Emerald Isle in the last half dozen years. Irish-born cops often return to touch the old sod, as if to reassure themselves it wasn't a dream.

I squeezed into a parking spot outside headquarters, left my DEA card and office phone number in the window. My '73 Chevy Nova is a New York car: safety-plated trunk lock, no hubcaps, and no radio antenna, and the hood is chained through the grille to the bumper for battery insurance. All exterior surfaces have been dented, scratched, rusted, or bled on.

I passed the line at the coffee truck and entered the building feeling sluggish and out of sync. I can't seem to adjust to day tours. My wife says that this job has made me too nocturnal to make it in the real world.

Gregory was at my desk, flipping through photos. "These three here," he said. "These guys were the three we saw dumping the barrel. I'll lay odds they dumped that fish on my car."

"We'll show them to Zipper," I said.

"I can't believe they did that to my car," Gregory said. "All freaking night I thought about it. I can't believe these guys, the balls and all."

The car didn't smell quite as bad. Three times we drove through a car wash on Bowery, paid for it ourselves.

"A man's car is his castle," Gregory said. "You don't fuck with a man's castle."

I said, "Murray Daniels and I are putting together a set of pictures for Zipper to identify. And we need to talk to your father, too."

"I knew you were going to say that," Gregory said. "Not today, okay, because he's just getting in. How about this. You drive the Buick out tomorrow, pick me up. Like it's informal."

I almost said "Why do we have to create an excuse to talk to your father?" But I understood something about the complicated expectations of parents and children.

After Joe left for JFK I stood at the window behind my desk, looking down at the line of red taillights moving smoothly in the storm-gray New York morning. In a vest-pocket park across the street, an elderly Oriental woman, in black pajama pants and a pink ski jacket, glided through the slow motion of t'ai chi as trash blew around her feet. A flock of homing pigeons, probably Zipper's, flew in circles over a roof near the river. Everything seemed so orderly from above. Everyone proceeding to their destination, silently, obediently, like a Catholic school fire drill.

The office was quiet except for the tapping of a typewriter. An undercover from the narcotics team was typing a supporting affidavit for a search warrant, copying from the model, filling in the blanks. My desk was piled high with boxes of evidence and case files.

I'd read the original investigative reports on Mulgrew's disappearance, filed ten years ago. Most of the steps taken appeared to be based on the assumption that Jinx had left the country. Although no airline reservations were found in his name, no one doubted his ability to obtain a phony passport. It seemed to me that whoever handled the case had smelled a setup and wasn't about to be embarrassed by the king of the bagmen. He must have figured that Jinx dumped his car in the fish market as a distraction for his vanishing act.

I tried to call Mulgrew's widow. No answer. Ellen Mulgrew, still listed at the same address, 61 W. 70th Street, same phone number. I called the 20th Precinct and asked them to ride by and check on her. We needed to interview her.

Besides Mrs. Mulgrew, the only substantive interview by IAD had been that of Detective Charles Spinelli and his wife, Donna Rose. Charlie Spinelli had been the recipient of the Honor Legion medal presented by Jinx that morning. After the ceremony they'd gone to a German restaurant around the corner from the Police Academy: Rolf's on East 22nd Street and Third Avenue. They'd said good-bye to Jinx outside the restaurant at 1330 hours, October 6, 1972. According to Donna Rose, Jinx was "three sheets to the wind." They were the last people to see him alive.

The pension section listed the retired Detective Spinelli as currently living in Tempe, Arizona. He answered the phone on the first ring.

"Way ahead of you," he said. "I got a duplicate set of the pictures we took at the ceremony."

Word had reached the desert. In every sun-baked hamlet in the South and Southwest, 1013 clubs have been formed, made up of retired N.Y. cops. They keep the grapevine alive.

"You still working with the Great Gregory?" Spinelli said. "That crazy bastard. Still digging up dogs?"

Spinelli told me he'd meet us at the Howard Johnson on Eighth Avenue on Thursday, December 16. He and his wife flew back to New York every Christmas; they had grandchildren on Long Island.

I hung up and began looking for the medical examiner's report, as Murray Daniels and the wiretap team came in, banging duffel bags off the wall and slinging more equipment than roadies on a Stones tour. They all wore blue nylon jackets with yellow stripes, borrowed from Ma Bell's attic. Hardware clanged on the front desks: cables, handsets, and one of the new pen registers capable of intercepting dialed numbers from either rotary or pulse phones.

"Where's the Great One, Anthony?" Daniels said. "Church or Brady's?"

Only a rookie would ask, out loud, where someone was.

"Court," I said. Never give up your partner to anyone.

"We brought cannolis from Ferrara," Murray said. "Help yourself."

Murray started pulling old file photos for me. I read the preliminary medical examiner's report. It stated that Jinx Mulgrew's remains were positively identified through dental records. A large-caliber bullet apparently punctured his skull near the left temple. The entrance wound measured 1.4 by 1.2 centimeters. The bullet traveled a downward angle, front to back, leaving a large, uneven exit wound in the occipital bone, near the right-hand posterior of the skull, below and slightly behind the ear. Apparently Jinx had been shot from above at close range.

No bullet was found in the body or in the surrounding debris, but the size of the wound indicated at least a .38-caliber. Jinx Mulgrew's .38-caliber Smith & Wesson service revolver was never found.

"I picked up a night lens," Murray Daniels said. "Let me know, I'll reserve the new surveillance van. I'm ready any night you need me."

In the gloom of the black-clouded day, I examined the seven pictures of Jinx Mulgrew lined up under the lamp on my desk. The NYPD required an official photo every four years. They served as undeniable evidence of a life of bad hours, bad booze, and bad faith. In twenty-eight years the full-cheeked boy with dark, wavy hair had turned into a hollowed-eyed man who'd found a watery grave. I wondered what my own collage would show.

Murray Daniels said, "Better get one of these cannolis before Gregory gets back. He'll inhale these things."

I took him up on the offer, then started opening the smaller of the two boxes of personal items seized from Mulgrew's locker in the 1st Precinct. It contained things taken from the shelf and floor of the locker; a yellowing voucher and inventory list was taped to the top. Both boxes smelled of a damp basement.

Murray Daniels put the cannoli on my desk. He pointed at the photos of the three men who'd dropped the barrel into the river. "You working these guys, Anthony?" he said. "Watch your ass. They ain't good citizens."

"You know them, Murray?"

He looked around the room to see if anyone was listening. "Feds do," he said. "We helped them put a camera on the towers of that church in Little Italy."

"Saint Patrick's Old Cathedral," I said. "They must be watching the Ravenite. These guys go to the Ravenite?"

He nodded, looking around. "Big power struggle," he said. "Different groups looking to take over the Genovese family since Sal Mags died. Picture of this geek on the wall in the plant. Crazy bastard, they say."

He'd pointed to the third man in the trio. Not Salvy, or the big guy who drove the forklift, but a hard-case with the face of an ex-fighter.

"The feds working the fish market?" I said.

"I don't think so. I'll try to find something out for you. Some of the feebs ain't too bad."

"Watch your ass with the feds, Murray."

"Hey, you and me are cops, in the same unit, and everything."

"Thanks," I said. "I have a feeling this case will be more trouble than it's worth."

"Nothing's easy," he said. "No simple answers."

I went back to the boxes of evidence from Mulgrew's locker, checking off each item: three packs of Kleenex, eighteen wadcutter bullets, a blackjack, one pair of green leather NYPD gloves, a Remington electric shaver, one nightstick, one daystick, six Trojan prophylactics, two pairs of black socks, three Bic pens, a bottle containing twenty-seven Bayer aspirin, eight Polaroid photos of an unknown nude female, and an Ace comb. No diaries, no address books, no notebooks, no keys.

I took the Polaroids and sat back with my cannoli. The woman was dark, Hispanic, late twenties, heavy-breasted. She sprawled across an unmade bed in raunchy poses, like a model in a layout for *Hustler*. Framed photos sat on a dresser behind her, paint was peeling from the walls. I made a mental note to clean my own locker and to avoid sweet, heavy pastry.

The photos didn't bother me; cops certainly weren't angels. What bothered me was the lack of notebooks. All cops kept extensive notes. I kept two notebooks myself: one speculative, where I could be free to write things I wasn't sure of; the other one official, sanitized for the eyes of defense lawyers. I was certain Jinx had kept a black book somewhere.

I didn't know where to begin with this case, because it appeared that all steps would be backward. In organized crime cases I usually started by trying to understand what had happened in the past. I began by listing the history of the people and the events. Then we went into the streets, started tailing, working on the three P's: people, patterns, and plate numbers.

Time was the problem here. Homicide's 24/24 rule was useless. The rule stated that the two most important time spans in a homicide were the twenty-four–hour periods immediately before and immediately after the killing. The twenty-four hours before the murder was the period when the fatal events were set in motion, the time when the killer appeared. The twenty-four hours after the murder were critical, because clues were fresh and alibis less set in stone.

In this case the corpse had aged for ten years; the crime scene was ravaged by the East River. Our only hope was to find witnesses and reconstruct the last hours in the life of Jinx Mulgrew. But a decade had passed, and memory was a poor foundation on which to build a case. And witnesses, if we found any, were sure to be hostile or, worse, vague.

Joe Gregory and I have a running argument. I say that the answer is always in the physical evidence. It is somewhere in handwritten notes, telephone records, conflicting signed statements, forgotten traffic tickets, canceled checks, Christmas cards—something tangible.

Gregory disagrees. He says you cannot solve human mysteries by comparing words on paper, because the answers come in bolts out of the heavens. He says it's like night shooting at the pistol range in the basement. You stand in the blackness, on the dirt floor, hearing only the breathing of the cop next to you as the smell of cordite burns your nostrils. Then the first shot explodes like a flare in a cave, a split-second blockbuster dazzle, and your target appears in a jagged-edged, white-hot spotlight. He says the answer will come. Wait for the muzzle flash.

8

"FAMILY IS so freaking overrated," Joe Gregory said as the Buick bumped over the rough cobblestone. He had returned from the airport around two P.M. and had been talking nonstop ever since. His father always seemed to do this to him. "The guy hugs me when he gets off the plane. Hasn't hugged me since grade school. Then he says, 'You're still drinking, Joseph.'"

"He could smell it. He's still a good cop."

We were in the fish market, with a picture album, hoping Zipper could make identifications.

"Maybe Zip's on the roof with the pigeons," Joe said.

"Try Beekman again," I said.

As we turned left I saw Zipper run across the street behind us. Gregory made a U-turn and came up behind him. Zipper was in a trot going up Fulton Street, looking over his shoulder. He saw us but kept on moving. It took us three passes before we got him in the car.

"You working out for the marathon or something?" Gregory said. "Everybody's a jogger."

Zipper didn't answer, he was breathing hard, sweating. We figured he was nervous about talking to us in daylight, so we drove over to the West Side and parked behind a construction trailer next to the fire boat station below Battery Park City. Gregory pulled a key out of his pocket.

"Ex-cop I know runs security," he said, shrugging. "I thought it might come in handy."

Inside the trailer, Gregory looked through the cabinets for teabags while Zipper and I sat at a table against the back window. Zipper wouldn't look at me. Kept rubbing his callused hands across the rough wood of the table.

"You okay, Zip?" I said. He nodded and tried to smile, but it was a child's attempt at a brave face. "Anybody say anything to you?"

"Don't talk to cops no more," he said.

"Who said that?" Gregory said.

Through the window directly behind Zipper I could see the Statue of Liberty. It occurred to me that this was the closest I had ever been to that statue. All these years in New York.

"Nicky Skooch," he said.

"He the one who dumped the fish on our car?" Gregory said.

Zipper nodded.

I opened the photo album and turned it around to Zipper. It was a collection of arrest booking photos and surveillance pictures, some thirty years old. Murray Daniels and I had researched every available intelligence report and picked anyone with a remote connection to the fish market.

Zipper hesitated at first, then acted as if playing a game. The book fascinated him, like an old family album found in an attic. He pointed to picture after picture, never stuck for something to say. He named names, sometimes moving faster than I could write. The only problem was, all he knew were nicknames.

"Santo Two Times, Jimmy Cadillac, Sally One Ball, Bay Ridge Charlie, Vinnie Crabs."

"Show me Nicky Skooch," I said.

He pointed to the guy Murray Daniels had warned me about. The crazy bastard, whose picture was up in the fed's plant, looked like a former pug.

Zipper identified all three men we saw dump the white barrel into the river. We compared booking photos to arrest sheets.

Salvy was Silvestro Magnani, two arrests for burglary, a dozen for theft and minor drug possession.

"Nicky Skooch" AKA Nicholas Sciotta, like Salvy, was a fish market strong-arm with a yellow sheet longer than a moray eel. But Nicky's crimes all involved the shedding of blood.

Ugo Bongiovanni, the one with the suit, who drove the forklift, had only five arrests: three for grand larceny auto at age eighteen, one assault, and one manslaughter. Nothing in the last twelve years. Zipper said Mr. Bongiovanni was the boss now.

"Not Mr. Rizzo?" I asked.

"Not no more," he said. "Now he has a fish business."

Joe Gregory said, "You hear anything, Zipper? About the cop we found in the river?"

Zipper looked down at his hands. Out in the river a dredge was sucking silt off the bottom of the Hudson, adding land for new Manhattan waterfront condos. A steady rhythm, a *whoosh* of steam, the clang of a hammer, was the only sound. Zipper spoke so softly, I had to ask him to repeat himself.

He said, "Nicky said they'll put us in the river, too."

"Fuck Nicky," Joe Gregory said, slamming his fist on the table. "Fuck Nicky, fuck Nicky."

"Koch bit Nicky," Zipper said.

"Good for Koch," Gregory said.

Thirty minutes later we dropped Zipper off at the *Titanic* Memorial. Before he got out he reached over the front seat and dropped a rolled-up twenty-dollar bill on Gregory's lap. Pigeon feathers were stuck in his cuff.

As we waited at the light at Fulton, watching Zipper walk to the river, the FPS car came around the corner. Nicky Skooch was driving, alone.

Gregory said, "He didn't see Zip get out."

I told Gregory to drop me off at my car. I'd had enough for the day—working days exhausts me. I made notes next to the pictures stapled to the case folder: dates, time, and source of identification.

"All three of these guys are from the Bronx," I said. "All Four Six and Four Eight Precinct collars."

"Bobo Rizzo's from the Bronx," Gregory said. "Makes sense. You pick guys from the neighborhood."

We wouldn't talk about Nicky's threat. You couldn't do this job if you allowed yourself to dwell on threats.

"Is that prick following us?" Gregory said, adjusting the mirror. We were a block from headquarters. The black Chrysler was behind us.

"Drive past my car," I said.

I wasn't about to let Nicky see my car. Any half-assed wise guy can copy your plate number, slide money under the table to the right person at the Motor Vehicles Bureau, and walk away with your home address. You protect your home address. No matter what, you protect that.

"The balls on this guy," Gregory said, watching the mirror, cigarette clenched in his teeth.

We drove past the parking lot, past the back door of One Police Plaza, the black Chrysler following. Joe stopped at the corner, I picked up the binoculars and turned around.

"He's smiling," I said.

We kept going straight, and the Chrysler made the right turn onto St. James Place. In three minutes he'd be on cobblestone.

"Not for long," Gregory said.

9

THE NEXT morning I rode all the way to Gregory's house with the Buick windows rolled down, trying to blow out the fish stink. The wind off New York Bay whipped funnel clouds of ashes and grit from the floor into my eyes and mouth. Brooklynites jogged along the concrete path beside the bay, ignoring waves crashing over the rail. More than any other road in New York, this part of the Shore Parkway reminds me I am traversing a city of islands.

Gregory rarely relinquished the wheel of the Buick to anyone; he had used a heavy contract to get it. The car had been confiscated in a drug conviction, and we'd driven it away from the courthouse before the engine had cooled, compliments of the CO of the motor pool. A man who honored his contracts.

In the NYPD you honored your contracts or you went through channels and waited. Our part of the contract was to discreetly provide the CO with the real story, when a cop, via mystery transfer, suddenly appeared in his garage. The motor pool was a notorious dumping ground for damaged cops who arrived packing rubber guns and carrying psychological or criminal baggage.

The CO wanted to know what he was getting before he read it in the *Daily News*. Discreet information was our stock in trade.

I went one exit too far and had to swing up the ramp to the Verrazano-Narrows Bridge, then back down to the cluster of brick and wooden frame houses that made up this part of Bay Ridge, Brooklyn. Every house on Gregory's block had a flagpole and was decorated for Christmas. Liam Gregory's Ford pickup was parked out front. Not a Honda or Toyota in sight. Joe was on the porch.

"You take good care of my car?" he said. He was wearing khaki pants and a blue sweatshirt with the NYPD logo over two uniformed pigs: "Pigs Are Beautiful." I hadn't seen one since the sixties.

As we walked through the darkened living room, past dark furniture huddled in the same position since the death of Joe's mother, he whispered, "He's downstairs," then loudly, "C'mon down, say hello to my dad."

We ducked our heads walking down the narrow steps. I could smell the musty dampness and fresh wood chips. Liam Gregory was bent over a table, cutting a thin strip of wood with a radial saw, the veins in his forearms bulging. Liam's pink scalp shone from perspiration, his thinning white hair moist. He didn't look up until we were almost on top of him.

"Anthony," he said, squeezing my hand in his callused paws. "How's that fine wife? And the granddaughter, my God, you don't look old enough. Should be old geezers like me with the grandchildren."

"He's building a trellis," Joe said. "Can you believe it? Like I'm going to grow roses or something."

"You could use a hobby," I said.

"I been telling him, try Florida," Joe said. "More ex–New York cops in Florida than Brooklyn."

"And listen to them crying about pensions," Liam said. "I love this work. I built this house, didn't I?"

"It ain't right, though," Joe said. "You worked hard all your life. You should be taking it easy."

Joe's voice sounded high-pitched, more youthful, in the presence of his father. Both directed their remarks to me.

"Talk some sense into him, partner," Joe said. "I'll take a shave."

He disappeared up the rough wooden steps Liam had built out of ammunition boxes discarded from Fort Hamilton. The specifications and count markings were printed in yellow on the underside.

"Grown children," Liam said. "Yours like that yet, Anthony? Act like they can't believe you've made it this far without them."

"They're not around enough for me to tell," I said, and leaned against the workbench.

"Maybe that's better," he said.

Liam sat heavily on a wooden swivel chair, next to a desk with framed pictures of Francis Cardinal Spellman and Joe, when he'd graduated from the Great Lakes Naval Training Station. A cup and saucer sat on the desk, a teabag drying inside.

"Well, get to it, lad," he said. "You're here to ask me about Jinx Mulgrew."

Liam Gregory was the original no-bullshit cop. I hadn't seen him in almost two years. He looked weather-beaten and heavier than I remembered, but healthy, more relaxed. Ireland had been good for him.

"Who killed him?" I said.

"You want I should deliver him to you in cuffs?"

"I can provide the cuffs."

"Bobo Rizzo," he said. "Or some other crony. All bastards, that crew. But you'll never make a case. A crying shame, too."

Water ran through pipes over my head. The hot-water heater had clicked on, casting a soft blue glow on the floor.

I said, "You think Jinx went to see Rizzo after he left the medal ceremony?"

"Makes sense. He was going to run. He was looking for every dime he could scrape together."

"You sound very sure."

"Common knowledge."

"What about specific knowledge?"

His swivel chair squeaked as he rocked back. The low ceiling was lined with beams and hanging pipes. A line of mason jars, containing screws and nails of various sizes, hung above his head, the lids nailed to the beams.

"Who have you interviewed so far?" he said.

"Not many choices," I said. "The Spinellis are flying in. We'll meet them tomorrow. Sidney Kaye won't return our phone calls. We can't find Ellen Mulgrew."

"Sid Kaye, don't trust that bastard. Sid and Jinx were a dandy pair. I warned them years ago, 'Stay away from those guineas.' But they loved flashing the bankroll. Thought they were men about town."

"Why, then, would the mob kill Jinx?"

"His usefulness had ended," Liam said. "Everyone heard the rumors about him going to the Knapp Commission. And I'm sure he went down to see Rizzo half-drunk, probably obnoxious. They killed him somewhere down there, some empty warehouse."

Liam squeezed a black sponge ball in his hand. "Arthritis," he said when he saw me staring.

"Damp Irish weather," I said.

"And New York is better?"

I watched his forearm swelling as he squeezed. Still not a man to fool with. A heavy punching bag, stuffing poking through rips in the leather, hung on a chain in the corner, next to a rusting weight bench.

"When was the last time you spoke to Jinx?" I asked.

"I'll tell you the God's green truth, Anthony," he said, raising his eyes. "Jinx called me a day or so before he disappeared. Wanted to meet me for a last drink—a last flute, he says—the night of the medal ceremony. I knew he was leaving then."

"You didn't tell IAD this."

"They didn't ask," he snapped.

It surprised me. I almost said I didn't think that mattered, but I just asked him to continue.

"Jinx said he'd be uptown, in Danny Boy's, by six. I waited until almost midnight."

"Long time to wait," I said.

He looked up at me with his priestly blue eyes, as if confessing a sin he had carried a long time. "I had ten thousand dollars in my pocket for him, Anthony. Almost every cent I had. He was a friend when I needed him, when Maire died. Friends help friends, no matter the problem. But he never showed up. Never saw him again."

He switched hands with the sponge ball. Started squeezing harder.

"I didn't think you were still that friendly anymore," I said.

"Why do you think I've made all these trips to Ireland? For the weather?"

"Are you serious? You're telling me you've been looking for Jinx?"

"You get old, you'll understand," he said. "You gather few friends in a lifetime. Fewer than you think. When Jinx didn't show that night, I figured he'd made a big score with Bobo, or couldn't face me to take my money. After I put my papers in, I had nothing better to do. I looked in every bog and every pub in that country. A man could hide for two lifetimes in Ireland."

Liam scuffed his feet on the rough concrete floor. He wore ankle-high, black leather lace-up shoes. "We had some times, me and Jinx," he said, smiling. His teeth looked yellow against the crimson Gregory complexion. "Every Saint Paddy's we'd march in uniform. Up Fifth Avenue, swigging Jameson from a billy club he'd hollowed out to a flask. One year he finds this midget woman, dressed in green. We took her to every bar on Second and Third. Jinx had her dancing on the tables, his leprechaun."

I could hear Joe walking heavily above our heads.

"I take it you haven't spoken to Ellen," Liam said. "His wife?"

"I've called, but I haven't gotten an answer. She wouldn't answer the door for the Two Oh Precinct cops."

"No wonder," Liam said. "The job treated her badly after Jinx disappeared. Like she was an accomplice or some such thing. The poor woman was the last person Jinx would confide in. Another woman, sure. Not his wife."

"We'll need to interview her."

"I'll talk to her," Liam said. "After the funeral. Ellen's a nice woman. Didn't deserve her treatment."

Joe yelled down the steps, said he'd start the car. He didn't say good-bye to his father.

"Florida, bejesus," Liam said, shaking his head. "You need a reason to live, Anthony. A good reason. People down in Florida are sitting on green benches watching their self-respect disappear. The worst thing you can do when you get old is to stop being tough."

Sun glinted off the looming structure of the Verrazano. Standing on the Gregory front porch, you felt like a toy soldier in plastic town under an Erector set bridge. Joe Gregory already had the Buick running. He adjusted the seat all the way back, as if he had the legs of a power forward.

"We learn anything?" he said.

"He says somebody in the market killed him. Probably Bobo."

"I agree. Without question," Joe Gregory said. "What do you say we get in early tomorrow, before we meet the Spinellis. Say around three A.M., make one quick sweep through the market. See if we can find Bobo."

"Your dad says Jinx was looking for cash to run with. He thinks he went to Bobo to make a score."

"My scenario exactly," he said. "Jinx is putting his boodle together, right? He gets a few highballs too many under his belt. Goes down to the market throwing muscle around, looking for a potful of cash. Rizzo says, 'Screw this arrogant SOB, who needs him?' They knew Jinx was history, anyway. Why give him a sou?"

"Your dad had ten grand, ready to give it to Jinx."

He looked at me twice, maybe to see if I was serious.

You can know a family all of your life and never be able to gauge how open they are with each other. What secrets they tell, which ones they keep.

"Well, well," he said. "What do we make of that?"

"I don't know yet," I said. "Misguided loyalty, maybe. It's a common malady with us. But let's get going. I want to stop at Macy's, do some Christmas shopping."

"Perfect," he said. "Perfect. I want you to look at those old men sitting on the benches holding packages. You know what word they got tattooed on the dead space across their forehead?"

"I can guess."

"It says RETIRED in big letters. You look close at Charlie Spinelli tomorrow. Tell me I'm wrong."

"I'm not Charlie Spinelli."

"Yes, you are, pally. Yes, you are."

10

As you approach South Street from the quiet darkness of the back alleys, you hear the roar of a thousand angry voices. It was shortly after three A.M. when Gregory spotted Salvy outside Jojo's, a sandwich shop no bigger than a phone booth. We stepped back under the covering of a construction walkway. The smell of Italian sauces, oregano, and garlic permeated the cold, damp air.

The fishmonger's lunch crowd lined up outside Jojo's. Two dozen burly, unshaven men in high rubber boots and greasy jackets stretched past the curb. Almost all of them carried a box hook hanging from straps sewn into their jackets. The box hook, a tool used for dragging boxes and crates, had the look of a medieval weapon, with its wooden handle and ten-inch deep curved steel hook usually honed to a point.

Salvy, leaning against the wall, was attacking an Italian hero sandwich, his greasy Mets hat pushed to the back of his head. Red sauce ran down his hand and disappeared into his sleeve.

"Hey, *paesano*," said a young guy in a greasy army field jacket with PFC stripes. "You eating your hand, it's fucking bleeding?"

Salvy held the sandwich between his legs. "This is bleeding," he said. "Bite this."

The PFC snatched at Salvy's sandwich and knocked it out of his hand. Salvy kicked at him, almost falling, buckles on his galoshes jangling. Then Salvy picked up the sandwich and threw it at the PFC, who caught it against his chest.

"They're doing lunch," Gregory whispered.

"I got your sausage, right here," Salvy said, grabbing his crotch. He pulled the Mets hat tight over his eyes, took the handcart from the wall, and bounced it off the curb. I noticed that the older guys in line were not laughing at him.

"Give him a good lead," Gregory said. "We can't possibly lose this guy."

Salvy turned left into the crowd on South Street. We waited a beat. A crab clattered across the plywood walkway, heading sideways toward Wall Street. Gregory stopped it under his shoe. "Give me that bag," he said.

I picked up a white Jojo's bag as Gregory held the crab at the center point of the shell behind the claws. The claws flailed when he turned it over for me to admire.

"Chesapeake Bay blue claw," he said. "Twelve ninety-five at Armando's. I used to eat these by the bushel when I was in Norfolk."

He dropped it into the bag and held it in his fist. He stepped down onto the cobblestone like Ward Cleaver going to the office. Out of the alley, I could feel the wind coming off the river.

South Street was a sea of bodies at this hour, but we found Salvy easily. He waddled past the loading docks along the row of dilapidated warehouses on the west side of the street. Pushing his handcart with one hand, he weaved between scales hanging on chains and boxes of crushed ice. He had a fat guy's walk, plenty of arm pump for propulsion. Walks are unique, like fingerprints. Better than a snapshot for spotting a creep in a crowd.

We ran across to the opposite side of South Street and acted like big-time buyers under the white glare of lights hanging from the canopy that covered the runway in front of the Tin Building. The din reverberated off the canopy and the long, open concrete warehouse. Fires crackled as wood burned in open barrels.

Behind us were the open stalls of sixteen wholesalers. A hundred men worked shoulder to shoulder, pulling and stacking crates of fish in rows fifty feet long. A man in a red wool cap brushed by me carrying a bleeding shark on his shoulder. By dinnertime tonight it would be masquerading as scallops at Armando's.

Salvy kept working directly across the street. We watched through breaks in the traffic as he scooped black-and-silver fish from boxes on the sidewalk, tossing them into the boxes on his handcart. He did this again and again, taking two or three from each one, skimming the top layer. He moved from stall to stall.

We kept pace as Gregory discussed the merits of the cod, hake, roughies, perch, and snapper with guys in rubber aprons and watch caps or yarmulkes. It smelled of smoke and diesel fuel and fish, raw with the stench of the sea. Then Gregory slapped me with his Jojo's bag and pointed. Salvy was talking to a small man in a black overcoat.

"Bobo Rizzo," I said.

I'd seen Bobo's face countless times over the years, through binoculars and in booking photos on the second row of a pyramid of snapshots thumbtacked to Eddie Shick's wall. Bobo puffed his cigar while Salvy talked, his mouth only inches from Bobo's ear. Someone held the door to R&B Fish, waiting for the Genovese capo to enter. Behind us, a truck whined in reverse. Then, abruptly, Bobo turned and walked away from Salvy, climbed the stairs into R&B.

"Salvy skipped R and B," Gregory said. "Didn't take one fish. Connected joint, guaranteed."

"Bobo's pissed about something," I said.

"Rizzo goes back, way back," Gregory said. "Ten years ago, when they whacked Jinx, he'd be calling all the shots."

"Maybe he still is," I said.

Rizzo had been the ruling force in the market for twenty years, since the death of Socks Lanza. Lanza, the Genovese capo, took over the fishmonger's union when the mob realized the power that came from being able to control the work force. Fish was a product so delicate, Lanza knew, that it would be destroyed if marooned for only a few hours. Lanza's union held the wholesalers by the throat. But Bobo Rizzo, during his creative reign, expanded the mob's power base enormously.

Salvy resumed boxing fish at the next place, Jimmy Gaeta and Sons. Workers walked by him. Salvy joked with them, enjoying himself, as if he were a popular guy. It looked normal.

Then Salvy picked up the pace. He had a full load and shifted to his top waddle speed, swinging halfway out into South Street. He made the left into Peck Slip. We looked for a break in traffic, pumped up with adrenaline, the cop's drug, all because of Bobo Rizzo, a made guy in the Genovese family. A case became more important when you could mention a known made guy.

We followed Salvy back to 14 Peck Slip. He leaned into his full load and pushed it up the ramp. We stood in the cold darkness across the wide street as Salvy dumped the crates among stacks of boxes and crates on the water-soaked warehouse floor.

"Look at all that freaking fish," Gregory said.

"I've always heard they skimmed," I said. "But there has to be hundreds of pounds of fish in there."

"Thousands, pally. They do this every night, we're talking millions of dollars a year. And nobody counted what this guy was taking. They ignored him, like he was invisible. The fat bastard took what he wanted. Like he deserved it."

Salvy stacked his handcart with more empty crates and hustled down the ramp, back to South Street, to where he'd left off.

"This is extortion, minimum," Gregory said. "They got the wholesalers shitting in their pants. They do what they freaking want here, like it's their little kingdom."

As we walked back to the car, Gregory handed me his crab in a bag and started making notes. The crab scratched for freedom against my leg.

11

CHARLIE AND Donna Rose Spinelli turned heads when they walked into the coffee shop of the Howard Johnson. They were deeply tanned and dressed in southwest pastels that looked cartoonlike on Eighth Avenue on a drizzly December morning. Donna Rose carried a navy blue quilted coat, but she was dressed in a pale green skirt and flowered blouse. She wore a green ribbon in her hair, which was a brassy red. Charlie, despite his tan and Hawaiian shirt, looked puffy around the eyes.

We waved from the back booth, but Charlie knew where to look. Cops learned as rookies in uniform to find the table with the best view. Never sit with your back to the cash register or the door.

Joe Gregory had known Charlie for years, from the Honor Legion meetings. Charlie had retired on the exact day of his twentieth anniversary in the job. Joe said New York lost a great cop and true wild man when Charlie Spinelli packed it in.

"Look at the tans on these two," Gregory said. "How's the Wild West treating you? Keeping busy? Getting along with the Indians and all?"

Donna Rose brushed off the seat with a napkin and

slid into the booth. "Everyone's so white in New York," she said. She squinted at our faces as if we were shiny moon people. "Charlie, can you believe how white everyone is? So deathly, deathly pale."

"Sun's bad for the Irish," Gregory said. "Fair skin, you know. I burn if I sit too close to neon."

"We're sun worshipers," Donna Rose said. "We have a built-in pool in our backyard. Right in the ground. We swim every day."

"Well, not every day," Charlie said.

"Oh, no," she said. "Some days we walk the mall, go to aerobics. We're active. Always on the go."

"We're busier than you think," Charlie said.

A deathly pale waitress, wearing black boots stained white from rock salt, stared at Donna Rose while pouring coffee. Charlie ordered bacon and eggs, Donna Rose a western omelet, disappointed they were out of jalapeño. We'd already eaten. Gregory sopped ketchup off his plate with my toast.

"Look at this weather," Donna Rose said. "You forget so quick. It never rains in Arizona. Only seven inches a year. Seven."

"Must be like a desert out there," Gregory said.

"Oh, no. You should see the greenery," Donna Rose said. "All the golf courses. Charlie's a good golfer."

Joe Gregory honked a laugh, a nasal blast of air. "Sorry," he said, wiping his eyes. Then, in a low golf announcer whisper: "Here's Charlie Spinelli, formerly of Safe and Loft, putting for birdie."

Donna Rose ran down their busy schedule, and Charlie smiled and shrugged. Outside, tourists hustled in and out of the hotel. Taxis triple-parked, oblivious of the horns, as new arrivals guarded their baggage on the curb.

"Christmas is the shits out there," Charlie said. "You got to admit that, hon. You don't even know it. People wearing shorts."

"So we come here for Christmas," she said. "But we'd never move back."

Gregory kicked me under the table. He was giving Donna Rose the full effect of his smily, "what bullshit" face. Mr. Congenial.

"Making any progress with the case?" Charlie said.

"We were counting on you," I said.

"Give me those pictures, hon."

Donna Rose rooted around in a large canvas satchel with pastel coyotes howling at a silver moon. The pictures were in an envelope that read "Osco Drugs, open twenty-four hours, senior citizen discount."

"These are yours," Charlie said. "The originals, for the case folder."

"Are you positive Jinx left alone?" I said. "In his own car."

"Tan Impala," Charlie said. "Thirteen thirty hours. Absolutely alone. I watched him pull away."

"He say anything at all about where he was going?" I said.

"I been racking my brain," Charlie said. "I'll say one thing for sure: the guy had the taste. He hadn't had his last drink for the day."

"Was he shit-faced?" Gregory said, looking up from the pictures.

I looked over at Donna Rose, but she was gazing around the room as if trying to remember if she had really once lived at this frenetic pace. The noise of traffic outside, constant sirens, the bustle of a midtown restaurant: people shouting in a dozen accents, the clink of cups and saucers, the *whomp*, *whomp* of kitchen doors swinging.

"We were dumping them pretty fast," Charlie said.

"He wouldn't let Charlie even buy a drink," Donna Rose said. "Kept peeling bills off a roll."

"He had a wad," Charlie said.

"Made the waitress stir his drink with her finger," Donna Rose said. "He kept rubbing his hands all over her hips."

"Guy was a pisser," Charlie said. "Had me roaring with stories."

"I thought he was a pig," Donna Rose said.

Gregory handed me the pictures. I had similar ones at home, standard promotion ceremony shots. The police commissioner stands in front of the flags, the new promotees line up with their families, ready to step in and pose with him. The detectives, smiling too broadly, look out of place in uniform, as if behind cardboard cutouts in a Coney Island carny. The wives, glassy-eyed, seem lost.

Most of the pictures were of Charlie. Jinx appeared in two: one inside, one outside. I handed Charlie a copy of his IAD interview and asked him if he could think of anything new.

"They were drinking way too fast," Donna Rose said. "Charlie had to take a nap when we got home."

"He mention the Fulton Fish Market at all?" Gregory said.

"IAD asked me that," Charlie said. "Bastards grilled me and Donna for hours. Seriously, hours. Then they called the next day, trying to trip us up. Right, hon? Tell you the truth, I honestly couldn't remember if he said he was going to the market or not. But I wouldn't have told those bastards if I did know."

"That Fulton Fish Market is so dirty," Donna Rose said. "That's the first thing we notice when we come back to New York. How filthy it is."

"One thing," Charlie said, "I didn't mention to anybody before. I tried to pick up the lunch tab, he wouldn't let me. He says, 'Don't worry about it, I'm about to come into some serious money.' "

I looked at the last snapshots of Jinx Mulgrew, taken on Third Avenue, in the rain. Donna Rose had taken them facing south, the red door of Rolf's in the background. Jinx and Charlie, hair wet, arm in arm, uniforms visible under open raincoats, smiling with the rubbery faces of the very drunk. Both pointed to the medal around Charlie's neck.

"I passed it off as the booze talking," Charlie said. "He always talked big money. But if I were you, I'd talk to Sid Kaye. Then I'd look at the fish market, check those joints down there. Somebody had to see something. Jinx was going to make a run for it, sure as shit. If he was looking for a bankroll, market's where he'd go. Remember what Willie Sutton said when they asked him why he robbed banks."

"What?" Donna Rose said.

The three of us said in unison, "That's where the money is."

I reached for the check, but Charlie covered it with his hand. Gregory pulled out his address book, began flipping through the pages. Joe's address book had a scuffed black leather cover, a strip of duct tape along the binding. Jammed between the pages were dozens of business cards, cocktail napkins, pieces of paper, and coasters with notes or telephone numbers. It was his

Rolodex and file cabinet all held together by a pair of thick rubber bands. Somehow he found a small calendar.

"We got an Honor Legion meeting January twelfth," Gregory said. "I'll pick you up."

Charlie took a quick look at his wife. She just raised her eyebrows as if to say "That's interesting."

"We fly back the ninth," Charlie said.

"Change your reservations," Gregory said.

"We got supersavers, you lose them," Charlie said.

We sipped coffee in silence for a minute.

Charlie said, "I miss the guys, the camaraderie. I even miss the rain. But I don't miss the job. Not one damn bit."

12

FRIDAY IS Leech's Day in the Fulton Fish Market, a day for paying and collecting. It was nearly dawn, and the three of us had been in the Tech Unit van for two cold hours. Gregory sat on the driver's seat, peering at 14 Peck Slip with expensive German binoculars. Detective Murray Daniels and I were in the back, separated from Gregory by a thick curtain. I squatted on a milk crate, holding the clipboard and watching my breath cloud in a cone of blue light. Murray, who'd been snapping pictures with a Nikon fitted with a sophisticated night vision lens, was pissing in a coffee can.

"What makes you think Sid Kaye will tell you anything?" Murray Daniels said.

"Ego," Gregory said, his voice muffled by the curtain. "Him and Jinx thought they were hot-shit cops. Sid'll love to show off. Show us what jerks we are. Especially me."

Zipper had told us that on Leech's Day Mr. Bongiovanni doled out a few bucks to the gofers and hangers-on. The rain thumped on the roof as Daniels tried to photograph men whose faces were hidden under hoods and hats. We were gathering pictures to show Sid Kaye, hoping he could point out a patsy, someone vulnerable we could squeeze for information.

"We could stay out here for weeks," Gregory said, "and not know who was who. Jinx and Sid were on the pad with these guys for years. Sid knows the scams, who the movers are, who the weak links are."

Our van was new, Acme Distributors painted on the side. The business address was a vacant lot. Murray Daniels spun around on the swivel stool, went back to facing the one-way window.

"The truth is, Murray," I said, "we're wasting our time."

Murray nodded, agreeing with me, as usual.

"You geniuses got a better idea?" Gregory said. "Let me know."

"We should be working the time frame," I said. "We know Jinx left the Spinellis at one-thirty, and disappeared before six P.M. He had to go somewhere. Somebody had to see him between those times."

"You pick six out of a hat, or what?" Gregory said.

"From your dad. He said he was supposed to meet Jinx at Danny Boy's for a drink by six that evening. But he never showed."

Something else Da forgot to tell his only son. Vince Salvatore said that Italian fifth cousins are closer than Irish twin brothers.

"So what's your point?" Joe said.

"Jinx was a drinker and ladies' man," I said. "He had to have other haunts, somewhere he went after he left Charlie. Bars, restaurants, girlfriends. IAD never backtracked."

"Nobody'd tell them shit," Murray said. "Might tell you, though."

"Maybe he came straight down to the market," Gregory said.

"Ask your father, Joe," I said. "He did a lot of drinking with Jinx."

"My old man," Gregory said, "always answers a freaking question with a question."

"Seems like a simple enough request to me," Murray Daniels said. "Does he know Jinx's favorite bars?"

"That guy," Joe said, "never gives a simple answer."

"That's the trouble with us cops," Murray Daniels said. "We ask simple questions, we expect simple answers. But there are no simple answers. Even when we successfully close a case, we still walk away from a mystery."

"You're so fucking deep, Murray," Joe Gregory said. "I'll be sure to write that in my diary tonight."

"Sid Kaye will know where Jinx drank," I said. "I'll ask him."

"Won't get us nowhere, pally."

"Like we're getting somewhere now."

The rain stopped, yet I could still hear the sound of the drops. I felt dirty, my mouth gritty. Dawn was a rude slap on a whiskered cheek, but in this weather morning came slowly between sooty pillars of steel and concrete. Grubby fingers fighting off the light.

"We know Jinx wound up down here anyway," Gregory said. "Am I right?"

"Eventually," I said.

"I rest my case," Gregory said.

I heard the click of Gregory's Zippo, smelled the lighter fluid.

"Let me ask you this," I said. "What happened to Jinx's notes?"

The van rocked as Gregory came through the heavy curtain and sat on the milk crate opposite me. His cigarette lit the dark contours of his face. "Now that's simple," he said. "Some cop grabbed them. Soon as they found out Jinx was dead, some slick bastard raided his locker and destroyed anything with words on it. Anything looked incriminating."

"How did they know he was dead?"

"You know what the hell I mean. When he was reported missing. Same thing, he was gone. His fellow thieves plundered his locker. Took anything looked incriminating."

I said, "I don't see him keeping notes about payoffs in his locker."

I could hear the roar of traffic building on the FDR, the pulse of the city beating stronger as the day began.

Murray Daniels said, "A truck just pulled up. I can't make out the writing on the side."

Gregory tiptoed back into the front of the van. I followed him and slid onto the passenger seat.

I wrote as Joe dictated what he saw through the binoculars. Two men in yellow rain slickers wheeling crates of fish down the ramp, tossing them into the old Ford panel truck. The name was too faded to read. Salvy waddled around the front of the warehouse, pointing and talking with his hands, directing. I made a note of the time, 0550 hours, and wrote down Gregory's descriptions. When Gregory was quiet I could hear Murray's Nikon click and the motor drive whir.

"This fish, I guarantee," Gregory said, "is going to Bobo Rizzo's joint."

Salvy slammed the panel truck door. Joe waited until he saw their exhaust smoke, then started our van. The battery was weak, it barely turned over. A fishy smell came from the heater as it blew cold air on my feet.

"We'll follow the fish," Gregory said. "Ride by Bobo's. Take pictures of the fish going in."

"Not with this camera, you're not," Murray Daniels said. "This setup sucks when there's the slightest movement."

Gregory left the lights off as he turned the wheels away from the curb. The wipers were set on intermittent. The worst thing about wipers on the intermittent function was the anticipation, like waiting for the other shoe to fall.

"Why don't you sit in the back, pally," Gregory said. "Let Murray sit here, use the other camera out the window as we pass by."

I climbed through the curtain as we started rolling. Murray Daniels passed me, moved to the front passenger seat. I sat on the milk crate, watching through the curtains.

The panel truck made a left on Water Street, then a left on Beekman. Joe followed, then paused at the corner of Beekman as the Ford's taillights disappeared left. Joe drove straight ahead another block, swinging in a wider arc.

Morning traffic on South Street was already bumper to bumper. We drove slowly past R&B Fish as their panel truck backed up to the ramp. Murray pointed the camera past Gregory's face and let the motor drive run. The long lens sat under Gregory's nose like the chinning bar in Shick's office. Salvy was standing on the platform, talking to Bobo Rizzo. Bobo's cigar burned like a lantern in the dark of the cloudy morning.

We drove back to the same spot opposite 14 Peck

Slip. Daniels put a new roll of film in the camera, handed the old through the curtain to me. Cold wind was blowing through Gregory's open window.

"Oh, shit," Murray said. "They made us."

I looked through the curtain. Gregory's window was rolled all the way down. Someone must have recognized him as we drove past R&B. Nicky Skooch was on the platform of 14 Peck Slip, pointing across at us.

"Nicky's pissed," Gregory said, laughing.

Nicky Skooch was furious, stomping around the platform. We could hear him screaming. He ran inside the warehouse, came out about a minute later with a red-headed guy we had not yet identified. They both got into the Chrysler, and Nicky made a sliding U-turn.

"Let's get these to the photo unit," I said. "We have enough to show Sid Kaye."

Gregory leaned down to start the van. It wouldn't catch, and began to smell of gas.

"Where did Nicky go?" I said.

"Took off down Water Street," Joe said.

"Where's he's going?" I said.

"Breakfast run," Joe said. "Something. How the hell do I know?"

I was concerned about Nicky, not worried. The mafia rarely kills cops because it's bad for business; they'd lose millions in street revenue in the all-out pressure that would come. But this new breed, you hear so many things about the Sicilian imports, the wacko generation. Ugo probably chased Nicky before he did something stupid.

"I'm starved," Daniels said. "Let's grab something."

Joe tried the van again, but the battery was barely audible. He waited a few minutes, tried again. Nothing.

Daniels picked up the radio to call for assistance, and Gregory grabbed his hand.

"Don't put it over the air, Murray," Joe said. "The ballbreakers'll hear it, and we got another thing to live down. I'll call by landline, they got a phone in the PO."

While Gregory walked toward the post office, I noticed the platform at 14 Peck had been quickly abandoned, the overhead door pulled down. Even in a surveillance van, in these neighborhoods, you expect to get caught.

Once, years ago, Gregory received information on a major organized crime meeting at the Ravenite Social Club. We put an empty TV box with a small peephole on the backseat of our car and I hid inside the box. Gregory parked the car directly in front of the club and walked away. I sat in the box sweating and waiting. I stared, for what seemed like hours, at the lace curtains and the small gold letters that said "Members Only." Finally a local boy, around ten years old, walked up to the car, looked directly into the peephole, his mouth against the car window, and yelled "Hey, cop, the meet is in Vegas."

Murray Daniels finished reloading his cameras.

"Why don't we use color film, Murray?" I said.

"Color film is for grandmothers," he said.

Gregory got in, slamming the van door. "Help is on the way," he said. "I found Nicky Skooch for you, pally. Around the corner. Other end of Water Street."

"Doing what?" I said.

"Probably shaking down fishmongers for Christmas gifts."

In the side-view mirror I could see freshly showered people driving to work. A few people walked by us carrying brown bags and the morning paper. Nothing made you feel more exhausted than clean people. I wondered how I ever did this for two and three days straight. Now I hoped I could make it home without falling asleep. All I could think of was my bed.

"Hope the hell they get here soon," I said, checking my watch. "I'm beat. Where did you say Nicky was?"

"Around the corner," he said. "You going to ask him for jumper cables?"

"No, I was just thinking. Are they in the car?"

"Must be in this building," he said, pointing behind us.

"These buildings are condemned," I said. "They're empty."

A single white feather floated in front of us, wafting gently in a winter breeze.

"Hey, Murray," Gregory said. "How come we spent all this money on a surveillance van and there's no bathroom?"

"No simple answer," he said. Something hard clinked off the sidewalk, like a small stone.

I looked across at the locked doors of 14 Peck. Then we heard the sound of pebbles tinkling off the truck, like sand in a windstorm.

I said, "These roofs connect, Joe?"

Gregory looked through the windshield, up at the building we were parked next to. "Get down!" he yelled a heartbeat before the thunderous thud of a million pounds of something slammed down on us. The inside of the van burst like a smashed paper bag.

In the ringing silence that followed I lifted my head slowly, expecting to touch the roof at any second. Dirt and dust rose in the air. I heard the whistling of air escaping from the tires. My lap was covered with glass. I could taste dirt in my mouth, feel it in my hair. Murray Daniels was hidden under sheet metal.

"Jesus Christ," Gregory said, and began yelling our location and "ten thirteen" into the portable radio. He forced his door open enough to squeeze out. Instantly I heard sirens in the distance and, closer, the sound of flapping wings. Gregory was running to the corner, his gun in the air. The entire front right corner of the van had been crushed down to the level of the dashboard.

With the sound of shattering glass still echoing in my ears, I worked my way from the back to the front seat, climbing over debris. Glass crunched under my feet. Murray Daniels was crumpled next to the console, his teeth protruded through his bottom lip. The top of his head was covered with blood. I tried to push the bent metal away from him, but he was wedged in by the collapsed front seat. I leaned in and spoke softly to him, unaware of what I was saying, hearing only sirens and the rush of wings flapping.

I felt a strange calmness as flashing red lights were all around. Someone helped me step backward down to the sidewalk. I straightened up cautiously, the ground still moving. Pigeons flew up from around my feet.

Emergency Service cops pried open the other door. In seconds they were strapping Murray onto a stretcher, slamming doors. The ambulance left for the four-block ride to Beekman Hospital.

I didn't look across the street to 14 Peck Slip; I wouldn't give them the satisfaction. Dirt was in my eyes and mouth, and I could feel blood on my forehead. I started pulling wire mesh away from the frame of the pigeon coop, freeing birds that had survived. My hands were covered with blood, the air was filled with feathers.

"Duty captain wants to talk to us," Gregory said, grabbing the sides of the coop. "This thing must weigh three hundred pounds."

"Nicky's car was gone, right?"

"Yeah," he said. "Murray Daniels is going to be okay, pally. Kids can pull through anything."

"No, they can't," I said.

Gregory pushed me aside and put his big hands into the wire of the pigeon coop and pulled away half the frame. Birds rolled onto the sidewalk. Some birds, like drunks, wandered in circles, trying to negotiate the cobblestone. Some disappeared under parked cars with that strange Charlie Chaplin walk. I felt warm blood running in a track down the side of my face. Above our heads, pigeons fell into a ragged formation, instinctively flying methodical circles around home.

13

THE MORNING sun shone through the branches of the Norway maple I had planted too close to the house. The light, through the curtains, made a dappled pattern on the kitchen table, tiny dots like a Monet. Leigh rolled the insulin bottle slowly between her hands; it clicked against her ring.

She said, "I called Laura Daniels. Her family's all there. I never know what to say."

"He's stable now. It's looking a little better."

"He's in a coma," she said. "Is stable supposed to mean something good?"

In all the years I'd known her, I still couldn't figure her out emotionally. Was she worried now or angry? It always seemed unfair that she should be angry at me for things I couldn't control.

"It was a freak thing, Leigh."

"They're all freak things," she said.

She held up the insulin bottle and drew the milky liquid back into the syringe. "Those two little kids," she said. "They have to be devastated."

I touched the cut on my head; a scab was already starting to form. Leigh flicked the syringe with her finger, working out an air bubble. She looked tired, her eyes dark underneath.

"Leigh, I really don't believe they expected to hit us. It's their wacky thinking, their idea of sending a message. I think it was supposed to miss, scare us. It just caught the corner of the van. They'll back off now."

My neighbor Kelly was in his backyard, pushing his twins on the swing set. I could hear their squeals as they went higher, faces barely visible behind thick scarves.

"You're not retiring now, are you?" she said.

"Not until this is over."

"What happened to Murray Daniels is not your case to investigate."

"That's not the point," I said. "I'm partly responsible."

"Oh, no, you're not. He knew the risks, Anthony."

She placed the syringe on the paper towel and put the insulin back in the refrigerator. She took two shots a day, eight units each. We took turns. I did the spots she couldn't reach, in order to move the injection sites around, so she didn't bruise too badly. She took a deep breath and put her hand on my back as she walked by. A gentle, lingering touch.

"I don't want to argue about this today," she said. "The Daniels's problems are a lot worse than ours."

We've been married long enough to appreciate the little touches that change the tone, avoid big arguments.

"I talked to Margaret yesterday," she said. "They'll be here on the twenty-fourth. Little Katie wants to see her Pop-Pop. I really don't see what that kid sees in you."

"Kids have instinct," I said. "They know the truly good people."

"Margaret said she spoke to someone in the community college there. They're starting a big criminal justice program in the fall. They said they'd love to have a New York City detective with a master's degree on their staff."

"Tell her to get a phone number."

"I think you'd like teaching."

"You sound like my mother."

"Kids like you. The girls certainly will."

She turned her back to me and pulled up her nightgown. I bent and wiped a spot with an alcohol swab, then picked up the syringe.

"Although your bald spot is getting bigger," she said, tapping the crown of my head with a fingernail.

"You're pretty rude," I said. "To a guy who's about to stick a needle in your ass."

I held the syringe like a dart, pumped three times, then plunged it into the soft white flesh she had squeezed between her thumb and forefinger. I pushed in the plunger, emptying the syringe, told her to relax, then pulled the needle out straight.

I said, "Are you breaking these needles off before you throw them away?"

"Stop being a cop, will you, please," she said. "For just five minutes."

"All neighborhoods have junkies, Leigh. They love to find a careless diabetic."

I broke the needle off the syringe and threw it in the trash along with the alcohol swab, a sphere of blood in the center like the Japanese flag.

"Let's talk about Jinx Mulgrew," she said. "Did he have a wife?"

"We see her this Thursday."

"Why wait so long?"

"It wasn't easy to get this interview. She was reluctant, and we didn't want to force it unless we had to. Liam Gregory talked to her for us, arranged the time."

"Did she remarry? Isn't there a time limit, when your husband's missing?"

"There is. But I doubt if she remarried."

I watched her as she washed the coffeepot, intent on the task as if it were spiritual. She had an ability to focus energy on each job, to concentrate on the thing she was doing at that moment and blot out the rest of the world. Not unlike Joe Gregory.

"Why wouldn't she remarry, Anthony?"

"Women of her type don't remarry. Besides, she wasn't positive he was dead."

"What did she think, he was on a world cruise and forgot to tell her?"

"I don't know what she thought. But wives of her generation are different. Marriage to them is a onetime thing, a lifetime commitment."

"Ten years? He doesn't write or call for ten years and she waits. That's not a wife, that's a saint."

"Some women don't know how to do anything except wait."

"Waiting is fine, Anthony. Up to a point. But no woman puts up with being abandoned."

I put my arms around her from behind and pressed her against the sink. "Or their bagels forgotten," I said.

"Especially that."

"I'll remember this week. We're working days."

"So you can Christmas shop on city time."

She turned around, smiling at her little dig. I put my

arms around her and touched my lips against her neck. The warmth of her body was a hearth, a sense of comfort, of permanence.

"I'm glad Margaret and Katie are coming home for Christmas," I said. "I just wish it wasn't such a long drive. I hate that Jersey Turnpike."

"You can't protect everyone," she said.

14

A**T TEN** minutes before noon, on the Monday before Christmas, the wind chill was in the twenties. Gregory and I cleared the revolving door of headquarters and stepped out onto the bricks of the plaza. I was on the way to meet Sidney Kaye, Mulgrew's former partner. Gregory was going to mass. Murray Daniels was comatose in Beekman Hospital.

Over the weekend Joe and I had talked to the 1st Precinct detectives investigating the Daniels incident. But we didn't mention Nicky Skooch and his threats. We couldn't prove anything at this point, and we didn't want two other cops questioning him, allowing him to strut around like a hero. It was personal now. We'd take care of it our way.

Sid Kaye worked as a uniformed security guard in the Woolworth Building. He agreed to meet me during his lunch hour at a bench in City Hall Park, providing I didn't bring Gregory.

"Sid's got a great act," Gregory said. "Don't let him sandbag you. Play to his ego, it's a big one."

Lunchtime bargain hunters hustled toward Canal Street to pick up discontinued hardware items for last minute Christmas gifts. City workers cleaned graffiti off an immense sculpture in the plaza: five rusting steel disks, said to represent the boroughs joined as one city. Gregory said it meant the five crime families joined as one mob. Joe flicked his quick wave and grunted a "Hiya, pally" at cops he knew from the job, or the building, or a dozen fraternal organizations.

"Light a candle for Murray," I said as we reached the church steps.

When we worked days Joe always made the noon mass at St. Andrew's. Everything he needed was within walking distance of One Police Plaza. Out the front door, only a two-minute stroll across the plaza to the oak communion rail of St. Andrews; out the back door, 119 quick steps to the scarred mahogany bar of Brady's.

"Murray's going to be okay," he said. "But, not for nothing, what the fuck you think you're doing? I hear you got an appointment with the pension section."

"How do you know?"

"I know," he said.

People were hustling past us, heads pulled into the collars of their coats. Nobody was eating lunch on benches in this weather.

"I'm curious," I said. "Just like to know how much I could get."

"Curious. You know what they say about curiosity."

"Better get in there before all the holy water is gone."

He walked up a few steps and turned to look at me. "You know, Ryan," he said, "you can't let a woman run your life."

A young Hispanic couple, fresh from the group ceremony at the marriage license bureau, posed coatless and shivering in front of the City Hall Christmas tree. She looked fourteen and hopeful, in a blood red taffeta dress; her hair was curled and piled high, so black it looked blue. The sullen groom wore a powder blue dinner jacket borrowed from a much bigger member of a mariachi band. A heavy gold chain dangled from his bony wrist, a Marielito tattoo on the web of his hand. Sid Kaye sat on a bench, watching the couple, his back to Broadway.

"I hear you're smart, Ryan," he said. "Not like that fucking rummy partner of yours."

"He doesn't drink that much anymore."

"He's not a caped crusader already, is he? Like his old man, the prick. That's the guy you should talk to, the old man. Never trust an ex-drunk, kid."

Sid wore a two-tone blue guard's uniform with a square badge on a big hat. His hairpiece stuck out from under the hat like a bird's nest wedged under the eaves of a split level in Levittown. I tucked my coat under me as I sat on the bench.

"What happened in the market?" he said.

"Something fell off a roof."

"I heard that," he said. "It's always the fucking roofs."

"How's the new job going?" I said. "I love the look of the Woolworth Building. Great building to work in."

"What, do I look like a shmuck to you?" he said. "This is a shmuck's job. I was a first-grader. I should have some cushy corporate security job, a three-hundred-dollar suit. I should be sitting back with a Cuban cigar, some secretary honking my root."

"Jobs like that are scarce."

"If you ain't in the right fucking clique, they are."

"What's the problem?" I said.

"Don't jerk me off, kid. You know what I'm talking about. It's ancient history. Once you get a B number, you're persona non grata."

A B number is an arrest number. Sid was arrested with Jinx, but he never did a day's time. He made a deal with the special prosecutor, giving up Jinx to get probation.

"You could do better than this job," I said.

"Not without the Retired Detectives Association. Not in private security in this town. See, you need contacts in Records and Intelligence, places like that. You got to be hooked into the pipeline. Nobody hires you for your looks, you need connections in the job. No connections, take a walk."

Sid had his cheese sandwich as predicted. Gregory said Sid had eaten a cheese sandwich for lunch every day since junior high. He held the bag and the aluminum foil between his legs as he ate.

"All this came down on you," I said, "when all along it was Jinx who IAD was really after."

"You're stroking me, but I'll tell you anyway. I got grabbed for bullshit. I had no idea that guy was a pimp."

A gang of pigeons crept up on Sid, pecking at sandwich crumbs around his feet. Birds bigger than the ones that fell from the sky onto Murray Daniels. They scattered, wings fluttering, every time Sid spoke.

"You don't believe that, Ryan. I can tell by your face. Swear on my mother, Jinx says the guy owes him money. He had a shitload of scumbag friends I didn't know. I'm standing there like Joe the Glom and the guy hands Jinx powdered money. IAD pricks are taking pictures from the roof and we're both collared."

A gust of wind blew leaves and newspapers down the path. The pigeons huddled near a trash can.

"Take my advice, kid," he said. "Watch the roofs."

"No shit," I said.

A young black man in a studded leather jacket walked along the edge of the park, whispering to passersby, "Grass, blow, grass, blow."

I said, "I guess you and Jinx didn't even hang out in the same places."

"You're some interrogator, you know that? What, are you from the Phil Donahue school? Ever hear of quid pro quo?"

"It's a homicide, Sid. A cop, your partner."

"Yeah, he's dead, and I'm alive. So what are you going to do for me?"

"My partner and I need information on his hangouts. Where would he go after the medal ceremony? What bars did he go to?"

"Your partner," Sid said. "He tell you the time he was a rookie working the circus at old Garden? We get a ten thirteen, cop down, and it's your partner. We pick him up, rush him to Roosevelt, like he's shot or something. We don't know; he's laying there moaning. Come to find out he hit himself in the nuts swinging his nightstick. An asshole, your partner. Like his old man."

I knew I was wasting my time. I hoped Gregory was praying I didn't catch a cold. I handed him the set of Polaroid photos of the naked woman, found in Jinx's locker.

"Nice set of jugs," he said. "Gregory's wife, right? I already bought a dozen wallet size."

"From Mulgrew's locker," I said. "Ever see her before?"

"No way. I never forget a set of tits."

I brushed the crumbs off the Polaroids, then took out a folder on which I had stapled the best of the pictures we'd taken in the fish market. I could see the muscles in his face relax. He must have been remembering the adrenaline rush of an investigation, the seductive street dance of cops and criminals. I wondered if the last surveillance pictures he had seen were of himself.

"Recognize anyone?" I said.

"Everybody's a photographer."

I pointed to a familiar face, and he didn't react.

"Bobo Rizzo," I said.

"No shit, Dick Tracy."

He stood up and brushed the crumbs off his uniform, and the pigeons charged. The remains of his cheese sandwich, carefully rewrapped in aluminum foil, sat in the rolled-up bag in his fist.

"Jinx was my partner, Ryan. And sometimes he was a space cadet. He was obnoxious, a heavy oiler, and he followed his cock around too much. But he never let anyone know his business. Kept it in his hat. Know what I mean?"

"Let me ask you a hypothetical question," I said. "Based on your expertise as a former first-grader."

"Shoot," he said, and pigeons scattered.

"If a corrupt cop, any corrupt cop, was looking for substantial money in the Fulton Fish Market, would he go there looking for Bobo Rizzo?"

"Yes and no," he said. "Think about the place. You don't shit where you eat."

"We talking shitting or eating here? Where did he pick up the money?"

"I hope this ain't leading to a fucking morality lecture."

"If he didn't pick up in the market, then where?"

"Go to the source, north by northwest."

"The Bronx," I said. "You ever go with him?"

"I hate the fucking Bronx, Ryan. Let me tell you, I never did anything heavy with him or anybody else. The market was his baby."

"You're not that naive, Sid. You knew where your envelope was coming from."

"Here we go, holier than thou. Next you're going to tell me you're Saint fucking Ryan. Never took a free meal, or a cup of coffee, or got drunk or laid on duty."

"There are differences, Sid."

"Oh, yeah, meat eaters and grass eaters, brilliant fucking concept. Let me tell you, Ryan, taking is taking. Everybody in this city takes in his own way. Everybody. Except that guy."

He pointed toward City Hall. At first I thought he meant somebody inside City Hall, but he was pointing wide to the left.

"And the only reason that fucking guy don't take," he said, "is because he's got his hands tied behind his back."

He was pointing to the statue of Nathan Hale.

"I'll give you a gift this time," he said. "But next time don't come empty-handed. Try that Italian restaurant on Arthur Avenue in the Four Six Precinct. Rizzo, all of them, used to hang out in there. What more can I do, run the investigation?"

"Watch the roofs, Sid," I said as he shuffled toward Broadway, head down, watching the sidewalk. Not watching the roofs. Not looking into the eyes of Nathan Hale.

15

THAT NIGHT I fell asleep suddenly, like a drop off a cliff. But no one slept through the shock of the telephone at three A.M. The receiver was moving to my ear while the ring echoed off bedroom walls. Leigh sat up rigidly, listening for a tone of voice, a hint of a name, parents, kids. Surely she hoped the tragedy was in my world and not hers. I said, "Yeah, yeah," into the phone while patting Leigh on the hip to reassure her.

"Who is it?" she finally said.

"Work," I said while the dispatcher apologized. She said she was instructed to notify me in case of any major crime pertaining to the Fulton Fish Market.

"Zipper," I said, stretching to hang up the phone.

"Who?" Leigh said. "Not another cop?"

"No, a civilian helping us with a case."

"An informant?"

"Yeah, an informant."

She rolled over and was almost back to sleep before I had my pants on. I kissed her cheek, and she mumbled, "Be careful," without opening her eyes. This was good. A cop's wife who couldn't sleep had big problems.

I called Joe Gregory from the kitchen, then took the

Major Deegan to the Cross Bronx, then the Harlem River Drive into the FDR, nonstop. At this hour the empty streets of New York become a Grand Prix for cabs, crooks, and cops. I drove unhindered, the lights of the city stretched out before me, past the UN, past Bellevue, past the Fulton Fish Market. I drove by Wall Street, a street named when a handful of the first settlers built a high fence to keep the savages away. Now neither fences nor walls could insure safety on streets purchased for so few trinkets.

My Nova flew on its own, like an old ranch mare, knowing the trails. I swung around the tip of Manhattan at the Battery, coming out of the tunnel on the West Side. Lady Liberty seemed to move farther away at night.

I kept telling myself that these things had nothing to do with me. Senseless violence occurred every night in the world we lived in. Then I wondered if I, too, so familiar with the terrain of that violent world, was cruising on automatic pilot.

I parked my car next to a line of Christmas trees leaning against ropes strung between telephone poles, the smell of pine surprisingly powerful. Two uniformed cops stood next to Styrofoam cups steaming on the roof of a radio car. They pointed down a flight of stairs to the basement. Under the Greenwich Bar.

The dark red outline on the faded linoleum could have been a spilled gallon of dago red. But I knew it wasn't. Zipper's body was spread-eagled by the TV. A dark purple wound in his left temple left no doubt about the MO. His hair was matted with dark dried blood. Gray hair. I'd never seen his hair before. The room smelled like food burning on the stove.

"This is nobody's fault," Joe Gregory said.

"Sure, right," I said.

Gregory said, "He took one to the head, small-caliber."

"Something burning on the stove?" I said.

"Garbage. This is the basement," Gregory said. "Garbage outside."

The photographer from Crime Scene Unit snapped pictures working in clockwise circles, getting progressively closer to the body. He knelt, he stood on a chair, he crouched over the body. Working as though it were a layout for *Vogue*. Detective Sylvia D'Angelo from the 1st Precinct sketched the room on a spiral pad, noting the spatial relationship of objects to the body. Photographs could be deceiving where depth was concerned.

"About two-fifteen," Gregory said. "Lady upstairs hears a dog barking. She says Zip's dog never barks. She hears a gunshot, calls nine one one. Uniforms outside were first on the scene."

"She see anybody?" I said.

"Sylvia says yeah, but she's scared. She's going back to talk to her again."

"Hot in here," I said.

"Close to the boiler."

In the windowless bedroom a metal single bed stood against a back wall. Next to the bed was a nightstand without a book and a Mickey Mouse table lamp. The lone dresser was untouched; they hadn't even tried to make it look like robbery. Magazine pictures were taped to the rough cement block wall: a black-and-white Ted Kluszewski, a Carl Yastrzemski. A picture of Pope John Paul II bore fresh Scotch tape.

"You knew the vic, right, Anthony?" Sylvia D'Angelo said. "He a CI or something?"

"I don't want to see it in the papers," I said. "The guy was a little slow, but he was decent. Not a lowlife."

She smiled and nodded as if she understood. We had worked with Sylvia on a stock swindle. Good cop. Even Gregory admitted that.

"Is this linked to the thing with Murray Daniels?" she said.

"Without a doubt," I said.

"You have any ideas on a possible shooter," she said, "you'll let me know."

"You need his name, Sylvia?" I said, pointing to the body.

"Poniatowski. It's all over the place. What I need is a next of kin."

"G-r-e-g-o-r-y," Joe said. "Put me down if you can't find anyone else. We might be cousins."

"Something's definitely burning," Sylvia said.

The medical examiner came down the steps. He wore gray wool pants and tassel loafers under a Burberry raincoat.

"What the fuck is burning?" the doctor said.

The smell was coming from the corner of the living room, near the radiator. Gregory walked over and pulled a stuffed chair aside, then the drapes.

"Jesus Christ," Sylvia said.

"Don't touch him," I said. "Call the ASPCA."

The room filled with the smell of burned hair and skin. A small brown-and-white dog trembled as it pushed back into the corner, against the radiator, burning and trying desperately to get away from us. Vacant-eyed, the dog shook violently as Gregory leaned down.

"Call the ASPCA, damn it," I said to Sylvia's partner. "Joe, wait. They know what they're doing."

Gregory grabbed the dog by his collar and pulled him away from the radiator. He lifted the animal and held it to his chest. The squirming dog smudged Joe's raincoat like a thumb signing the cross with holy ashes.

"The keys are in my pocket, pally," Joe said. "Manhattan Animal Hospital, Twenty-ninth and First. We'll be there before those guys get out of bed."

There was something different about lower Manhattan at night. More than the deserted, cavernous streets. Ghostly clouds of sewer gas rose from the pavement, hinting at some conflagration below. Traffic lights clicked nervously, performing to an empty house. It had the sense of a city abandoned, waiting for Armageddon: too bright to be so empty. Joe Gregory said that the lights are brighter down here because they're closer to the Battery.

"Is this Koch?" Gregory said.

"Koch is a Doberman," I said. "Koch is the watchdog in the club. This is Zip's mutt, I don't know his name."

I drove up the ramp to the FDR. To our right, bridge and boat lights twinkled, reflecting in the dark river.

"After Christmas," Gregory said, "we go back on nights. Nail these scumbags."

Gregory murmured to the dog as I drove through the red light on First and turned into the hospital driveway. The dog was breathing more slowly, soothed by his words. Knowing he was in good hands.

16

THE MORNING of Thursday December 23 we jumped traffic lights all the way up Twelfth Avenue, then turned east up the Fifty-seventh Street hill. We were working days before Christmas, trying to get through all the routine steps in the investigation before we went back on nights.

We'd stopped by the hospital, but nothing had changed. Inspector Neddy Flanagan had arranged a private room and nurse for Murray Daniels. Neddy was the Mother Teresa of the NYPD, somehow arranging the best hospitals, doctors, and special care for cops and their families. But now we were late, and Mrs. Jinx Mulgrew was waiting.

"She was a cop's wife," Joe Gregory said. "She'll wait."

We passed the DEA office at the triple nickel, 555 W. 57th Street, passed the CBS news center, then over the crest of the hill at Tenth Avenue. Sunlight flashed between the high rises, in staccato bursts, like the flashbulbs of a gauntlet of paparazzi.

"Speaking of waiting," I said. "How long is Vince Salvatore going to make us wait on that white barrel?"

"After Christmas, he says. Lot of guys on vacation."

"Then the river will be too icy, some other excuse."

"What can I tell you?" Gregory said.

The Buick windshield was streaked with slime and soot. Ashes, crumbs, coffee lids, and cigarette butts littered the floor. Cops' cars, like taxis and the cabs of long-haul truckers, were homes and took on the unique smells of the people who inhabited them. Ours smelled like the fish market. Tires threw fish slime up into the undercarriage, where it was absorbed like rustproofing, for the life of the vehicle.

"Maybe if we have the car steam-cleaned," I said, "it'll get this smell out."

"It's atmosphere," he said. "People pay big bucks for atmosphere."

I'd spent a sleepless night trying to find a reason why I shouldn't feel responsible for Murray and Zipper. Like all investigators, I knew there was no such thing as coincidence; everything was cause and effect. But one advantage of being a cop was that it provided an avenue to absolution. Or at least a back street to revenge.

The Crime Scene Unit had found a partial bloody print on a doorjamb in Zipper's house. Sylvia D'Angelo was checking it against the prints on file of a list of names I gave her. We offered to help, but Eddie Shick said to work on our own case, informants were expendable.

"Goddamn sun, you can't see shit," Gregory said, peering through the streaks, cigarette clenched in his teeth.

I said, "The mistake we made was letting that FPS car see us talking to Zip. Sloppy, very sloppy."

"They killed him, we didn't," Gregory said. "They

knew he was a few nickels short of a quarter; no way he could hurt them. But they don't give a rat's ass about that. All's they know is they see him talking to us and it might be trouble for them. So they whack him. Now we owe them double."

A small platoon of hot dog vendors filed out of a garage near Ninth Avenue, marching toward midtown to take battle stations for the lunch wars. Under orange-striped umbrellas they leaned into the weight of metallic carts that glinted in the sun. As we drove across Ninth Avenue Gregory jerked his thumb toward Fifty-Eighth Street, Roosevelt Hospital.

"If I get shot around here, bring me to Roosevelt."

He was always adding to the list of things I should do if he was shot, especially his approved hospitals list: Bellevue on the East Side; Harlem Hospital if we're uptown. They knew gunshot wounds. No designer hospitals, please.

"Don't take me to Beekman Downtown for bullet wounds," he said. "Only if I take a heart attack. They specialize in cardiac, because of Wall Street."

"What about ulcers?"

"Cops don't get ulcers, they give them," he said. "Besides, Roosevelt's where they took John Lennon."

"That's a good reason."

"And you can sell my glasses," he said.

John Lennon's little round eyeglasses had become a cop story, the kind Gregory loved. The story is this: A uniformed cop from the 20th Precinct was at the shooting scene in front of the Dakota and picked up the dying singer's glasses. He later quietly sold them for four figures to a Beatles' collector. He wasn't caught until after the sale of the fifth pair.

"After Christmas," Gregory said, craning his neck, looking up for street signs, "we'll get even with these bastards."

Seventieth Street between Columbus and Central Park West is a picture-postcard New York street, lined with brownstones, bushes, and BMWs. Small white Christmas lights laced the bare trees. Number 61 was in the middle of the block. A dozen steps up to oak doors, a polished-brass knob. Gregory rang the bell.

A tall woman appeared in the spotless glass of the door. She had white hair, pulled severely back into a bun, cheekbones and posture that said money. I introduced myself, but Ellen Mulgrew stared at Joe Gregory.

"I know who you are," she said to Joe. She was still staring as I apologized for being late. Still staring when I shook her outstretched hand. A hand stronger, more callused, than I expected.

"Are you a gardener?" I said.

She gave me a wide-eyed look as if she were waiting for me to say something else. I thought I might have insulted her.

"Sometimes," she said. "I go through periods where gardening interests me."

The house smelled of pine and seemed airy, but it was too warm. She took our coats and vanished into a walk-in closet.

"This is a wonderful house," I said. "Probably worth a great deal now that the West Side has come back so strongly."

As she closed the closet door she looked around as if considering this for the first time. We were in a small alcove with a round window that looked out over the street.

"My father's money bought this place, Detective. Long before I met John." Her face flushed a little. Her complexion had the blush of fresh air mistakenly attributed to country people.

"I didn't mean anything by that," I said. "I apologize if you thought I meant something else."

"My father was Michael Harding of Fenrich, Smith and Harding. I have this house and a substantial trust fund."

I didn't expect this woman. I expected one of the cops' widows I'd met at a hundred wakes. Some frumpy, frightened woman worn down from a lifetime of waiting for her husband to return from a crime scene, or a drinking bout, or another woman. She turned and walked down the hall with the athletic gait of the people who walked this city every day of their lives.

The living room seemed as if it should have been roped off. The furniture was fragile and delicate, something out of a museum. A sofa and chair had a burgundy covering, patterned with small flowers. The arms and legs were a thin, curving dark wood. Framed photographs covered much of the wall space. A large Oriental rug covered the floor, a path worn to the window.

"Who's the photographer?" I said.

"My husband," she said, sounding as if she expected me to know that. "He took his own, and collected as well. That's a Lou Stoumen you're looking at. It's one of John's favorites."

It was a black-and-white overhead shot of Times Square in the rain, 1940. Mickey Rooney was appearing in person at the Loew's State, *Gone With the Wind* at the Astor, too rainy for smoke rings from the Camel sign.

"Forty's the year Ryan was born," Gregory said. "It rained all that year."

Ellen smiled for the first time. Not a smile, just a crinkling around the eyes. She kept her hands behind her back snapping her thumb's nail with that of her index finger. In the quiet I could hear the near imperceptible click.

"Well, shall we sit?" she said.

Joe and I sat on the sofa. He tugged his jacket, pulled his tie, and sat up straight. He seemed uncomfortable, too big for this delicate setting, like a parent at a kindergarten desk. The dark coffee table shone with furniture polish, reflecting light from several small lamps in the room. Everything was glossy, immaculate.

Although we hadn't asked, she began telling us of the last time she saw her husband. Ellen Mulgrew told the story, looking at Joe Gregory, while I made notes.

It was the same story she had told investigators ten years ago: Jinx left that morning around nine A.M., on his way to the Police Academy for the ceremony. He was wearing his uniform, she had sewn the new NYPD patch on it that morning. He seemed to be in a good mood, happy about presenting the medal. It was the last she'd seen of him.

When she finished I asked, "Where do you think he might have gone in the afternoon? Did he have a favorite bar or restaurant he always talked about?"

"Once he walked out that door, he could have gone to Tahiti for all I knew." She looked at me, her head held firm. The clicking of the thumbnail started.

"How would you characterize your relationship?" I said.

"How would you characterize yours?" she said, pointing to my wedding ring.

"Close," I said. "We talk, I tell her things, some things about cases, places I go."

"Does your wife know where you are now?" she said.

"Good point," I said. "But she knows where I stop to have a drink. She knows who my friends are."

"Oh, really," she said. "Well, I didn't. I'm sure he had plenty of friends. But I didn't know them."

"You sound bitter," I said.

"Do I? Well, I'm not. I think bitterness is such an ugly quality."

I wanted to tell Gregory to jump in any time he felt like, but he stood up and walked to the piano and picked up a photograph.

"Did your husband keep any notes, Mrs. Mulgrew?" I said. "Did he have a desk somewhere, any files he kept?"

"A file cabinet, in his darkroom," she said.

"Darkroom?" I said. It wasn't mentioned in the IAD report. "May we see it, please?"

She stood and rearranged the frames Joe had picked up, then pointed upstairs. The darkroom, adjacent to a bathroom at the head of the stairs, was the size of a walk-in closet. The door had a hasp and probably had once been padlocked, but it didn't appear to be forcibly removed. The red light above the door still worked. Ellen Mulgrew didn't come up with us, she waited at the foot of the stairs.

Dust rose in a shaft of light when the door unstuck and slammed back. The inside light didn't work. A table ran the length of room along the right wall, a small sink in the back. A two-drawer metal filing cabinet sat next to the sink at the dark end of the room. The room smelled stale and metallic, the way your hands smell after counting coins.

I held the door open with my foot and tried to read over Joe's back as he thumbed through the files. Light from the hall was all we had. The top drawer was half-full. Both drawers were sloppy, papers shoved into folders, creased and wrinkled.

"We need light," Gregory said. "We'll get this file somewhere we can read, some place we can breathe." He walked out to find Mrs. Mulgrew.

Above me, blackened negatives hung curled in decay from a nylon rope; others had fallen to the table. I reached into the back of the cabinet to see if anything had been wedged behind files. As I pulled my hand out, the tops of my knuckles touched paper. I squatted and saw something wedged into a crack in the metal. It was a small envelope.

Gregory was talking to Ellen from the top step, "This room might be dangerous. We'll come back and clean this up, throw these old chemicals away."

"That isn't necessary," she said.

Inside the envelope was a black-and-white photograph of seven men posing in front of a fishing boat. The only one I could recognize, in the dim light, was a young Jinx Mulgrew. I stuffed it into my pocket.

"To tell you the truth," Gregory said, "there's some old pictures in there, guys my father might know. He might enjoy seeing them. If it's okay with you."

"That would be fine," she said. "That would be fine."

"We'll dump those old chemicals when we come

back," Gregory said. "Clean out all the old junk in here."

Ellen Mulgrew retrieved our coats from the hall closet. She had buttoned them all the way up before she put them on the hanger. When we walked outside I turned to say good-bye, but she'd already closed the door.

17

After leaving Ellen Mulgrew, we drove back downtown. It was late afternoon and snowing lightly when we walked into Brady's Bar. I loved the feel of bars at Christmastime. Sinatra was on the jukebox. The ceiling was crisscrossed with red and green Christmas lights that would stay up until St. Patrick's Day. The air was warm and damp and smelled of cigars, pine needles, and wet wool from a dozen damp overcoats. The crowd at the bar was three deep with guys from headquarters, jammed hip to hip, belly to the wood. And Brady's was a cop's bar: no ferns, no quiche, no lawyers.

Gregory went straight to the bar. I walked back into the empty dining room, laid my raincoat across the back of the last booth. On days like this the coat rack was buried under more beat-up London Fogs than a Columbo look-alike contest, and you could easily leave with a worse raincoat than you came in with. I knew, because I'd done it.

I slid into the booth and snapped on the light. Inside the envelope, in addition to the fishing photo, were several negatives that appeared to be of the same picture. Seven men, holding beer bottles, posed in front of a white fishing boat, the *Montauk Queen*. All seven looked wrecked from a day of fishing and drinking. I recognized two of them: Jinx Mulgrew and a thinner, dark-haired Bobo Rizzo. Behind them, a shark hung from a hook. The shadows of dusk striped a wooden dock.

Gregory came back with a couple of glasses and two Molson ales and a Guinness Stout.

"That was quick," I said.

"Brady, that asshole," he said.

"What's wrong?"

"He's breaking my balls about this case. I tell you one thing: You show me one ex-cop who isn't bitter about retiring, and I'll personally handle your send-off racket."

Johnny Brady now called himself a restaurateur, but before he retired he was a big man in plainclothes. We could only guess where his down payment came from.

"He's worried," I said. "He spent some time in the First Division, same time as Jinx."

"So did a hundred other guys. They ain't breaking my balls."

"Not yet," I said.

Gregory put on his glasses and held the photo directly under the bulb. Joe was the one who taught me always to look for pictures. He'd said we should give all the criminals cameras, they loved to frame themselves.

The Brady's Bar wall, stripped to the original brick, was filled with black-and-white photographs. Above us were the booking photo of Willie Sutton and a picture of a young Detective Brady. He was squatting over the body of a mobster with a black hole in his face, pointing at something with a pencil: an entrance or exit hole.

"This is Jinx here, with the Greek fishing hat," Gregory said.

"Anyone else?"

"This is many, many moons ago."

The bar was decorated with things Johnny Brady had "found" throughout his career. The benches, once church pews, were a blond wood, with high curved side pieces. The tables, from a Chinese restaurant, had small flower designs inlaid in the plum-colored tile. A round stained-glass window was directly above the booth. I could hear the bass boom of laughter from the bar.

"This is Sidney Kaye," Gregory said. "Looks different without his rug."

I downed the ale in two swigs, refilled the glass. The first one of the day is always the best.

"And Neddy Flanagan," Gregory said. "His Holiness, right here."

"Where?" I said, and pulled the picture around.

I wouldn't have recognized Neddy. His hair was dark, cut in a flattop; the smile was something I'd never seen before. But it was his outfit that fooled me: a matching cabana shirt and shorts. Everyone else was in T-shirts.

"We have problems," I said. "Look at the guy in the upside-down sailors hat. Next to Neddy."

"Looks like a ginzo," he said.

"Put white hair on him, like Jerry Vale."

He stared, concentrating, as I listened to Sinatra imbue a Christmas song with irony. "Have Yourself a Merry Little Christmas." Nobody understood the mood of a song like Sinatra.

"Bobo Rizzo," he said.

"Look like buddies, don't they?"

"They looked shit-faced," he said.

"What was Neddy doing there?"

"Years ago," Gregory said, still staring at the photo, "Neddy was a fishing nut, a freaking fishing psycho. Any precinct fishing trip, Queens, Bronx, wherever, he'd be there, pole in hand."

"But he stopped doing that," I said. "When? What about the clothes? When did he start dressing like the monsignor?"

Gregory sat back against the straight-backed pew, his face half-hidden by the overhanging light. The flame from his lighter rose behind the lamp. Smoking was Gregory's stage prop as well as his habit.

"You trying to say Neddy killed Jinx?" Gregory said. "Then had a radical personality change? I think not."

"Why was this envelope hidden in the cabinet? Coincidence? It's not inconceivable that Jinx was blackmailing Neddy."

"For what? What could Neddy give him? Besides . . . kill him over it?"

Gregory poured a couple of ounces of Guinness stout into my ale and his. It sank like sludge in the Kill Van Kull.

"Let's ask him," I said.

"Let's hold off a little while before we step on our cocks."

"Until we make first grade," I said.

"Give me a break, will you? What I'm saying is let's get something we can hang our hats on before we dump his career down the hopper. We can discreetly ID the other guys in the picture. We need a little more before we start making accusations."

Crosby sang "White Christmas" in those smooth, lazy

tones. I wondered why rock music had decided the vocalist needn't be talented. Gregory kept squinting at the picture, looking for someone else he might have seen at a racket, or the firing range at Rodman's Neck, or a bar stool in some local cop bar, or a parade detail, or the long benches in criminal court.

"Don't tell Eddie Shick about this picture," Gregory said. "He'll make a beeline to Neddy."

"What then? Back to the market, right?"

A pink neon beer sign flickered on the side of Gregory's rough face, making his eyes appear even darker. He raised the beer glass and drained it. "We got a score to settle down there," he said. "We do nothing else, we settle that score. We owe Murray that, anyway."

I put the picture in the envelope and slid it back into my shirt.

Gregory said, "First let's try Sid Kaye again. He knows things. Knowledge is power."

"But he wants things. Things we can't arrange."

"Nothing we can't arrange, pally. I'm about to call in a long overdue contract."

Gregory took out his ancient leather address book and wrapped the two rubber bands around his fingers. Then he put on his glasses. Guys like us first notice our eyes are going bad when we can't read a telephone book in a bar.

"Sid was a brother officer," Gregory said. "Now he's on the balls of his ass, doing square badge security jobs. Living like a freaking rag man in Queens. He deserves a break."

I told Joe to call Vince Salvatore while he was on the phone. Remind him about the white barrel. Then I watched the Great Gregory waving his arms, making gestures with his hands, talking to the phone as if the instrument were a person. He was a telephone detective, an artist on the wire.

Over the years I had become more cautious on the phone, always hearing a low buzz or someone's shallow breathing. I'd spent hundreds of hours in damp basements listening to wiretaps and bugs. Now whenever I'm on the phone I see a middle-aged white man wearing earphones, in a tiny room clouded with cigarette smoke. He listens quietly, listing my sins on a lined yellow pad.

While Gregory talked I went to the bar, ordered another Molson. Patti O rapped her knuckles on the bar to let me know it was on her. An old detective sitting next to me, with a web of fine crimson lines across his nose, moved off his stool, walked to the other end of the bar. He wasn't being polite; I knew why he moved away.

"No thanks," I said. "Only women and drunks sit in bars."

I stood with my foot on the rail and listened as Shanahan from Missing Persons told a story about a girl he met when he was a foot cop in the Bronx. She was a big girl with the wild, boozed-out look of Janis Joplin. She wore a whistle around her neck and a necklace heavy with the brass collar numerals of dozens of NYPD precincts. She said she was working hard to increase her collection. He paused to properly describe what she offered for his. I stood shoulder to shoulder with my people. Glasses in hand, we listened to the story of our life.

18

The day before Christmas was bright and sunny. I took Sidney Kaye to lunch at the Twilite Inn on Dover Street. Somehow Joe Gregory had worked out a private security job for Sid. I was supposed to extract our part of the contract.

"Ryan, tell me this ain't a bullshit job," Sid said as we walked in. "I'm not a gofer, some shit like that."

"You're an investigator, Sid. The largest private security firm in Brooklyn. Handle cases, the works."

The Twilite Inn is a mom-and-pop restaurant hiding under the Manhattan approach to the Brooklyn Bridge. Its clientele is mostly graying New York men, searching for the place they came from. Out-of-towners who accidentally turn into Dover Street back out immediately, positive the road goes nowhere.

But the elderly couple who own the Twilite aren't out to get rich on tourists. They don't advertise, the place needs painting, the tables don't match. Some silverware says "U.S. Army," some says "Bickford's." But there's no wine steward, no menus, and no patience for complainers.

"I hate bullshitters, kid," Sid said. "Never let your mouth write a check your ass can't cash."

"We're not playing Santa," I said. "We expect a return."

The place smelled of pine and garlic. Every Christmas the owners cleared out half a dozen tables to make room for a Douglas fir. Needles were all over the floor.

"I don't do names," Sid said, jabbing me with his finger. "No cops' names."

We picked up plates and stood in the lunch line of stockbrokers and sewer workers, guys from Con Ed and Ma Bell, investment bankers and off-duty bartenders, all filing into the step-down kitchen, where they served directly from pots on the stove. Sid put his silverware in his shirt pocket and inhaled the aroma of real food. He could pass on the cheese sandwich when someone else was buying.

The line circled around the old woman obediently, as if she were the housemother in a middle-aged Boys' Town. She knew everybody's name; some guys ate more meals here than at home. Today's lunch was the Christmas special: roast turkey, stuffing and mashed potatoes, string beans, cranberry sauce. I ordered two beers, then grabbed a corner table near the Wurlitzer with the old records.

"Tell me what you know so far," Sid said.

I told him about our surveillance of 14 Peck Slip. About watching Salvy take thousands of pounds of fish a night, then deliver it to R&B Fish. I showed him the pictures Murray Daniels had taken, but he bitched about the poor quality and said something about lots of new faces in ten years.

"R and B Fish is mob owned," Sid said. "Stands for

Roberta and Barbara, Sal Mags's two daughters. Stolen fish is sold through R and B."

Sal Magliozzi had been the boss of the Genovese family until his death six months ago—oddly, by natural causes. Within days after his death the Ravenite Social Club bricked over the front windows, preparing for war.

"The club above Fourteen Peck Slip," Sid said, "is like a clearing house for money, everything. A command center for all the scams, union problems, that shit. Rizzo runs the show from upstairs, in the Box Hook Club."

"Rizzo's not there anymore, Sid. A guy named Bongiovanni seems to be the boss."

"Big guy, big head, right? I know him. Used to be muscle. When this happen?"

"I don't know," I said. "What does it mean?"

"Rizzo used to be there every night. Figure it out yourself."

Sid sipped at his brew, then wiped his mouth with the napkin he'd stuck in his shirt collar. A white-haired man in a trench coat and fedora stood over the jukebox, staring vacantly out the window, as if there were some better place to be. He was deep in reverie, his lips moving in some long-gone conversation. Vaughn Monroe sang "Dance Ballerina, Dance."

"How much money are we talking about?" I said.

"Total?" he said. "Fulton Fish Market does about five hundred million a year. But who really knows? It's a big cash business. Figure tapping alone: Jinx estimated the club steals over three thousand pounds of fish a night. Just that, you're talking ten grand nightly."

"Any of the wholesalers ever complain?"

"Give me a break, Ryan. Nobody down there is losing money. Price of fish goes up."

Two guys in suits walked through the door with a woman in a suit. Conversation stopped for a second as everybody looked up at the woman. Three assistant DAs, slumming.

"You got your parking contracts," Sid said. "And the unloading scam, the security scam, and on and on."

"Why is unloading a scam?"

"Trucks come in from the ocean," Sid said. "Have to be unloaded, right? The unloading crews charge each truck so much, like a buck a crate, to unload. But if you're a driver, don't hold your breath waiting. Know what I mean? And then, you're going to love this. They charge each buyer to load the fish into his fucking truck. Same fish, same deal: no service, pay with a smile."

A big-band song was playing. The old man in the fedora swayed, eyes closed.

"What's the union role in this?" I said.

"What do you think it is?"

Sid rolled his eyes up toward the high tin ceiling. Two fans turned slowly in the smoky haze, one directly over Sid's head. He watched it warily, as if it were the blade of the guillotine. The line from the kitchen stretched past the men's room.

"It's all illegal as hell," Sid said. "Problem is, you'll never get a complainant. Wholesalers, truckers, everybody's scared shitless. You need the feds, Labor Department. Better yet, the IRS."

Sid ate with his arms around the plate, as if afraid someone were going to snatch it away from him. He ate like he talked, in quick, furtive movements, eyes rolling around the room.

"How would you handle this case?" I said.

"I'd go after the bosses," he said. "They'd be the only

ones with knowledge about who whacked Jinx. You check out that restaurant I gave you? The one in the Bronx, down the block from the Sons of Sicily?"

"They hang out in half a dozen locations up there. Which one are you meaning?"

"The one Sal Mags owned, on the corner. What the fuck you waiting for, Ryan? Somebody to come in and give himself up?"

Sid was smirking and chewing. On top of the world.

"Tell you a story about this guy Bongiovanni and that restaurant," he said. "Bongiovanni was a punk. A car thief and consignment guy when he was a kid in the Bronx. Then this one day he's hanging outside that restaurant, and this old Italian guy in an apron comes running out. He's chasing this black kid, or Puerto Rican, I heard it both ways. The old man's screaming, saying the kid ate clams, refused to pay. Old man grabs the kid, begins to hit him. Kid pulls a knife and stabs the old geezer. Bongiovanni comes to the old man's rescue. When the cops show up the black kid is dead on the sidewalk. Suffocated. Whole clam shells stuffed down his throat. Ugo tells the cops, 'Hey, you know niggers don't know how to eat clams.' Ugo does forty-nine months in Attica, comes back a legend in the neighborhood. The old man was Sal Mags's father."

"How fortunate for Ugo."

"Sal set him up working for Bobo," Sid said.

"What did Bobo think about that?"

"Hated the bastard," Sid said. "Ugo was a mover, started mooching in on a lot of Bobo's action. Blood started flowing the day Ugo came. If he's running the market now, you can bet your ass he's getting complete cooperation. Vicious bastard."

"Maybe Bobo wants to get back at him?"

"That's good," he said, holding a forkful of mashed potatoes. "You're thinking now. Maybe there's hope for you yet."

"Ten years ago Bobo was the boss in the market," I said. "Maybe he's bitter about being replaced."

"Wouldn't you be? Bobo didn't do the hit on Jinx himself, either. The contract probably went to some button man."

"Some ambitious bastard like Ugo Bongiovanni," I said.

"Adds up. He was the muscle. You got a point, kid. About time."

I still had half a plate of food. Sid Kaye had managed to talk and eat everything on his plate plus all the bread.

"Whatever happened to Mulgrew's notebooks?" I said.

"I got no knowledge about any notes. Never saw the man write note one. Kept it all in his head. I shit you not."

"If Jinx didn't keep notes," I said, "how did you know he wasn't screwing you on the pad money?"

"You didn't know the guy, you wouldn't say that. I'd sure as shit rather be in a foxhole with him than your partner."

It always amazed me. Sid was walking the line between confessing enough to win salvation, while avoiding the near occasion of disloyalty. Disloyalty to a job that had dumped him after stalking him from the roofs.

I said, "You're still stroking me about one thing, Sid. We both know he had to give his partner a phone number, where to reach him. A bar, a woman's apartment."

"Who remembers phone numbers? The guy liked broads. Don't make him a bad guy. Broads brought down a lot of guys in this job. Sometime ask your partner's old man, that holier-than-thou prick, why Jinx threw a punch at him in Brooklyn."

"Over a woman?" I said.

"What else, a fucking ham sandwich?"

He stood up, wiped his mouth with the napkin, and threw it on the plate. "You know the problem with your generation, Ryan? You think you invented everything, including fucking. I just hope you ain't blowing smoke up my ass about this job."

"The job is legitimate," I said.

"No job worth anything is legitimate. I got some shopping to do, couple of suits. Maybe we'll talk later."

"Count on it," I said. "We're not even."

Sid opened a pack of Rolaids and popped two in his mouth. "I got this guy in Chinatown," he said, crunching antacids. "Good suits, cheaper than wholesale. I'll get you his card."

"No thanks, Sid."

"Suit yourself. Buy fucking retail."

"Have a Merry Christmas, Sid."

"Don't get sucked in by that Christmas shit, Ryan. It's just another reason to watch the roofs."

19

THE SILENCE of the cold Christmas afternoon was broken only by the shrieks of children. I walked around the outside of the house with my granddaughter on my shoulders, checking the roof for signs of reindeer hoofprints or sled tracks. Out in the street Kelly's kids raced in circles, chasing a remote-control Corvette. The thump-thump of a new basketball echoed from a driveway somewhere. I told Katie the brown stain near the chimney had to be reindeer poop, and I watched her reflection in the window as she stared, her eyes the immense, deep brown of Leigh's.

I ducked through the doorway as Katie rang a hanging bell. The smell of turkey still filled the house. I could hear the voices of my wife and daughter over the pots and pans at the sink, discussing a trip to Murray Daniels's house. Leigh had made a tree ornament for Laura and had toys for the kids. I took Katie's coat off and hung it in the closet.

"Last chance, Anthony," Leigh said from the kitchen. "Sure you don't want to go?"

The last time I saw Laura Daniels was the day it happened. I tried to visit Murray often, but my visits were usually late and Laura had gone home. Christmas Day was not a day I wanted to see Murray Daniels's family.

Margaret said, "We'll leave Katie with Dad. Make them both happy."

I plugged in the Christmas lights and sat on the floor. They started blinking again. After a few seconds they stopped blinking, then they started again, a will of their own. Katie dropped Chutes and Ladders at my feet, sat down opposite me. Despite all the new toys, she seemed more thrilled with the stash of old games she'd discovered piled in the hall closet. I couldn't remember playing half of them with Anthony and Margaret.

Margaret was telling Leigh about the teaching job in the community college. She asked Leigh if she really thought I'd like it. Leigh said it would be a very big change.

Joe Gregory thinks I'm too influenced by the women in my life. He'd be at Brady's today, watching a football game on the tube. The place would be crowded with cops, as it was every holiday, especially family holidays: Christmas, Thanksgiving, and Mother's Day.

Katie flicked the metal spinner again, getting three jumps instead of one up the ladder. After we came into the house she went into my dresser and took out one of my old T-shirts to wear as a nightgown.

"Your turn, Pop-Pop," Katie said.

"Finally," I said.

I spun and moved to a chute, slid down, all the way back. I grabbed my head and cried in disgust, and she laughed. She laughed at everything I said; it always surprised me. She was the only one who thought I was funny. I wondered when I'd stopped being funny to the rest of my family. The tree lights started blinking again. Leigh and Margaret whispered.

For Christmas I had given Leigh pearl earrings and a long red flannel robe. She'd given me a copy of *The Stories of John Cheever* and a clock that told the tides.

"I won," Katie said. "Let's not play again."

Katie pushed the game aside. The floor was covered with doll clothes. Sometimes I found it hard to believe that I was a grandfather. But I'm one of the few able to put panty hose on a Barbie doll. Katie yawned and crawled up, wrapping her arms and legs around me. Last night I'd stayed in bed with her until she'd fallen asleep, assuring her that Santa would find her here, because this was her home, too.

"We're going," Leigh said, putting on her coat. She wore her new earrings and a scarf Margaret made.

"You don't have to hold her all the time, Dad," Margaret said. "You can put her down."

Leigh didn't say good-bye. She was not happy about my working nights next week. I'd promised it would only be for a week, two weeks tops. She was worried about my working long stretches of nights, because she knew it was easy to lose touch.

It happened to cops all the time: guys work all night, sleep all day. They lose track of wives, kids, days, months, lies they've told, bars they can't get back into, women they've screwed, stories about them that aren't true. I'm older now, past those days.

This big house was the problem. Leigh never complained when the kids were home, but now the house is too quiet, too empty. She'd begun hearing tapping against the window, house noises she had slept through for twenty years. And Margaret and Katie were going back to South Carolina on Wednesday.

I carried Katie to the rocker, feeling the warmth of her body. I didn't like to admit it, but I couldn't remember many moments like this with my own children. Moments that I was so acutely aware of their love. I was too busy with cases or night school, or else I was hung over. Their loss, my loss. Katie sighed and held my shirt in her fist.

20

On a foggy Thursday morning, the next-to-last day of 1982, Joe Gregory and I rode the ferry over the choppy two-thirds–mile channel from City Island to Hart Island. Behind us, City Island was a part of the Bronx that looked like a New England fishing village. Looming ahead lay the wasteland of Hart Island, for over one hundred years the potter's field for the city of New York. I held on to the cold metal railing as City Island and our brown Buick faded to gray in the mist.

The only vehicle aboard the ferry was the morgue wagon, an eighteen-foot Ford truck. In the rear of the truck the body of Casimir "Zipper" Poniatowski was stacked in one of fourteen adult pine coffins that cost the city of New York $32.90 each, including tar-paper lining and zinc nails.

Sixto Caban, the wagon driver, assuming we were special guests, recited the VIP spiel as we approached the windblown and strangely primitive island. Seagulls, smaller and whiter than those at the fish market, flew escort.

Sixto said, "Nobody allowed out here, usually."

"I'm a cousin," Gregory said.

Sixto thought we had influence. All we had was a dozen roses: six red, six white, wrapped in blue.

"Not even relatives," Sixto said. "They start that, they got problems. You know how many they got buried here? Over a million."

"Over a million served," Gregory said.

"I swear," Sixto said. "Bodies decompose. They redig a spot after twenty-five years. Start all over."

Sixto said that more babies were being buried every year now. Three coffin sizes: adult, infant, baby.

"Let's stand over there, Joe," I said. "Out of the wind." I was tired of Sixto's speech, tired of bad news.

"Wind's coming off the starboard," Gregory said, but he followed me. "She gave you a book, I can't believe that," he said. "What the hell kind of Christmas gift is that? You want books, go to the library. Read it once and it's over."

"You collect records, I collect books. I'll enjoy it."

It became quieter after they cut the ferry motor and we floated to the dock. I could hear the gulls again.

"Maybe you enjoy reading too much," Gregory said. "Case in point: Neddy Flanagan's file. Now you're sneaking down to Personnel Records to read shit."

From across the bay, at the NYPD outdoor firing range at Rodman's Neck, came the sound of a hundred guns in staccato bursts, like firecrackers on Chinese New Year's.

"I don't understand you sometimes," he said.

"Just being thorough," I said.

"Just being stupid," he said. "I know about it, you can bet your ass Flanagan does."

No one greeted us when we slammed into the dock. The three of us got into the truck and bounced over the dirt road of the island. I sat in the middle, holding the clipboard with the roster of names, listening to the coffins sliding around in the back, screeching against the sheet metal floor.

To the north I could see some abandoned-looking institutional buildings; otherwise the island was starkly bare. Less than an island, it seemed more like an empty lot surrounded by water. We drove over a small hill. The ground on either side was covered with scraggly low shrubbery and a few willows.

We stopped and I jumped down, still holding the clipboard. Sixto backed the truck up to a large trench about ten feet deep, some of it filled and covered with loose dirt. The wind made the only sound.

"I talked to my old man," Gregory said. "He says Jinx was always disappearing in the Bronx. Says he liked the Spanish broads."

"Maybe we can find a girlfriend," I said.

"Maybe he was banging Carmen Miranda," Joe said. "Chiquita Banana or somebody."

Sand was blowing across an empty baseball field, the wind from the northeast off Long Island Sound blowing in the faces of a gang of a dozen men carrying shovels, walking toward us. They wore sweatshirts with pro football logos or old fatigue jackets over their prison uniforms. Forty-eight prisoners from Riker's Island functioned as gravediggers and custodians.

"You looking for waterfront property, Ryan?" a squeaky, familiar voice said. "This I can arrange, for the right price."

I put on my glasses to see which of the crew was talking.

"What kind of cop are you, you don't recognize me?"

"Willie Flat Nose," I said. "The worst bookmaker in the Bronx."

Willie Greco was a sports book we had grabbed in a Bronx wireroom in 1977 or 1978 during one of the Yankee-Dodger World Series. He was a smart guy, used call forwarding, kept moving the wireroom on us. But smart guys always outsmart themselves.

"Who died, Gregory's favorite uncle?" Willie said. "That cheap prick wouldn't spring for a chink funeral."

Gregory was smiling for the first time that day. He grabbed the little bookmaker's hand and shook it as if he were family. "We put you here, Willie?" he said, still smiling.

"You shitting me? I never did time for gambling. I'm in for alimony, but I'll do the time before I pay that slut a dime. Hey, ain't that a country-western song?"

Sixto took the clipboard from under my arm. The crew had begun to pull the pine boxes from the truck.

"Who do you like in the Super Bowl?" Gregory said.

"Skins big time," Willie said. "What's the spread now, still a field goal and a half?"

"You're asking us?" Gregory said. "You must have a sheet going here."

I heard the clank of shovels and the counting one, two, three, *heave*, as the prisoners passed the caskets down into a thirty-foot-square trench that looked eight to ten feet deep.

"No more booking for me," Willie said. "Too many headaches. Too much bullshit, dealing with fucking deadbeat gamblers. Got a straight job. I'm out of here Monday. Work release."

"Who you bullshitting, straight job?" Gregory said. "They're getting you out for the Super Bowl, the NC double A's, hockey playoffs, the NBA finals. It's the bookmaker's season."

"I ain't shitting you. Bronx Best Carting is my sponsor. I'm a fucking sanitation engineer."

"A garbage man, you?" Gregory said. "The cans are bigger than you."

"Tell this asshole, Ryan," Willie said. "The company's legit."

"Legit, yeah," I said. "Five trucks, fifty drivers, all on work release."

Again the long burst of gunshots echoing from the police range. I know this drill: ten shots timed in thirty-five seconds. An eerie silence follows the thunderous explosion of the first five shots as everyone reloads against the pressure of the clock ticking. Then a single shot from a practiced gunslinger, then a few more from the competent, then the rapid burst of *ack-ack* from a hundred guns held by the average cops.

Gregory said, "Maybe we ought to talk to Corrections before Willie gets out. Nip this injustice in the bud."

"Go ahead, break my balls," Willie said. "And I'm such a sweetheart, I even had a holiday gift for you. Georgie K in the sixth at Hialeah, this very day. Don't say I never gave you nothing. Now it's been nice chatting, but I got to bury stiffs."

Willie started to climb down into the ditch, but Gregory put his arm around him again, held him tight, like two old buddies grab-assing.

"Sal Magliozzi's family still own the restaurant you guys hang in?" I said. "The one on a Hundred Eighty-seventh Street, down from the Sons of Sicily?"

"Fontana's?" Willie said. "Don't ask me. Who knows

who owns anything anymore? Maybe Coca-Cola, or IBM. Some parent company."

"You ever see Jinx Mulgrew in Fontana's?" I said.

"I heard you found that prick snoozing with the salmon."

"Who put him there?" Gregory said.

"Who gives a shit?" Willie said. "He was a scumbag shakedown artist. Never honored a contract in his life."

"Ever see him in Fontana's?" I said.

"First of the month, like clockwork. Or when he had his load on, wanted to impress some broad. Order top shelf and expect it on the muscle. We used to spit in his fucking minestrone, the prick."

"Anybody with him?" I said.

"Only one I remember was that Puerto Rican broad. Redhead, big tits. From that bar, used to be on Webster across from the Pepsi plant."

The wind changed direction. I could smell the salt in the air, taste it on my lips.

"Rizzo kill Jinx?" I said.

"Get outta here," Willie said. "Why? No reason why. You couldn't convict Rizzo if he did do it. Which I doubt. He's senile."

"He's running a business," I said.

"He's running shit," Willie said. "They give him that office on South Street for show. A bullshit thing, for his honor."

"Ugo Bongiovanni runs the market now?" I said.

"You tell me," he said. "I'm a bookmaker according to you. But I do know enough to get out of the fucking rain. You two dopey bastards are going to wind up picking more than pigeon feathers out of your hair. We're burying this poor bastard, ain't we?"

"What poor bastard?" I said. "What did you hear?"

"I hear a lot of shit," Willie said. "Shit you don't want to know about. I'll tell you this: You guys keep fucking around with the wrong people, forget about it. I'm Met Life, I ain't writing no policies on the two of you."

The little bookmaker pulled away from Gregory and scrambled down into the huge ditch. He disappeared around coffins stacked three deep, ten across, one hundred forty-eight to a section. No privacy for the poor even in death. I walked up to the edge of the ditch.

"We're going to screw up your work release," I said.

"Do what you gotta do," he said. Then he cupped his ear and said, "Can't hear in this wind."

Willie began digging furiously. I looked out past the baseball field with its rotting bleachers, salvaged from Ebbets Field when the Dodgers fled to the coast. The bleachers faced south, looking out over the whitecaps of the sound, back toward Flatbush. When I turned around Joe Gregory was climbing down into the ditch, carrying the roses.

The coffins were laid out according to a master list, an inventory of bodies to be kept in some file cabinet, in some superagency. There were no grave markers here, no flags or wreaths, no mourners. Sixto Caban read from the list of names on the clipboard to make sure they were in order. All sounded vaguely familiar, names on mailboxes, in phone books, or announced from the pulpit during the banns of matrimony: Olga Davis, Iris Figueroa, Precious Freeman, Jesus Medina, Casimir Poniatowski.

There was no John Doe or Jane Doe sung out in Sixto's broken English. I had thought we were burying the nameless, the homeless: anonymous people who found eternal peace next to a shopping cart in the doorway of an abandoned factory. But we were not burying strangers.

At Gregory's direction the prisoners stood, hats off and heads bowed. He placed the roses at the foot of Zipper's casket and saluted. Then he fired five shots, emptying his gun, into the air. The echo skipped across the water, like a stone we couldn't see.

21

On the way downtown we stopped at OTB and put fifty bucks on Georgie K in the sixth at Hialeah. That left us with seven dollars between us, so we decided to wait for the results. Joe drove by the Pepsi plant on Webster Avenue, looking for the bar Willie had talked about; but apparently it had been torn down. So we picked up two cans of Schaefer, two slices of Sicilian pizza, and then parked across the street from Fontana's Restaurant.

Fontana's, on the corner of Arthur Avenue and E. 187th, was the fanciest of a dozen Italian seafood and pasta restaurants in the four-block area. Next door was a novelty store with the green-, red-, and white-striped flags. Hats and T-shirts said "Kiss me, I'm Italian."

"These neighborhoods," Gregory said. "The only ones in the Bronx holding out. The Jews ran to Co-op City, the Irish ran to Long Island or Rockland. You got to give that to the guineas, they stayed to fight."

This was among the last safe neighborhoods, and security was assured by the Sons of Sicily Social Club. Most of the marauders who ravaged the crumbling Bronx had learned the risks of invading this neighborhood. Junkie burglars who didn't get the word regularly "slipped" from the roofs of five-story walk-ups in this area and died when they slammed onto immaculate sidewalks, swept every morning by old women, dressed in black, who saw nothing.

"What I'm thinking now," Gregory said, "our target got to be Bobo. He's still got a lot of old friends over on Mulberry Street. With all that's going on, Ugo trying to take over the family and all, maybe we present Bobo with the opportunity to get Ugo out of the picture, he'll jump at it."

"Willie says he retired."

"Everything Willie says is bullshit," Gregory said. "These guys don't retire. They don't even go on vacation, for chrissakes. All they got is the mob. You watch. We get him right, he'll do it."

A teenage boy in a black leather jacket and black high-tops slapped a pink Spalding off the brick wall directly behind us. He had appeared within minutes after we parked, probably sent by the men in silk suits in the Sons of Sicily Social Club. This is a neighborhood of shopkeepers, construction workers, and generations of wise guys. If you weren't born here, you were the enemy. Two men in suits, sitting in a dirty sedan, were obviously behind the lines.

"Bobo lives on Staten Island now," I said.

"They got a bridge now, pally."

The red café curtains of Fontana's parted momentarily.

Gregory said, "We got to do something bold to goose this case. You can't go through life with your balls taped to your leg."

"Are you saying we should flake Bobo?"

"No, we'll get him right," he said. "We stay on his ass enough, he'll fuck up."

"Why don't we just shoot this lookout?" I said.

The kid playing handball stepped into the doorway of a deli but kept watching us. Salamis, cheeses, and Italian breads hung in the window. Gregory looked at me with pizza grease running down his chin.

"What's your bright idea?" he said. "Your goddamn bar lead went down in flames."

"Not the barmaid, though," I said. "Sid Kaye said that Jinx picked up the pad money in the Bronx, maybe right here in Fontana's. Willie Greco said he came here with the barmaid. Maybe Jinx came here after the medal ceremony, maybe she was with him."

"Lot of maybes," Joe said. "Okay, Jinx comes here, then what? They blow him away, pour concrete, then cart him all the way to lower Manhattan. No way. They'd have dropped him close by. Harlem River, Hudson, maybe."

"How can it hurt to look for the barmaid?"

"Good luck," he said. "You ever hear that old saying: 'It's like trying to find a Puerto Rican barmaid in the Bronx'?"

"That's a country-western song," I said.

Georgie K came in at eighteen to one. We pulled onto the Cross Bronx, heading to Brady's with cash in our pockets and the taste in our mouths. On the way downtown we stopped at the state liquor authority. The bar across from the Pepsi plant had been called La Copa de Oro, Webster Avenue and E. 178th Street. The last owner was Reuben Soto, 1925 Grand Concourse. They gave me a copy of the file, no problem. The problem was the place had burned down two years before Jinx disappeared.

We walked into Brady's, and Gregory went to the bar to settle his tab and buy a round of drinks. When Joe Gregory had money you could hear it sizzling in his pocket. I went into the back room, but our booth was occupied by a certain lieutenant in a madras blazer, holding an empty martini glass to his nose.

Eddie Shick said, "I waited for you in the office, but I forgot this was your office."

"It's only an annex," I said.

Shick looked worse than usual; his psoriasis was erupting into red blotches on both sides of his nose and on his eyebrows.

"I'm not going to have problems with you, am I?" he said. "Tell me I'm not, Ryan."

"How about another silver bullet?" I said, pointing to his glass.

"Sit," he said. "What I'm going to say to you stays in this room."

He looked around as I slid into the booth opposite him. "From now on," he said, "you need something from the ninth floor, you ask me first. You don't bypass the chain of command to go through personnel files. *Comprende?*"

If Eddie Shick knew I went through Neddy Flanagan's personnel file, the entire NYPD knew. Shick was always the last to know. He'd been our boss for five years. I couldn't remember ever doing anything he told us to before, but I knew he was deadly serious now.

"Understood," I said.

"Hallelujah," he said. "I'm a happy guy when you agree with me."

Patti O'Brien came to our table, drying her hands on a red apron that said "Fuck Christmas." Gregory sent her back; he wanted the drinks rolling quickly. She took the empty glass from Shick's hand.

"The big spenders have arrived. Drink up, right, Lieu?" she said.

Patti and Joe Gregory were an on-and-off thing, more off these days. To my knowledge she was the only woman Gregory ever dated whose paycheck didn't bear a governmental seal.

"Now give me some good news," Shick said, and checked out Patti's ass as she walked away

Patti had black hair, green eyes, and porcelain white skin. Joe said she had Sinn Fein tattooed in kelly green, for dramatic contrast, on her pearly ass. The Irish had the best coloring.

"Wadda ya got so far?" Shick said.

"A dead informant, a cop in a coma."

"What about Mrs. Mulgrew?"

"Nice lady, neat housekeeper."

"Don't be a wise-ass, Anthony," Shick said. "It's not your style."

Gregory sat next to Shick and put his arm around him. I knew he was feeling for a wire.

"I got news for you two," Shick said. "I'm too good to you, I know." He scratched the back of his hand and looked around the room.

"Take this to your graves, understand?" he said. Then he whispered, "Feds got a wire into the Ravenite."

"We know that," I said.

"You know this, wise-ass?" Shick said, getting louder. "Nicky Skooch's been bragging about dropping the pigeon coop on Murray Daniels. You know the feds got him cold? You know that, smart-ass?"

"Shit," Gregory said. "They're going to take him, right? Snap him up from right under our noses."

"Give me a little credit here," Shick said. "Neddy Flanagan and me are working a deal so's the First Precinct gets the collar. Feds'll let us use their tapes. But we need to wait on their timetable. They want the wire to run as long as it can."

We all stopped talking when Patti put the martini in front of Shick. He had it to his lips before the glass had a chance to make a ring on the table.

"So give me something on Jinx, anything," Shick said as he scratched at his cheek, leaving fine flakes caught in his beard stubble. "Some good word I can take back."

"We're going to start tailing Bobo Rizzo this week," Gregory said.

"No help," Shick said. "I can't spare nobody. That's the deal. We ain't turning this into a three-ring circus."

"We don't need help," Gregory said.

Shick said, "Let me say this again, then, are you making any fucking progress?"

"*Nada,*" Gregory said.

I wondered why there was no Sinatra on the jukebox. Somebody always played Sinatra when Gregory walked in.

Shick said, "Aren't you supposed to sprinkle a little sand on the floor before you do the old soft-shoe?"

"It's not required," Gregory said.

"Lieu," I said, "does it make sense to you that we didn't recover any notes from Mulgrew's locker? Maybe you can ask Flanagan to check with IAD."

"You having a midlife crisis, or what?" Shick said. "Why you always asking questions that can't be answered? Maybe Jinx wasn't the type of cop who kept notes. You can get hung by your own notes."

"Boss is right," Gregory said.

"Cut the bullshit," Shick said. "Work on Rizzo. He has status, all the big bosses know his name. We'll call him the prime suspect."

"Let's drink to the prime suspect," Gregory said, raising his glass.

Shick held the stemmed glass in his short, smashed fingers. "I'll tell him you're working an angle on Rizzo. He suggested that anyway."

"Who?" I said.

"Who the fuck ya think?" he said, and drained the glass.

Shick left when it was his turn to buy; went to the men's room, then walked out the door. Joe and I were alone in the back room just before last call. I could still taste the cheeseburger Patti O fixed us during the late news.

When you'd been drinking for a long time, people suddenly appeared before you. Poof, a puff of magic smoke. Patti O appeared, holding the phone.

"Is Ryan here?" Patti said, looking at me, her hand over the mouthpiece. I didn't even hear it ring. "Is Ryan here?" she said, louder.

"Who is it?"

"A woman."

"He just left," I said.

Patti relayed the message in her soft brogue, then: "Is Joe Gregory here?" she asked, making her eyes big. The last few stragglers at the bar watched Gregory stand up, knock a chair to the floor, grab the phone.

A bar at this hour is the domain of hard drinkers drowning their blues in amber, seeking climax to the night. People talk aloud, laugh, cry, sing to anyone, no one. The last semiconscious act of a drunk is to locate someone willing to punish him. Thus a cop's bar at this hour, stocked with guns and fueled by booze and paranoia, becomes a place waiting for a tragedy to happen. Gregory's dollar's worth of Sinatra was the only sound coming from the bar. "Stormy Weather."

"Sylvia D'Angelo," Gregory said, smiling. "Who'd you think it was? Your old lady, right?"

"No, Chiquita Banana. What did Sylvia want?"

"She says she struck out on the partial print, but the old lady upstairs says she saw two heavyset guys leaving in a big dark car. Think big."

"You're thinking the FPS car," I said.

"Guaranteed."

Billy the porter banged chairs upside down on tables, drowning out Sinatra and a bar argument over the new mass. Drunken arguments always covered three subjects: religion for sots; politics for the merely tipsy; women for the drunks.

"You know why women don't like this job?" Gregory said. "They can't control it."

"I thought you said women loved cops. You always say a woman on the street will walk up to a cop and start talking. Something she wouldn't do to a stranger."

"I didn't mean women this time," he said. "I meant wives, cops' wives."

Billy held the broom with hooks the government issued him to replace hands lost fighting in Europe. Now he was sweeping under church pews in a bar on Pearl Street.

"Cops don't work at the office," Gregory said. "The little woman can't call or drop by to see if you're banging the secretary. We're out here at night rubbing up against women they ain't going to bump into at the Christmas party, or nine o'clock mass, or the PTA. They're out in the suburbs, we're here in the Big Apple, all night. Different bars, different women. They don't know shit about where we are. Only what we tell them."

"Is that what bothered Maureen?"

"Every freaking thing about the job bothered Maureen," he said. "My old man said she wasn't cut out to be a cop's wife."

Someone was dropping coins in the phone, asking for the number of the Vatican.

"My old man says that a man's work is everything," Gregory said. "I believe that. Everything else will let you down. Your wife, your kids, your health, all let you down. But your work will always be there. Am I right?"

"This a retirement lecture?"

"Just shedding some light," he said. "All cops' wives want them to get out of the job. But why should you? Why leave a job you like for something you don't like? Play golf in the hot sun like Charlie Spinelli? Be miserable just to please them? Women want something they can control. What you want don't mean shit."

* * *

"Serious talk tonight," Patti said, pulling our bar bill from under the cash register. The bar had emptied out. Billy locked the door behind each soul who staggered out solo under the starless sky. "But then you two have serious problems."

"We got no problems, Patti," Gregory said.

We both slid a five under the ashtray for Patti. She "forgot" to ring up two of every three of our drinks. We tipped big in order to pay small.

"Look at your tab," she said. "A lot of your friends rejected your sweet hospitality."

Patti stood on her toes and held Gregory's face in her wet hands. "I don't want anything to happen to this ugly face," she said.

"A sad freaking day," Gregory said, looking at the tab, "when you can't buy your friends a drink. What the hell are they thinking, anyway?"

I knew what they were thinking: traitors always had deep pockets. Patti rolled the two fives and put them into a tip jar jammed with bills. She plunged her hands back into the sink. Glasses clanked against the sides of the tin tub. We walked out in the night.

It was a strange feeling to step out into the night after entering a bar in daylight. Like Rip van Winkle you stood there, surprised and lost, looking for clues, unsure of how long you've been gone. I heard the metal on metal of Billy's hooks snapping the deadbolt behind us. I felt locked out.

22

WE SPENT the month of January tailing Bobo Rizzo. We began on January 6, the Feast of the Epiphany, a gray, windless day on Staten Island. Al Carrol, Bobo's driver, sat outside Bobo's house reading *The Wall Street Journal*. We watched through binoculars from a driveway on the next block.

"He don't look senile to me," Gregory said as Bobo came out of the house. "Old age don't change these guys. Crooks till they die."

Tailing mob guys is a delicate business, because they assume they're being followed. They keep their eyes on the rear-view mirror, taking mental snapshots of the group of cars behind, looking for the same car riding in the pack too long: the wolf, stalking. So we begin tailing with small goals and at a distance, noting departure times, driving style, the pace, the routes, the stops.

"He'll screw up," Gregory said, "My old man told me that one time Highway locked up Bobo for throwing slugs in the bridge toll basket. The prick had eighty grand in the trunk. It's in their blood. They'll drive ten miles out of their way to buy a pack of untaxed cigarettes. They don't change."

Bobo's driver was an old dice game lugger. A lugger's job was to pick up dice players waiting on a prearranged street corner, then drive them to the secret location of the floating game. Guys like Al Carrol were paid to shake a plainclothes tail and avoid leading the cops back to the game. Rules of the road be damned.

Gregory anticipated Al's first move. As soon as Bobo got in the Lincoln, Al floored it for two blocks. Midway down the second block he made a screeching U-turn and came back against the one-way, past Bobo's house again, then made a left toward Victory Boulevard. Bobo read the paper. We stood pat in the driveway.

The second day we picked him up on Victory Boulevard and followed him to the Verrazano Bridge. The third day we waited near the bridge. That's the way it worked: it was progressive.

We spent the entire month of January waiting for him to screw up. But Bobo always went straight from home to R&B Fish, to an office upstairs in the counting rooms. The counting rooms overlooked the action on the floor below, where fish was bought and sold. Bobo didn't do much counting; he never spent more than two hours before adjourning to the Paris Bar.

From the Paris Bar his schedule varied. Every Friday and Saturday he left the market early to go to Elizabeth Street, an all-night card game. Every other night except Wednesday he went to Little Italy to a restaurant or to the Ravenite Social Club.

On Wednesdays, however, he left Al Carrol behind and took the Lincoln to shop for a whore. That was the screw-up we'd been waiting for.

On the first Wednesday night in February we were

parked in the market, under the FDR Drive, almost out of the rain. Although we'd used up almost two-thirds of our ninety days, we weren't getting any pressure from above. Shick said everything was copacetic.

Gregory angled the Buick so we were facing uptown, watching the dimly lit Paris Bar through the rear-view mirror. Rainwater, draining down from the highway, beat a tattoo on the trunk. Joe took pictures off the mirror while we waited for Bobo Rizzo to leave for his Wednesday blow job.

"Remind me to reverse the images," Joe said.

"I don't know why you're bothering. This distance, the weather. You don't have enough light."

"I got faith," he said.

I slid down on the seat and closed my eyes, listening to the click of the Nikon.

"Call me when he comes out," I said.

Gregory was still snapping pictures off the mirror when Bobo appeared in the light of the doorway. The Lincoln, parked half on the sidewalk, bounced heavily to the pavement.

Bobo was a terrible driver but an easy tail. He'd cruise Bowery, then lower Third Avenue, then the West Side, slowing down for every walking female. But Bobo never took the first hooker, as if he needed more than one bid.

Streets were deserted in the downpour. The rain forced Bobo all the way up Tenth Avenue to midtown, where he found a big girl in a red Tina Turner wig, tan leather pants, and gold lamé jacket, standing under the marquee of a closed theater. We followed them to the West Side, to the river. He pulled underneath the West Side Highway and killed the lights.

"Give him five," Gregory said. We had timed Bobo three times, watching cheap wigs bob up and down over his sixty-five-year-old crotch. The capo averaged thirteen minutes from cash to climax.

Gregory put a fresh roll of film in the camera, then looked for a place in his raincoat to pin his shield. I clamped the turret light on top of the car and checked my watch. We gave Bobo an extra minute and a half of ecstasy because traffic was too heavy to get across.

"Now," I said.

The Buick slid on the slick roadway, skidding to a stop inches from the Lincoln's bumper. I went to the driver's side, Gregory took the hooker's door. Hookers always left their door open in case they had to bail out.

Bobo's door was unlocked, too. He'd been leaning against it and fell halfway out when I swung it open.

"Police," I yelled, propping Bobo up with my knee. "Don't move."

I held Bobo's head upright so he couldn't duck the camera, then angled the flashlight like the lighting man in a porno film crew. The car heater blasted on max. Flash from Gregory's camera lit the front seat in white-hot light, over and over and over. The girl, on her knees on the floor, struggled to get up, but Gregory's foot was on her back. The overheated Lincoln smelled of perfume and sour sweat.

"Oh, shit, oh, shit," the girl said, trying to yank her halter top over her small breasts. Her scuffed platform shoes banged under the dash as she looked up, grimacing from the lights, protecting her face with hands that could have palmed Bobo's head. Huge hands. Rough stubble of beard showed between long fingers, through layers of pancake makeup. Gregory leaned in to get a close-up on the face of the prostitute, who clearly was not a lady of the night.

"What's the problem, Officer?" Bobo said. "Some trouble? Me and my girlfriend were talking."

He arched his hips off the seat, trying to get his pants up. Bobo's face was gray, but he was relieved it was only the cops.

"You have a right to remain silent," Gregory said.

"Shit, fucking shit," the hooker said, not using a falsetto, just a soft southern baritone.

Gregory was saying "Get the fuck out, honey." Vic Damone crooned "On the Street Where You Live" from speakers tuned too heavily to bass. Gregory pulled the hooker from the car and stood him up straight; he was well over six three in platforms. The car motor was idling quietly.

"If you cannot afford a lawyer," Gregory said, "one will be appointed for you."

"I know you two shitheads," Rizzo said, pointing at me. The old man shoved his shirt inside his boxer shorts, then somehow kept pulling it back out.

"Get out, Bobo," I said. "Fix your pants."

"You got a warrant?" he said. "I don't go nowhere unless you got a warrant. Bring me to the station house. I can call my lawyer from the house."

I turned the car off and pocketed the keys, then pulled Bobo out. His arm felt thin and flaccid.

"Is this like a fucking deal, man?" the hooker said. " 'Cause I don't know nothing. This is a john, that's all I know."

I patted Rizzo down, feeling his old-man bony hips. "Is there a gun in the car?" I said.

"Fuck you," Rizzo said.

I reached under the seat and pulled out a bottle of Carlo Rossi Rhine. The bottle clinked against something as I shoved it back. I felt the cylinder of a revolver and pulled it out by the barrel: a brand-new Ruger .38 revolver. Gregory shoved the hooker into the Lincoln and handcuffed him to the steering wheel.

Bobo was still trying to adjust his shirt and pants as I pushed him into the backseat of our Buick. We got into the front seat, and Gregory slammed the door hard.

"We got you cold, Bobo," Gregory said, waving the gun.

"You got no probable cause," Bobo said.

"We got Melvin there," Gregory said. "And photographic evidence."

I took the gun from Gregory, made a note of the serial number, and placed it on the seat between us.

"C'mon, lock me up, assholes," Bobo said. "I'll be out in an hour. My age, what the fuck I got to worry about? I should be proud."

"Proud?" Gregory said. "We drop some copies of these off at the Ravenite and a set down at the Paris. You and that faggot, that walking disease factory."

"This is a shakedown, am I right?" he said. "A fucking shakedown. How come I ain't handcuffed? How much you want? Let's get it over with."

"Put your money away," I said. "Answer a few questions, that's all."

"Take my money, you'll get more. Look at this fucking car you drive. It stinks like shit in here."

"It's up to you, Bobo," Gregory said.

"Roll a window," he said. "I don't breathe so good."

I rolled the window down. The hooker was waving,

yelling something I couldn't hear. Bobo pulled a comb from his pocket and began smoothing his hair back. Gregory leaned down and picked something up off the floor.

"Ask already," Bobo said. "I can listen."

"We got a proposition," Joe said. "A simple exchange of favors. We quit breaking your balls, you give us who killed Jinx Mulgrew."

"What the fuck is a Jinx Mulgrew?"

Gregory said, "A set of pictures to your wife, to your kids, the *Staten Island Advance*, the guys in the Ravenite. Guys in Patsy's won't let you touch the silverware again."

Bobo put the comb away, went back to scratching at his crotch. Gregory bent over, stretching his leg as though he had a cramp.

"This the cop from the river?" Bobo said. "Got whacked a long time ago, am I right?"

"October 1972," I said.

"I knew this guy, he was a ballbreaker," he said. "But you're asking me ten years ago. I can't remember my last shit, for chrissakes."

The hooker was yelling louder, saying he was cold, wanted the heater turned on.

"I don't want her to fuck up my car," Rizzo said. "Wait a minute, 1972. Seventy-two I was in Danbury. Twenty-three months on income tax. All year I was there."

Gregory looked over at me as if it were my fault. I hadn't noticed it in the file. Joe turned his face away with a look of pain.

"I'll check that," I said.

"Check and double-check," Rizzo said, laughing. "You guys scared the shit out of me."

"You thought it was Bongiovanni," Gregory said. "Looking to get rid of you completely?"

Bobo laughed and coughed, the color beginning to come into his face. He checked his pants and shoved more shirt down, then pulled and scratched, adjusting himself.

"That cop was a greedy bastard," Bobo said. "I always heard that. How much you want for those pictures? Coupla sheckles in your pocket, have a nice dinner on Bobo?"

"Leave it to me in your will," Gregory said. He reached over the seat and handed the Ruger back to Rizzo. "You're a dead man, Bobo. This gun has no firing pin."

"Bullshit," Bobo said, and cocked the hammer. The firing pin was gone. The cylinder was fully loaded, but without the firing pin nothing would strike the primer cap of the bullet. The gun was useless.

"They're setting you up, Bobo," Gregory said. "Ugo wants all you old bastards out of the way."

"Nobody sets up Bobo Rizzo," he said. "No son of a bitch whatsoever."

"Maybe you need new glasses," I said. "Look at that gun."

"Give us the guy who killed Jinx," Gregory said. "You were in Danbury, you got nothing to worry about. We'll solve your problem, and we both walk away happy."

Rizzo looked out the window at his car, then back down at the gun. "I don't know who iced that cop," he said. "My hand to God, I don't know."

"Think about it, Bobo," Gregory said. "Ugo ain't good for business, draws too much attention. We know some people on Mulberry ain't happy with him."

"You know shit," he said.

"We know he told Nicky to drop that pigeon coop," I said. "That cop is still in a coma. We don't just forget that, Bobo. And you know it."

"I'll give you half a yard for those pictures," Bobo said.

"We don't deal with cop killers," Gregory said.

"Hey, this is Bobo you're talking to. You know that's not the way I do business. Never once did I have a problem with cops when I was running the show. Never once."

Bobo motioned for us to step out of the car; he knew that cars, when wired, made perfect sound stages. We all buttoned our coats in the cool wet night. Above us was one of the last sections of the crumbling West Side Drive. Traffic sloshed by in the rain.

"Some people," Bobo said softly, "fish business ain't good enough for them. They got ambitions. I'll do this for you: You give me the film in that camera, I'll make some inquiries. No guarantees."

"We need guarantees," I said.

"Take it or leave it," he said.

Bobo turned south, the tires of the Lincoln hissing. I could hear a siren coming from midtown, over near the Lincoln Tunnel entrance. Gregory and I stood against the Buick and watched the hooker take long strides toward 40th Street, the click of heels echoing off the buildings.

"It's like betting on the Red Sox," I said. "You know they can do it, but you know they won't come through."

"He'll do it," Gregory said.

"How did you break the firing pin?" I said.

"Church key," he said, pointing to the can opener lying in the coffee lids and napkins on the floor.

We got back into the Buick. I shoved the equipment under the seat. A precinct radio car drove by, pretending not to notice us, probably bringing the spaghetti pots back to Mamma Leone's.

"We'll back off for a week," he said. "Let Bobo have some room to work. We'll work on your bullshit Bronx barmaid idea."

We turned south toward lower Manhattan, in the same direction as Bobo, who was undoubtedly going for a double Sambuca at the Paris. We were all heading downtown for a drink. That's what we all did when the game ended: went to our own bars for drinks and a couple of laughs, rehash the story. Rain fell into the Hudson River, somewhere in the darkness, a few yards to the west.

23

On Friday Gregory and I headed north like people with a country home. I'd located the owner of the bar across from the Pepsi plant where Mulgrew's girlfriend had been a barmaid. SLA records had listed Reuben Soto, the owner of the former La Copa de Oro, living at 1925 Grand Concourse, the Bronx. Soto had moved and left no forwarding address, but I contacted the fire insurance company listed on the records. A check for twenty-three thousand dollars had been mailed to Soto at 18 Brenda Drive, Warwick, New York. When I called, he almost begged us to ride up and see him.

"This car still stinks," I said.

"I got it washed, what more can I do?"

"Clean the crap off the floor, open a vent."

Warwick, New York, is seventy miles northwest of the city, on the New Jersey side of the Hudson. As soon as we crossed the George Washington Bridge our car seemed too polluted for the environment.

"Smell the air up here," I said. "Smell the difference?"

"Smells too raw or something, too thin."

"That's clean air," I said. "No carbon monoxide."

"Don't knock carbon monoxide," he said. "It's the

reason we don't have no flying bugs in the city, no mosquitoes. First mosquito bite I ever got in my life was on this side of the river: Asbury Park, New Jersey. Carbon monoxide's okay in my book."

We lost radio contact before we were out of Fort Lee, then rode in the strange silence. For all these years the crackle of the radio had always been in the background, part of our world. We were struck dumb by its absence.

When we stopped at a light in Paramus, I shoved Bobo Rizzo's arrest sheet in front of him. "The IRS collar isn't even entered," I said. "How could we know he was in Danbury in seventy-two?"

"Goddamn feds, empty suits," he said, reaching into the bagel bag. We'd just bought half a dozen for the trip. They were still warm, fresh enough to eat without butter.

"The feds worry me," he said, chewing. "Sneaky bastards are going to snap Nicky Skooch up without telling us. They'll call a press conference, we'll see it on the news. I don't want that. Not yet."

"They went to a lot of trouble to get the wire into the Ravenite," I said. "If they take Nicky, they blow the wire. And they're not going to do that. Besides, Flanagan made a deal. They'll call us first."

"I don't trust the bastards," he said. "Case in point: Little Augie's card game."

Little Augie's card game was a classic example of the lack of law enforcement cooperation. We'd received information that Big Augie Costanza was setting his son up with a midtown card game. Little Augie was a little slow, so Dad wanted something easy for him to do. Joe and I figured if we got close to Little Augie, we'd make a case on Big Augie, a Lucchese capo. So we wired Gregory, and he went undercover as a high-roller.

The game was in an expensive brownstone on a tree-lined street on the Upper East Side. For five long nights I sat outside in the car, listening to Gregory raise the pot with the city's money.

The fifth night had begun to hint at a beautiful dawn, the sun just beginning to show pink over the East River. I poured the last coffee from my thermos and opened the *Daily News*. Inside the brownstone, the game was straight poker.

Little Augie bragged about knowing Joe Namath, kept showing an autographed football he had. One of the card players, a guy Gregory thought he recognized, said that when he was in college he could throw a football seventy yards in the air. The same five guys had been in the game every night, drinking, getting friendly. I sat up straight, anticipating Gregory's response.

"Bullshit," the Great Gregory said, "I got a double sawbuck says you can't reach two sewers."

Everybody started yelling, laying money this way and that way. Chairs were scraping, plastic chips rattling off the table, everybody laughing, putting on their coats.

It was just before six A.M., the street was deserted. But I was parked only twenty feet from the building entrance; I needed to be close for clear reception on the wire. The front seat of the car was filled with equipment. I threw my coat over a Tandberg reel-to-reel tape recorder and shoved a flashlight, walkie-talkie, and head-set under the seat. I started the engine when the door to the brownstone opened.

Gregory came down the steps, flipping the football, followed by guys with cigars putting on hats and gloves.

I pulled out of the parking spot, no lights on, just as they reached the street. But as I drove to the corner I noticed four other cars pulling out in front of me, all male drivers with hair disheveled as if they'd been sleeping.

During the next week we identified those four cars as belonging to the FBI, Manhattan DA, Brooklyn DA, and N.Y. State Organized Crime Task Force. Everybody in the game was a cop. Everybody was wired. Everybody was playing too close to the vest.

The part of that story Gregory loves, though, is that all the investigators filed reports saying they lost money in the game. Nobody ever won for Uncle Sam.

"What happens if your car breaks down out here?" Gregory said, pointing out at the fields and wooded areas along the road. "See a pay phone anywhere? I don't."

Cows, horses, deer stood in green fields along highways through towns named Sloatsburg, Tuxedo, and Monroe. Less than an hour from Manhattan and we drove for miles without seeing a house. Less than forty miles separated gangs from herds.

Reuben Soto's street was a curving line of high ranches with newly staked trees and enough lawn in front for weekend landscapers to create unlikely gardens. Dolls on lawns, tricycles turned over in driveways, swing sets in the backyard, were evidence of a street full of children. Soto was waiting at the picture window.

"Officers," he said, smiling as if he were glad to see us. *"Mí casa."*

Soto was small, gray-haired, with thin legs and a distended belly. His olive skin had a hint of the yellow complexion of alcoholics whose plumbing had gone bad. He spoke in short sentences, laboring to breathe, whistling through his nose on intake. We walked slowly up one flight into a room decorated in Early American, a fireplace roaring. I sat next to him on a couch patterned in Minuteman and British militia. The coffee table was dark pine, shaped like a gear in a watch.

"Always glad," he said, "to help . . . New York's finest. I had . . . so many friends . . . on the force."

Bar owners always had plenty of friends on the force. Next to cops, we knew more barmen than any other single occupation.

"Do you remember Jinx Mulgrew?" I said.

"I read . . . in the paper," he said. "So sad. Such a fine gentleman."

"You knew him, then?" I said.

"Even after . . . he goes downtown . . . he comes in . . . once a month . . . sometimes more. Dewar's and water. Always."

"When was the last time you saw him?"

"No more . . . after the bar burns down. . . . I quit bar business . . . my health . . . not so good," Soto said, tapping his chest.

I could hear someone in the kitchen, water running. The house smelled medicinal, like Vicks VapoRub.

"Did Jinx ever bring anybody with him?" I said.

"He meet . . . someone in back . . . my special table. . . . Funny man . . . like to eat Spanish food."

I handed him the photos. Soto tilted his head back to use the bifocals.

The photos were glued to a manila folder. On the official department photos I covered the collar brass: Neddy Flanagan, Sid Kaye, and a half dozen other ex-plainclothesmen. On the booking photos I covered the B number: Rizzo, Bongiovanni, Salvy, Nicky Skooch, and several known market hoods.

It was a good, well-matched lineup of similar faces, cops and crooks: middle-aged men with fleshy faces, thinning hair parted on the side. The same hard, knowing expressions, the same secrets behind shrewd eyes.

"This is him," he said. "Funny man . . . like Jinx." He pointed to Sid Kaye.

"Take a good look on this line," I said, and waited. "How about him?" I said finally, pointing right at Flanagan. Gregory raised his eyebrows at me.

"Is this . . . big man?" Soto said.

"No, not that big," I said. "About my size."

"Maybe . . . I think maybe once," Soto said. "Not sure . . . please."

Joe Gregory said, "You're not sure about that guy, but Jinx and Sid Kaye came often."

"Sid . . . Chivas rocks . . . top shelf."

"What about a barmaid?" I asked. "Jinx went out with a barmaid."

"Immaculata Perez," Soto said quietly, looking back toward the kitchen. "Officers . . . I will not . . . testify. . . . I am not well enough."

"Is she a big girl, big chi-chis?" Gregory said.

"Sí," he said, kissing his fingertips.

I handed Soto one of the Polaroids of the naked woman from Mulgrew's locker. He held it for a long time, nodding his head, his eyes getting moist. Then he reached into his wallet and pulled out a dingy business card with a Playboy bunny logo: McGuire's Yankee Lounge 5587 Broadway.

On the way out we walked past the kitchen. A gray-haired woman smiled sadly at me, then went back to her dishes. Soto walked to the car with us as if he wanted to go back to the Bronx. But the walk of twenty-five feet had winded him. The bar business kills. I kept taking deep breaths, sucking in the clean air.

"Immaculata ... please ... don't tell her ... I ..."

Gregory took one of the Polaroids, slid it into Soto's pocket, and patted it.

"Here," he said. "We lost this one."

24

THE LAST light of a cold February Saturday faded across our kitchen cabinets. It was my forty-third birthday, and the house was quiet except for the sound of Leigh chopping onions on a wooden block. A birthday card, in green and red crayon, had come in the mail: Love to Pop-Pop, Katie. A crayon stick figure, a man with dark hair, holding the hand of a little stick figure girl.

"This barmaid," Leigh said. "What makes you think she can help you?"

"Maybe she can't," I said. "Only thirty days left, we have to try something."

The kitchen stayed bright later into the evening, since I had cut the maple branches Leigh said were tapping against the window. Leigh's hands were in that spotlight of fading sun, working the knife in short, sure strokes. Her hands were sinewy and strong, with age spots like freckles on the back and short nails with clear polish. She always wanted to grow long, glamorous fingernails and paint them red, but they never had a chance.

"Will they extend the case?" she asked.

"Only if we come up with something solid. They want to close this, it's making people nervous."

"You should have looked for the girlfriend a long time ago," she said. "You listen to Joe Gregory too much."

Leigh said all the signs pointed directly to a woman. She said that some drunken cops, especially Mulgrew's type, looked for the bimbo first. I've heard that cops' wives take on their husbands' cynicism, but I hoped Leigh wouldn't become bitter, wouldn't lose her gentleness. Maybe we expected too much of the people who love us, wanting them somehow to remain our oasis.

"Who is that big blond kid, across the street," I asked, "always working on the Mustang?"

"I think he lives in the Tudor."

I put my cold coffee in the microwave, then walked over to the counter, trying to get a look at her face. She was barefoot, wearing only the red flannel robe. I put my arms around her, but I already knew her mood. In a long and close marriage the defense of ignorance does not apply.

"I used to know everybody on the block," she said, "when the kids were small."

Leigh had surprised me as I worked on the computer upstairs—she was naked under a long Yankee T-shirt. We made love quietly, but with an intense need to find something, feel good about something. Lately I had become aware of a melancholy after sex, a surprising sad emptiness.

"Every kid in the neighborhood used to be in here," I said.

"Not when you were working nights, sleeping. The kids wouldn't dare make a sound."

She put the knife down, put the onions back in the bag, and went to the refrigerator for the celery. She was an orderly person, consistent in the way she did things. A place and time for everything. The microwave buzzed, and I took the cup and set it down quickly; the porcelain handle burned my fingers.

"Run some cold water on your fingers," Leigh said. "I told you not to put the cups with the hollow handles in the microwave."

"I admit it's not a good job for family life," I said as the water ran. "The hours aren't good for raising kids."

"Don't blame the job," she said. "A lot of cops make out fine."

"Are you saying it's me?"

"Don't get defensive, Anthony. I don't want to argue with you."

"We can't just drop it here," I said.

She took the chopped onions and celery and scraped them into a green Tupperware bowl. She handed me a small towel and took a deep breath.

"As a matter of fact, it is you," she said. "If you treated it as just a job, fine. You work, you come home, fine. But you and Gregory act like it's a game and nobody really gets hurt. You hang out all night, drink, then go play cops and robbers with the Mafia. Well, people do get hurt, Anthony."

"I know that," I said. "I know that very well."

Shadows moved over her face. I almost said "Don't worry, it's nearly over," but I held back. Never make promises you can't keep.

"Organized crime intelligence is no more dangerous than any other investigative job," I said. "We work too many nights, I know. But that's the way it is."

"You work nights, I work days. It's not a good way to live."

"We could live differently," I said. "Have more friends. Socialize more."

"Your friends, Anthony, not mine. Only your friends."

"What's wrong with my friends?"

"Nothing. Some of them are nice, sweet guys. But most of them can't carry on a decent conversation with someone who isn't wearing a gun. Nor do they want to."

"Everybody's friends are from their job."

"What happens to my friends? You think they're all naive or stupid. And people sense that around you. Around cops." She turned back to the counter and began pulling dishes from the cupboard.

"You're right," I said. "I know that. All I can say is I'll try to be better, more normal, like your friends. I can be as boring as the next guy."

"See what I mean?"

"That was sarcastic, sorry. But I mean it, Leigh. This has been a tough month. Everything will be better when this case is over. I'll put my papers in, go teach somewhere."

She took a deep breath, walked over to me, and put her arms up high around my neck. "Let's stop this," she said. "Just listen to me a little, okay? I'm just talking now, just blowing off steam. I know you can't fix everything. I know there are no perfect solutions. Just listen to me."

"Let's go to the movies," I said. "We haven't been to the movies in months."

"Stop, please. I'm just a little down today. I don't know what's wrong, but I'll be okay. So relax, be quiet."

"Maybe we should get a dog," I said.

"Anthony," she said, "set the table."

25

JUST BEFORE midnight on upper Broadway the air was full of the spicy licorice smell of anisette cookies wafting down from the Stella D'Oro bakery. McGuire's Yankee Lounge was in the northwest corner of the Bronx, just a few blocks from the bakery and Van Cortlandt Park. Well within walking distance of its main source of revenue, the 50th Precinct. We'd made the trip for three consecutive nights, looking for Immaculata Perez. All we'd accomplished was to make the natives restless.

"Stella," Joe Gregory yelled. "Stella." But his Stanley Kowalski was drowned out by the el on the way to E. 242nd Street, thundering overhead and showering sparks into the night.

The smell of stale beer replaced sweet aniseed as we pushed through the door. The sound of "Young girl, get out of my mind . . ." filled the narrow room. At the far end, a burly guy who looked like an overweight Gerald Ford hugged the jukebox like a hot date. He couldn't have been more than in his early thirties, but cops who worked revolving shifts aged in giant steps. A .38 Smith & Wesson Chief's Special stuck out under his red sweater. A string of linked deer pranced across his back.

McGuire's was a long, railroad-car-style joint with a J-shaped bar to the right and barely space to stagger from stool to men's room. Locals avoided cops' bars, so McGuire's was empty except for Gerald Ford and a trio of gum-popping precinct groupies waiting for their heroes from the four-to-midnight tour to roll in. We took the corner stools near the window so we could see the length of the bar.

Immaculata had finally come to work, and we made her easily. The copper hair was too electric not to be nylon. Her breasts, under the tight black sweater, hung suspended somehow, like the upper deck in Yankee Stadium. She strutted the length of the bar toward us, clicking her stiletto heels over drainage boards, Miss PR on the runway in Atlantic City. The cop groupies glanced at us and whispered nervously, positive we were Internal Affairs. Even the groupies feared IAD.

"Can I help you?" she asked, pronouncing the last word "ju."

"What kind of bottled beer?" Gregory said.

Immaculata whipped through her interpretation of German brand names. One of the groupies went to the pay phone to alert the precinct. The strangers, again, had entered their sacred gin mill.

"You from the Five Oh?" she said.

"Downtown," Gregory said. "Organized Crime Control."

"OCCB don't wear suits," she said.

"We got them wholesale," I said. "In Chinatown."

"You IAD, right?" she said.

"We're not IAD, Immaculata," Gregory said. "We're

working the Jinx Mulgrew homicide. We're here to see you."

She walked away mumbling in Spanish as her ass fought to break out of the tight black skirt. In bars like McGuire's the sexiest barmaid worked the midnight shift. Immaculata was a little heavy for those skirts now, not the headline act anymore.

"Immaculata," Gregory yelled. "Get us a Bud and set the house up. On me."

The groupies whispered to Gerald Ford, who was charged with enough liquid bravado to flash a menacing glare. Immaculata called us faggots in Spanish and began popping bottle caps, backing up full drinks on the bar.

"On the big shots," she said, pointing.

She strolled back toward us with a long neck wrapped in each hand, a ring on every finger, including the thumb. She banged the bottles on the bar and took a twenty from Gregory.

Joe slid a Polaroid on the bar. She didn't touch it at first, then picked it up and looked at it for a long time.

Gregory said, "We got more where that came from." He held the set of pictures up to his face, fanned out like a poker hand.

"Shit," she said, and let a burst of Spanish hang angrily in the air. "How you get this?"

"What are you worried about?" Gregory said. "You look great. I'm going to pass these around."

"Young Girl" began again for the third time since we walked in, but nobody was listening; they were watching us.

"No," she said softly, dropping Joe's twenty back in a wet spot in front of him. She raised her arm and jiggled a dozen bangle bracelets back toward her elbow. "I get off at twelve. Nevermore Lounge. You know where?"

Gregory said, "No later than twelve-thirty."

At midnight a younger version of Immaculata, in tight jeans and red halter top, took over behind the bar. We finished our beers as cliques of off-duty cops, in leather or canvas windbreakers and flannel shirts, streamed through the door, forewarned of our presence. One of the brave ones held his nose, saying, "Something stinks in here." Anyone in a clean shirt was IAD to precinct cops.

We took second drags on the anisette air as we walked up Broadway. Gerald Ford lurched out just ahead of us, got in his Pinto, pulled out in front of the number 24 bus, and aimed himself at the suburbs.

"When you're not drinking," the Great Gregory said, "drinkers are scary."

We were drinking a little more these days, but not as much as we used to. In the lost years we began lunch in the back of Brady's with a round of Bloody Marys. We drank our way through the workday and wound up in some bar like this in Queens, or Brooklyn, or maybe here. I always have an eerie feeling in places like this, that I've been here before, and it wasn't a good time.

The Nevermore Lounge was a cheater's joint on the Grand Concourse near Fordham Road, across from Poe Park and the farmhouse where Edgar Allan Poe once lived. We took a booth in the dark and private back room. The booths were softly padded puffs of red vinyl, with crested buttons, cozy love nests with candles in Chianti bottles on each table. A couple sat, side by side, in the far back booth.

Ten minutes later Immaculata slithered in with the static swish of nylon thighs. She slid in next to me, close enough to make hip contact, and ordered a Bacardi 151 and milk.

"This is bullshit, man," she said, adding a "g," "mang." Her voice was deep and resonant in the quiet room.

"Murder isn't bullshit," Gregory said.

"I didn't kill nobody. Don't give me that shit, or I call my lawyer. I don't need to take no shit. I didn't do nothing."

Immaculata rooted through her purse, finally pulling out a pack of Marlboro filters. Her perfume was strong enough to force shallow breathing.

"You and Jinx were pretty tight," Gregory said.

"No law against fucking," she said, and lit her cigarette from the candle. Close to the flame I could see a layer of thick pancake-type makeup, but when she sat back in the dim glow of candlelight she looked dark, plush, exotic.

"Relax," Gregory said. "We know you didn't kill Jinx. Just tell us how you met him."

She touched a red fingernail to the corner of her red lips, picking off a flake of lipstick.

"I first meet Jinx, I was fifteen, dancing go-go in the Orchid Lounge on Tremont. Jinx knows the owner." She rolled her eyes upward. They disappeared under heavy lashes.

"Fifteen?" I said.

"I look older," she said, cupping her breasts.

"You ever meet any of his friends?" I asked.

"When I work in La Copa he bring guys in."

"Cops or mob guys?" I said.

"Cops," she answered. "Shit, I'm not crazy."

Her perfume seemed to be getting stronger. I moved away a little, and she gave me a pouty look. "When was the last time you saw Jinx?" I said.

The couple in the back stood up, walked arm in arm to the jukebox, and began dropping coins. Immaculata watched them. "I don't think I saw him his last day," she said.

"How do you know it wasn't his last day?" I asked.

"You give me bullshit, motherfucker." She snatched her purse off the table and began to slide out of the booth.

"You want bullshit," Gregory said, reaching over to grab her arm, "we'll give you bullshit. How about we subpoena you at McGuire's, let them think you're working for IAD? You know what happens to you then."

I said, "All we want is some simple information. Were you with Jinx in October of 1972?"

"I don't know, man. Last time he come to my house he's in his uniform. Drunk, talking shit."

"In uniform." I nodded at Gregory. The medal ceremony was the only time Jinx had been in uniform in a decade. "What time did he get there?"

"Afternoon, I think. When I'm getting ready for work. I work then at the Homestead, near the Four Eight Precinct."

"What shit was he talking?" I said.

"Shit. You know, bullshit. He's drunk. Drunk bullshit. He only stay a few minutes, maybe a half hour."

Barry White whispered intimacies from the jukebox as the couple behind us danced, barely moving. Immaculata watched as they scuffed across the grit of the unswept wooden floor.

"Where was he going when he left you?" Gregory asked.

"I don't remember."

"Maybe you remember a place on Arthur Avenue and One Hundred Eighty-seventh Street?" I said. "Italian place."

"Where?" I saw the look on her face; her mouth parted a little wider.

Gregory said, "We have a witness saw you there."

"Fontana's," I said.

"I think so," she said. "Yeah. Sometimes we go to that place. Jinx don't like to pay for nothing. He was cheap, like that. I don't know. Listen, we did shit together. We go to bars, to restaurants, to motels, good times, shit like that. We did shit, but fun. You know? He never say his business."

I handed her the lineup folder.

"Too dark in here," she complained. "I don't know, man. It was a long time ago."

"Who did he meet in Fontana's?" Joe asked. "Take a good look at the pictures. Snap that light on, pally."

Immaculata looked briefly at the folder, then stared at the couple dancing. The man was white, balding, the woman dark-skinned, with a swirling, lacquered hairdo. Her arms wrapped tightly around the man's neck.

"That's all," she said. "Let me think later. I don't feel good now. You can believe me."

"Did Jinx keep notes, a notebook?" I said. "Like a school notebook, or a police notebook?"

"Yeah. Like a book for school," she said. "His memory, he say."

"Where did he keep it?" I said.

She shrugged. "In his, what you call it? Brown, like a businessman."

"Briefcase?" I said.

She grunted a yes, finished her drink, slid out of the booth, and tugged her skirt down over her thighs. Her drink had left a white milk line on her upper lip. She blotted it with a wide, pink tongue, big enough to cover her nose.

"Should we ask McGuire for your home address?" I said.

She gave us the address, no phone. "I don't feel good," she said. "No bullshit."

"You could feel worse," Gregory said. "Better think hard."

We both watched the movement of her ass as she walked out the door.

"She knows more," I said. "It was all over her face."

"What the hell kind of perfume is that?" Gregory asked, smelling his sleeve. "We're going to have to burn our clothes."

The couple in the back had disappeared down into the booth. We could hear breathing, the rustle of clothes.

"I knew he kept notes," I said. "We need to get back inside Mulgrew's house. Get that file cabinet."

"I'll lay odds on one thing," Gregory said, still watching the door. "That woman doesn't own a piece of white underwear. Nothing but red and black. Always wears a garter belt, guaranteed."

26

WE SPENT a few days trying to catch up on paperwork. It was not unusual for us to fall a week behind, but Shick had apparently caught some flak from Neddy Flanagan. Headquarters cops lived and died by paper.

Saturday morning I parked my Nova in a spot on Seventieth Street just vacated by a Volvo with a full ski rack. Gregory was late, so I waited in the car. I was about three car lengths from the corner of Central Park West, about half a block away from the Mulgrew house, on the opposite side of the street.

Out of habit I checked the visual angle: trees were bare, the view unobstructed. This was a bad habit. I did this too often when Leigh and I were going somewhere, to visit or shop. I parked fifty yards away and looked up to read the sight line, as if on a surveillance job. Leigh would just sit there shaking her head, waiting for me to return to the real world.

The West Side yuppies were going to brunch. A tall guy in a designer army field jacket skipped down the steps of a brownstone, clutching *The Times* under his arm like a diplomatic pouch. I was dressed in jeans, a paint-spotted sweatshirt, and an old ski jacket. I cracked open the car window an inch and ripped a pie-shaped piece off the coffee cup lid. Cops didn't do brunch.

Legally we were walking on eggshells. If we did find something incriminating in the Mulgrew house, we would then have to apply for a search warrant, saying it was discovered accidentally. A judge might buy our Good Samaritan story, if we swore the evidence was found in close proximity to the area we were cleaning. But cops knew that coincidence resided alongside intuition on the bottom of the credibility scale. We would never get it past the guys in Brady's, who'd know we had manipulated the aging widow of a stand-up guy. Socially we'd be in quicksand.

I'd just finished scratching out the DD5 on our interview with Immaculata when Gregory parked his dad's pickup at the hydrant in front of Mulgrew's, flush on the bumper of a Mercedes 350-SL. Liam Gregory had never owned any vehicle except a pickup truck. Several times we'd used the truck to move Joe's belongings from Levittown to Bay Ridge and back. Joe wore a Brooklyn Dodgers hat and Auto Crime Division coveralls. He was swinging a paper bag.

"You think our cars are safe in this neighborhood?" he said, getting in.

He opened my glove compartment and set two containers on the shelf, then noticed my cup steaming on the dash. "Took care of yourself, I see."

"How are we going to handle this?" I asked.

"I'm along for the ride. It's your baby."

"Oh, really? When did I get sole custody?"

"What exactly you looking for?"

"Notebooks, address or appointment books. Best case

would be a marked-up calendar indicating where he'd be that day."

"What happens, we come up with a list, naming names, guys on the pad, some shit like that? Going to be names of guys we know, guys we drink with."

"We'll worry about that when it happens."

"Hear me out for a second," Gregory said. "We need some empathy here. A lot of those guys ... before the Knapp Commission; I ain't got no patience for guys stealing since Knapp. But back then, those guys got involved in pads and shit, not because they were bad cops. They went along because there was no other way. It was the norm."

"We didn't go along," I said.

"So what then? We knew about the pads. And we kept our mouths shut. Now we nail them for shit we knew about fifteen, twenty years ago. Not for nothing, but that's freaking hypocritical. I don't know about you, but I plan to be a forty-year man. And I don't want to be treated like a leper for the rest of my life."

"You saying you're not going in?"

"No, just that we need to understand that we're human. Humans sometimes miss things when they're searching. See what I'm saying?"

"I see," I said.

"It's the right thing to do."

Ellen Mulgrew greeted us at the door in a gray wool dress, a green silk scarf around her neck. She barely said hello, nervously flicking at loose strands of hair, pushing them behind her ear. She took my old, ripped jacket and walked to the closet, where she took a padded hanger and carefully inserted it into the sleeves. Then she zippered the jacket all the way up and hung it on the bar. Gregory asked for a broom and followed Ellen into the kitchen.

"I'll work alone, I'm used to it," I said, and walked upstairs carrying the pail and bags of brushes and rags.

The stairs on either side of the runner had been waxed to a dark oaken shine. I opened the door to the tiny darkroom to let it air out for a few minutes and walked quietly into the master bedroom.

The bedroom floor was covered with a large oval braided rug. A faded orchid chenille bedspread covered the double bed, but there were no sheets, no pillows. Two dressers, dark oak with mother-of-pearl knobs, sat on opposite sides of the room. The tall one was bare. On the smaller one sat only a statue of the Blessed Virgin, her arms outstretched. Dust rose from the floor in a beam of sunlight. A framed needlepoint of Ireland with two counties outlined hung on the wall, the only personal item. The room had an eerily vacant feel.

I searched quickly. Closets and dressers were bare. I reached under the dressers and bed for a briefcase, for papers, for any sign of life. But nobody had lived in this room for a while. I heard Joe coming up the stairs, singing "Doobie, doobie, doo . . ."

"Not started yet?" Gregory said. "Must be a city worker."

"This is very kind of you," Ellen said from the bottom of the stairs. She took a rare look up at me. "Both of you."

"Our pleasure," Gregory said. "You may have to excuse my pal Ryan, though. Manual labor's not his thing. He's a heavy thinker."

I made five trips to the truck, carrying plastic bags filled with trays, bottles, and boxes of chemicals, dumping them all into the back of the pickup. It took both of us to carry the old metal file cabinet out of the dark-room. I backed down the steps one at a time, listening to Joe grunt like a sumo wrestler.

"I should have brought my old man's dolly," Gregory said.

"You should have brought your old man," I said.

We carried everything out of the room, cleaned the table and the shelves. Then we scrubbed the walls of the darkroom and mopped the floor.

"Where can he dump this dirty water?" Gregory asked.

"In the basement," Ellen said. "There's a deep sink."

Water splashed, cold and brown, down into the base-ment sink. I squeezed and twisted the mop under the flow. The floor was an uneven concrete; a heavy wooden beam ran down the center of the ceiling. A short flight of concrete steps with ramps on both sides ran up to a double door, out to the backyard. Stacked against the rough stone wall were two suitcases, one with a piece of an Aer Lingus baggage tag.

My hands burned from chemicals or disinfectant. I dried them on my pants and turned the luggage tag. The flight number was ripped off.

Along the far wall a workbench of thick heavy wood ran the length of the room. Gardening tools and uno-pened packets of seed lined the workbench. On the floor near the steps were two long boxes, emitting strong fumes of mothballs. Both boxes were full of men's clothes.

I walked to the top of the stairs and asked Ellen if she wanted us to throw out those old clothes.

Gregory said, "I know just the mendekin who can use them."

"What's a mendekin?" I said after we parked in the circle in back of headquarters.

"Look it up," he said.

I'd followed him downtown. We parked close to the building so we could lug everything up the back elevator. Headquarters was empty on weekends.

"You mean that bum you always talk to?" I said. "The guy who's always on the corner?"

"Brownie's not a bum, he's a mendekin. Take him off my income tax every year. He signs a receipt."

"IRS accepts that? How do you list it?"

"Brownie slash mendekin. Madison and Pearl streets. Five hundred dollars."

We carried the file cabinet and clothes into the equipment room in our office and opened the cabinet immediately. Somebody had already been through it; folders were empty, papers and pictures jammed in.

"These files have been checked," I said. "Nothing here."

Gregory seemed relieved and left to pick up lunch. While he was gone I called for a passport check on Ellen Mulgrew. I was just starting on the clothes when Gregory returned.

"Roast beef. The way you like it," Gregory said. He laid a brown bag and two empty coffee cups on the metal cabinet, then ripped open the bag. The smell of garlic filled the room. The windowless equipment room was only seven by ten, with beige metal walls and the constant rush of air forced though ducts in the ceiling.

I asked, "Is there a bedroom downstairs in Mulgrew's house?"

"Next to the kitchen," Gregory said. "I saw it when I got the broom. Why?"

"Curious," I said.

I opened the box of clothes, and my eyes watered from the mixture of garlic and mothballs.

"Feds called back for you," Gregory said. "I took the message. No record of a passport on your lady."

I could hear the air *whoosh*ing; it seemed to get stronger at times.

"Ever notice about the feds?" he asked. "They always have to get back to you. They never give you an answer when you call. It's always 'I'll get back to you.'"

I began pulling clothes out of the box.

"Whose passport you working on, anyway?" he said. "Is it a secret, or what? Just something else you're curious about?"

"Ellen Mulgrew. Suitcases in her basement with an Aer Lingus tag. Just wondered when she'd been flying."

"Could belong to Jinx," he said. "Luggage from years ago."

"I didn't see a bit of dust on either one."

"She's Mrs. Clean," he said. "Dust don't get a chance to hit the floor."

"Forget it, Joe. She doesn't have a passport, so the point is moot."

"Moot," he said. "The point is freaking moot."

The clothes boxes contained a dark tweed overcoat, a dozen sport or suit jackets, as many pairs of pants, an olive-colored raincoat, six pairs of shoes, and one pair of cowboy boots, the toes curled up enough for a genie. I felt the lining of a blue suit, shiny from wear.

"Checking the linings for Nazi microfilm?" he said.

The inside lining of the suit jacket was scored with cuts, threads hanging. Jinx must have worn a shoulder holster. You could always tell a cop's suit jacket. The hammer of the gun rubbed the satin lining, scratching fine scars in the fabric. A lifetime spent wearing a gun left its mark.

"We can always beat it out of her," Gregory said. He held up a small rubber daystick, an eight-inch-long rubber club used by cops walking a foot beat on day tours. The theory was that day tours were less dangerous and a small club carried in the back pocket would suffice.

"That's the flask your father was talking about," I said. I unscrewed the false top and looked in, finding only the smell of old whiskey.

"Maybe there's a secret message in there," Gregory said. "We can use our decoder rings."

"Guys who keep this much stuff do not misplace things, Joe. Look at this jacket. He probably wore it to his prom."

"His notes are long gone, pally. Face it."

I rubbed the lining of the raincoat against the outer shell. A large dark food stain ran down the front.

"All I ask," he said, "is that we don't go overboard looking for corruption. If it's there, okay. Otherwise . . ."

I threw the raincoat in the box, put the cover back on, and slid it under the wire team's workbench. Gregory opened a paper bag and took out a Coke bottle filled with amber liquid, a cork in the top.

"I got us a flute of Johnnie Black," he said. "We can have a cocktail during the inquisition, can't we? A coupla dinosaurs like us, working the weekend. We deserve a highball."

Knowing what a flute is dates you in the job. It's just a soft-drink bottle filled with booze. I can remember midnight tours in the precinct, at three or four in the morning, a sergeant would tell a rookie to "get a flute for the lieu." He meant find a friendly bartender in some friendly bar.

Desk lieutenants then were imperious, white-haired Irishmen in starched white shirts, looking down from the raised precinct desk. All night long they wrote in the blotter with fountain pens, recording the sacred precinct events in a formal, elegant hand. I remember, as a rookie, stepping up behind the desk and pouring Scotch into a coffee cup, like an altar boy pouring wine into a chalice. The old lieutenant didn't even look at me, just continued to write in that big green book, solemnly, as if it were the word of God.

Maybe having a head filled with all these old things roots you too deeply in the past. Sentiment works like the tide, beating you back. Maybe you reach a point in your life when links to the past outweigh hope for the future. Maybe I'm destined to be a cop forever. A lot of maybes, Gregory would say.

"I think it's time we went back on Bobo Rizzo," Gregory said. "He should have something by now. Day tours are making you paranoid, anyway."

"I'm going to inventory this stuff Monday."

"Oh, for Christ's sake," he said. "It'll take all day."

"Then let's try Immaculata one more time," I said. I picked up the coffee cup and felt the good burn of Scotch in my throat.

"You're just like that broad, pally," he said. "A real piece of work."

27

On Ash Wednesday we left for the Bronx after the noon mass at St. Andrew's. Gregory's forehead was crossed with the black smudge he'd leave there all day.

"Bottom line is we still got three weeks," he said. "If Bobo Rizzo don't come through, we go after Bongiovanni. Or Nicky. I got plans for Nicky."

Immaculata's five-story walk-up was in a ravaged beige brick building that faced the no-man's-land of Crotona Park. The glass front door panel had been replaced with a piece of plywood with more spraypainted signatures than the Declaration of Independence. "Candy 178" had scrawled his John Hancock across the center in swooping red curlicues. No names appeared on the mailbox; some doors had been pried open and left hanging. The hallway, lit by a bare bulb on long wire, reeked of urine and stale fried grease.

"Always the top floor," Gregory said.

I'd forgotten the noise, the constant din, like a cell block: pots banging, men yelling, women crying, the sounds of children on their own. And faintly, in the background, a TV laugh track.

We walked up five flights, staying to the wall, listening

for a sudden scramble of footsteps. We'd both worked in ghetto precincts and knew enough to walk up slowly. Never arrive winded, pulse pounding. Trails of dried bloodstains diminished as we climbed the stairs. Immaculata's apartment was 5B, hand drawn on the metal door over peeling green paint. Gregory banged on it. Cops banged on doors in the Bronx out of necessity and because of adrenaline.

"Who?" a female voice asked. "Who?"

"Look out the peephole," Gregory said.

I could hear footsteps padding down the long hallway and voices, one certainly a man's. Out of habit we stood at each side of the door. Never stand directly in front.

"What a piece of work," Gregory said.

"Give me ten minutes," the woman said.

"Five," Gregory said.

"Go get coffee and come back?"

"We're not walking five flights," Gregory said. "Tell him we'll turn our backs and he can leave. We won't peek."

"No, no," she said. "You leave."

Gregory slammed the side of his fist against the metal door. It shook in the frame, echoing throughout the building.

"Tell him we'll have that goddamn Pinto towed away," Gregory said.

We'd recognized the Pinto from McGuire's Yankee Lounge. In this part of the Bronx the PBA decal and the "America: Love It or Leave It" bumper sticker was out of place among pink pimpmobiles and Chevys up on milk crates.

Gregory was breathing hard, even though we'd walked up slowly. Headquarters cops didn't get to climb stairs every day. He put a cigarette in his mouth and flipped open the Zippo; the flame lit the darkened hallway. All around us peepholes clicked open. You could feel the eyes, sense the fear. But these women, alone behind metal doors, were not afraid of cops; they were just trying, somehow, to protect children. In this death trap that had seen too many waves of immigrants, they had sniffed the air and found the smell of lighter fluid.

When I was a brand-new cop, I was overwhelmed by the sour stench of rotted food, the rats scratching behind the walls, cockroaches scurrying when the light was snapped on. A veteran cop told me not to lean against the walls inside the apartments, because that was how cockroaches got in your clothes. After that I felt them crawling on me the rest of the night. Twenty years later that seemed like such a petty worry.

The door flew open and the Gerald Ford look-alike ran down the stairs, still tucking his shirt in. Immaculata stared at Gregory's forehead.

"What's that black shit on your head?" she said.

Immaculata wore a pink satin peignoir with puffy white balls on the sleeves, underneath that only a black Jack Daniel's T-shirt and red bikini panties. She sat on the couch opposite me and tried to fold her bare brown legs under her. Fresh scarlet lipstick stained her coffee cup and cigarette. Her perfume drifted in a mist, like tear gas in the wind. She laughed when Gregory told her that her boyfriend look satisfied.

"Tommy's good people," she said. "Takes me nice places. Empire State Building, you know that place?"

"The place where King Kong died." Joe sat across from us in a plum-colored BarcaLounger. Immaculata's electric red wig was hooked over the chair arm like a nylon pelt. An empty Wise potato chips bag was on the floor.

"He usually don't stay all night," she said. "His wife, you know. He lives in Pearl River, upstate."

Pieces of lint were stuck in her black hair. She sat against the arm of the sofa, facing me, and shifted to extend her legs across the cushions, one foot against my hip. She cocked her right knee and smiled as she adjusted her red panties. I noticed a large bruise inside her upper thigh.

"I'll bet Jinx took you to nice places," I said.

"Jinx took me the best places I never went before in my whole life. We went to the Bahamas once. When Jinx wife was in the hospital getting that thing. You know. Where they cut a woman's insides so she can't have no more babies."

"A hysterectomy," I said.

"He tell his wife he have to go pick up a prisoner." She laughed and began rubbing her bruised thigh with her free hand. I could see teeth marks.

"The light is good in here," I said. "Good enough for looking at these pictures again."

"You can see everything," Gregory said.

I handed her the folder with all the pictures.

"I can't remember shit," she said. "I knew a lot of cops."

"Look close," Gregory said, "like your life depends on it."

"Names, shit . . . who remembers? Sid, this is Sid."

"Sid Kaye," I said. "Anyone else?"

She shook her head no.

"We'll have to keep visiting," Gregory said.

She smiled at me and let the tip of her pink tongue peek between her lips. "So?" she said. She angled her knee to show more red nylon crotch.

"We'll have to hang around the bar," Gregory said. "In case you suddenly remember something."

"How about this guy?" I pointed to Flanagan.

Gregory said, "Jesus Christ."

"Maybe," she said. "I don't know. Jinx don't tell me his friends. I don't ask."

I heard a rooster crow in an adjacent apartment. The South Bronx was the home of the fighting cock.

"Can I use the bathroom?" Gregory said.

When the bathroom door closed Immaculata pushed next to me and touched my hair, just flipping it with her fingers. Then she kissed me lightly, as if to feel my lips.

"*Qué lindo,*" she said, and stood up and walked toward the bedroom. The bedroom had a wide opening where a double door must have been.

"You married?" she asked. I showed her my ring. "Your wife is married, but you're not, right?"

She glanced over at the bathroom door, then stepped back into the bedroom, removed the peignoir, and pulled her T-shirt over her head. She stood in the doorway and sucked her stomach in. Her breasts were wide and full; her waist in proportion looked tiny. She looked again toward the bathroom.

"You like?" she asked. "Maybe someday we have coffee, alone." Her hands looked small, kneading those brown breasts, dark nipples rising between blood red fingernails.

I said, "Jinx was a lucky guy."

"You know it, baby," she said. She lifted her right breast and bent her head and flicked her pink tongue over the nipple.

I was about to show her Neddy's picture again when the toilet flushed; she grabbed a blue oxford shirt someone had left behind. Gregory looked at both of us, did a double take. Then he held up a small glassine envelope with a small amount of white powder.

"Look what I found," he said. "Time to hear your rights."

"Bullshit," she said, forgetting about buttoning the oxford. "That's fucking bullshit. No drugs in there."

"Cuff her, pally," Gregory said.

"She'd like that," I said. I reached in my suit pocket, knowing that I'd left them in the Buick. I made a mental note to begin carrying cuffs, then I started to recite *Miranda*.

"You put drugs there," she said. "You not supposed to do that shit no more."

"Anything you say may be held against you," I said.

"Okay, stop, motherfuckers, stop," she said. "I don't go to no court."

"No court," I said, "I promise."

"You promise shit," she said. "No court, right? Or else I get my lawyer."

"I swear," I said. "Tell us who Jinx met."

"Bastards," she said, sagging onto the BarcaLounger. Gregory said, "Don't bullshit us this time. Tell us about Fontana's."

"All I know about that place," she said, "Jinx check his coat and briefcase with the waiter. We eat dinner, have some drinks. Then we leave. Money is in the briefcase."

"How do you know that?" I said.

"Jinx count the money as soon as he gets in the car."

"Did he ever give you any?" Gregory asked.

"No," she said, then, *"Poquito,"* holding her thumb and index finger about a quarter inch apart. "For rent. I live on Morris then. Nice place. We go there, he count the money again, put it in envelopes. Then we go to the bar and wait for Sid."

"Who did he meet in Fontana's?" Gregory said.

I handed her the lineup folder. She looked at me and flared her upper lip like Elvis.

"Mellow Head," she said, pointing to Ugo Bongiovanni. "He's in the restaurant, talks to Jinx. But I don't testify against Mellow Head. Those people, shit. Mellow Head blow my ass away."

"You mean melon head?" Gregory said.

"Jinx call him Mellow Head, I think. Jinx didn't like him."

"The last time you saw Jinx," I said, "that time he was drunk and in uniform, was he going to Fontana's to meet Mellow Head?"

"He want me to go, too, but I have to go to work. And he was drunk, I told you. Asshole drunk."

"Did he ever take you to the Fulton Fish Market?" Gregory asked.

"No way, José," she said. "What the fuck you think? It stinks down there."

28

WE DROPPED Immaculata at a rice-and-beans joint on the corner of Crotona Avenue. Then we stopped at a hot dog wagon on Tremont, picked up four Sabrett dogs with onion sauce and two Yoo-Hoos. Joe said as long as we were in the Bronx we should cruise by Fontana's. I asked him what he'd put in the glassine envelope.

"Talcum powder," he said, handing me the envelope.

"Smells like that perfume she wears," I said. "Maybe we should sprinkle this around the car, get the fish stink out."

"Remember the miracle of Forty-second Street?" he said, wrinkling his ash-smeared brow.

I had a ton of stories with Joe Gregory. A lifetime of stories. A few years ago we were working with the Mayor's Commission for a Better Times Square, conducting raids, trying to shut down the peep shows and porno parlors. I wrote warrants, Joe was with the street team, gathering evidence. He kept telling me about Daisy May, a stripper who defied the laws of nature as well as man. According to Gregory, Daisy would puff on a corncob pipe and blow smoke rings the size of a Hula Hoop through her vagina.

I made a point to go along on the raid. We sat in the back while Daisy interacted with several members of the audience. In her big finale, she wafted a dozen smoke rings out into the crowd. We threw the house lights up during her first curtain call, and as I walked up to the stage I noticed that guys in the first three rows were covered with white. Their faces, hair, and clothes were all thoroughly dusted white; it looked like a school for mimes. Talcum powder. The miracle of Forty-second Street had been blowing talcum powder.

Joe parked across from Fontana's Restaurant, using the braille parking method. Without looking, he backed up until he hit the car behind, then drove forward to tap the one in front. One more rear tap, one more front, and we sat back to eat our hot dogs and stare. The smell of onion sauce covered the fish stink.

We were parked a total of half a minute when the door of the Sons of Sicily opened and the kid with the pink Spalding appeared behind us, resuming his eternal handball game. Ugo Bongiovanni's black Mercedes was in front of the restaurant.

"Before this ends let's drop something on Ugo's car," Joe said. "Like the body of Nicky Skooch."

I was beginning to feel the rush that came when the chase heated up. We were getting closer to knowing about Jinx Mulgrew's last hours. We figured that after he left the Spinellis, at Rolf's Restaurant, it took about forty-five minutes to drive to Immaculata's. He probably arrived at her place around two-fifteen. Say an hour of play with Immaculata, then a fifteen-minute ride to Fontana's.

"Figure Jinx got here at three-thirty," I said.

"At the latest," Gregory said. "Maybe he didn't walk

out of here; got rolled out. What do you think? We getting close?"

"We're doing good. But we're going to come up one piece of evidence short of a case."

"Case needs a goose. That's all," he said. "You got that picture of Jinx?"

"Why?" I said.

"I'm going to shake the trees."

One of the things I both loved and hated about working with Joe was that he never thought things over for long.

"Let's not screw up now," I said.

"Screw what up?" he asked. "We got three weeks left. What have we got to lose? These guys ain't going to roll over on the word of a Puerto Rican barmaid. Besides, we owe these pricks, the shit they pulled. The only thing these mutts understand is fear. And it's our duty as cops to instill the fear of God in them."

I should have said, "Tell me exactly what you plan to do." But I knew he didn't have a plan. I gave him the picture, then slid everything under the seat, trying to control what I could control. Never leave anything visible in a car: binoculars, files, portable radio, clipboard, lottery tickets, loose change, stale doughnuts, anything that might tempt a junkie to break your window.

Gregory asked the lookout to look out for our car, as long as he was looking out. The kid gave him the Italian salute, slapping his biceps hard enough to bruise.

Fontana's was in that lull between lunch and dinner when restaurants cleaned the ashtrays, filled salt shakers, and changed to the expensive menus. Ugo Bongiovanni, Nicky Skooch, and two unknown males in Qiana shirts were gathered under a cloud of cigar smoke at the small service bar near the window. Nobody was sitting at any of the two dozen tables covered with white cloths. Bobo Rizzo was not in attendance.

Ugo was wearing a green sports jacket, even uglier than the one they gave to the winner at the Masters. His white shirt, open at the collar, showed one solitary gold chain with a small horn. Ugo was as big as I thought, but a lot of his bulk looked like upholstery, not muscle.

Nicky looked lean and hard. He wore his shirt open, showing off a tight gold necklace. On his chest I could see the top of a tattoo: a hand, reaching upward toward his throat.

We stood at the opposite end of the small service bar and waited for a bartender. Through a small window in the kitchen door I could see someone on the wall phone. Dishes and silverware rattled. The wise guys ignored us. Then Gregory banged his fist down on the bar.

"You need a rap sheet to get served in here, or what?" he said.

"Gentlemen," Bongiovanni said, turning slowly as if he'd just noticed us.

"When does the rest of the entertainment get here?" Gregory asked. "You guys are the mariachis, right?"

"This is not a drinking bar," Ugo said. For a big man he had small hands, neatly manicured, clear polish. "Dinner begins at five. We'd be happy to serve you then."

"I'd eat dog shit before I'd eat here," Gregory said.

"Perhaps then I could suggest the Blarney Stone on Fordham Road," Bongiovanni said.

I had seen Joe's tough-guy routine before, and it always made me uncomfortable. I felt as if I'd just tagged along to hold his coat.

"Maybe you're right, Ugo," Gregory said. "At least I'd be eating with honest workingmen."

Nicky Skooch was yanking at his pants and breathing hard through his mouth. The two unknown males whispered among themselves. Nicky had the collapsed face of an ex-boxer: swollen eyelids and puffy skin quilted with scar tissue. I noticed the bulge of his ankle holster.

"I don't believe we've met," Ugo said.

"Cut the bullshit," Gregory said.

"We've not been introduced," Ugo said.

Gregory flipped his shield and ID card quickly and naturally, as if merely opening his hand. I didn't identify myself, but I stepped up, shoulder to shoulder with Gregory.

"What can I do for you . . . officers?" Ugo said, glancing at me, sizing me up. Gregory handed him the picture of Jinx. Ugo looked and immediately said, "I do not know this gentleman."

"You're a lying sack of shit," Gregory said.

"Jesus fucking Christ," Nicky Skooch said, getting close to hyperventilating. Ugo turned and glared at him, and Nicky stormed into the kitchen, banging both swinging doors.

"Sorry," Ugo said calmly. "I truly wish I could help."

"Think ten years back," Gregory said. "Think trash can, put a little cement around him."

"I have no idea what you are talking about," Ugo said, handing the picture back to Joe.

"Look at it under the light," I said, trying to salvage something. "You do know him."

"Excuse me a moment," Ugo said, and walked into the kitchen. Nicky was shouting into the wall phone in the kitchen.

I remembered that you could get hurt shaking the trees, especially if you stood directly underneath. It had happened to us before. I took a breath and whispered to Gregory, "You've made your point."

Gregory winked at me. I wondered if he'd forgotten the night in Archer's Ringside Lounge when we had to pry Hurricane Jackson off him.

Ugo returned with a bottle of red wine, slid three glasses from the overhead rack, and set them on the bar. "We have gotten off on the wrong foot," he said. "Perhaps you will kindly do me the honor of sharing a glass of wine, and I will look again at your photograph."

He put the bottle on the bar and found the corkscrew next to the wet sink. Ugo poured wine in the three glasses, then picked up the picture. Nicky was still on the kitchen phone.

"I must apologize," he said. "I once met this gentleman. A police officer, am I correct? I did not recognize him at first." Bongiovanni studied my face briefly, then said, "I read of what happened to him, but I have no idea how he died. If I could help you, I would, gladly."

The wine had the bitter taste of altar wine. I thought if we could calm the situation, we might be able to get something out of this. Ugo might slip and give us a missing piece.

Gregory picked up the glass of wine and raised it to Ugo. "Well, I guess that's it, then," he said. "The word of a dumb guinea, cop-killing bastard is good enough for me. How about you, pally?"

I flinched when Joe threw the wine; it was like something Bette Davis might do. Nicky Skooch burst through the kitchen doors and made a charge toward us. Ugo put his hand up, but it took the unknown males to stop

Skooch. Red stains ran down the front of Ugo's white shirt. Then Gregory threw the glass into the mirror, and glass shattered; red wine blurred our reflection. Ugo stood frozen, staring at Gregory, perhaps wondering if you could kill a man wearing ashes.

"C'mon, Nicky," Gregory said, backing into the middle of the dining room. "Face to face, you fucking coward."

Gregory, jacket off, called Nicky out onto the center of the floor. The unknowns fought to hold Nicky, their feet sliding on the waxed tiles. Nicky looked as though he'd had more than a few fights, and a pro had a huge advantage. But I'd seen Gregory fight. Furniture broke, someone got hurt. His was not a sweet science.

But there'd be no fight today. Ugo said something low and in Italian, while patting Nicky on the face. Nicky laughed, straightened his shirt, and left through the front door. Ugo waited until the door closed behind Nicky. He continued speaking in Italian to the unknowns. I could remember my grandparents talking conspiratorially in that warm, musical language. The only word I understood was "Irish."

"You come into my place, my house," Ugo said, daubing at his shirt, "and you show me no respect." His tone was calm but with the strained, surreal pitch of pure rage. "What then, gentlemen?" he said. "What then?"

"We'll see how they respect you in our place," Gregory said. "Riker's Island."

There may have been times when I was happier leaving a bar, but I couldn't recall one. A light rain had begun to fall; wipers slapped on passing cars. I pulled up my coat collar and looked at Gregory while we waited to cross the street. His face was an iridescent red, coated with a patina of sweat. It glowed in the reflection of traffic lights and rain. But something was wrong, something was different in the street.

"Grandstand bullshit," I said. "Stupid goddamn hot dog bullshit. You blew our hand, whatever chance we had."

"See how pissed they were."

"Not that pissed. Hurricane Jackson wouldn't have taken that much shit from you."

Someone locked the restaurant doors behind us, pulled down the shades.

"Listen to me," he said. "We got them over a barrel. Ugo can't come after us, because the bosses won't stand for it. Whacking us makes him look too psycho to take over the family. But he can't let us push him around, either, because he loses face. Follow me?"

"Follow you? What possible line of reasoning could you have to follow?"

"We'll see some fireworks now," he said as we started across the street to the Buick. "Let the games begin."

Then I realized what was wrong. The kid with the pink Spalding wasn't there. It was a moment of epiphany that coincided with the crack of the shot.

You are never more focused than when your life is in danger. In the silence of slow motion I saw my foot in the air, taking its time to come down on the yellow center line. Then Gregory fell, bringing me down with him, slamming my knee into the pavement.

Instantly I did a push-up, feeling the damp grit of the road in my palms, seeing each pebble and grain of glass as if under a microscope. Next thing, I hung in the air like a bag of laundry, the Great Gregory with a handful of my coat and ribs. We reached the car hearing shots ricochet. Gregory threw me down on my knee again.

Out of the corner of my eye I'd seen a muzzle flash from the roof of the Sons of Sicily. Two more bullets ricocheted, sending sparks off the buildings behind us. I crawled on one knee to the passenger door before I realized I had locked everything up. I'm so goddamn neat. Gregory sat against the front wheel as I rummaged in his pockets for the key. The right leg of his gray pants was soaked with dark blood.

I opened the door, knocked over a half bottle of Yoo-Hoo, pulled the portable radio out from under the front seat, and called in a 1013. Assist patrolman. Within seconds I heard the first siren.

The shooting stopped, but traffic was still moving down the street. Nobody saw anything in this city. Warm blood trickled down the numbness of my knee. Gregory flopped facedown across the backseat, mumbling. I leaned in to see how he was. Blood was pooling on the tan upholstery under his leg.

"I solved one mystery," Gregory said. He held up a white Jojo's bag, fuzzy, crawling with ants and bugs. "The smell."

Inside the bag was a blue claw crab from the Chesapeake Bay who'd spent the winter in our Buick. I flipped it into the streets of the Bronx, then daubed at blood on my knee with a napkin covered with onion sauce. And listened to the convergence of sirens.

29

"Don't take me to Fordham," Gregory kept saying to the two cops helping him to the radio car. "Ask my partner. He knows my hospitals downtown."

He had been hit in the upper thigh. When he slid onto the backseat of the car, he lifted his right leg with two hands, showing a blood-darkened tan argyle sock.

"We don't go into the city," the sergeant said, slamming the door behind him.

I stayed behind to search with the 46th Precinct detectives. The muzzle flash I saw had come from a roof near Belmont Avenue and the Sons of Sicily Social Club. My knee stung, kept sticking to my pants, as we climbed the narrow interior stairway to the roof.

This had been the first time I'd been ambushed, and I had reacted as taught in the academy twenty years earlier: I got behind the front wheel to let the engine block provide cover. But sometimes ricochets fooled you. The bullets caromed wildly, echoing off the steel and concrete of a city, until, as in a room of mirrors, you believed they were coming from all directions. Sometimes it came down to a lucky guess. Sometimes you hid in full view.

We walked every inch of the flat, spongy roof of the Sons of Sicily, scanning the faded tar paper, especially near the east side parapet. I stood at the spot where the shooter must have leaned over the wall with his elbows resting on the coping as he'd framed two aging cops in his cross hairs. There were no coffee cups, no cigarette butts, no shell casings, no threads of a sniper's jacket snagged on rough concrete. The cleanest roof in the Bronx.

From the roof I could see down Belmont Avenue where Dion and the Belmonts once doo-wopped under streetlights and middle-aged men still bet bankrolls on stickball games played between parked cars with sewer covers as bases. The fire escapes were lined with plants in clay pots and string mops drying. Sheets, blowing on a third-floor clothesline, snapped in the wind.

In the bare backyards of the private houses, dogs of a thousand bloodlines rooted in the dirt under the scaffolding of grapevines, next to brick barbecue grills, huge picnic tables, and rusting swing sets. It was quiet enough to hear the soft cooing and fluttering of wings from a pigeon coop on some other roof.

Afterward we walked out of the front door as a half dozen old men on mismatched wooden chairs sat around a deck of cards. They nodded politely. An espresso machine wheezed on the bar.

Gregory was already out of surgery when I arrived at Bronx Municipal, already on the phone in the nurses' station. He was surrounded by a phalanx of silver-haired Bronx brass synchronizing the story in their notebooks.

"They're admitting me," Joe said, holding his hand over the receiver. "Un-freaking-believable. I had beer can cuts worse than this."

"You calling Shick?" I asked.

"Calling my old man first, before he hears it on the radio. He's not home, wherever the hell he goes all day."

Bronx Municipal admitted Gregory, more alarmed by his blood pressure than the bullet wound. The bullet had penetrated the flesh of his upper thigh. The angle of the entrance wound showed that the trajectory was upward. The bullet had ricocheted into Joe's leg.

I called Leigh and told her I was fine, but the television news would probably blow it out of proportion. It was nothing. She was quiet and calm, but I knew her pauses were too long, her silence held a heavy weight: the weight of two decades spent anticipating such a phone call. She said, "Be careful, I love you." After I hung up I could still hear her silence.

A nurse wheeled Gregory to his room.

"We got them worried," he said.

"You think so?" I said. "Ugo didn't look like a worrier. Look at me. This is the face of a worrier."

I waited until he was set up in his room. The drug they'd given him had begun to take effect; he began mumbling and smiling as he did sometimes when he was sleepy drunk. The last thing he said to me before he fell asleep was, "I love this freaking job, pally."

The cross of ashes still covered his forehead.

I knew it was useless to go back to Fontana's. They'd all have alibi's, visiting priests or sick relatives. So I drove to the fish market to look for Rizzo. His car was parked in front of the Paris Bar. I leaned against the Lincoln and waited; the hood was still warm. Al Carrol was on his usual stool; I knew Bobo was around. I watched a cat gnaw on a fish head in the gutter as the

FPS car cruised slowly by. A redheaded guy was behind the wheel. Finally Bobo came out of R&B Fish and started walking toward the Paris Bar. I pushed myself off the Lincoln and walked toward him. My knee was still stinging from the fall.

"Don't do this to me, kid," he said out of the side of his mouth. "Not here, please."

"You want me to put my arm around you and act like we're buddies?"

"I want you to disappear. I had nothing to do with it. My hand to God."

"Get in the car, Bobo. You don't have an option."

"Cuff me," he said. "Whack me around, cuff me."

I was pissed enough to take him up on the offer. I retrieved my cuffs from the glove compartment, then slammed him over the hood of the Buick, and it rocked with the blow. Bobo was a sinewy old man who had assumed this position before. He played the role all the way, twisting and kicking for the benefit of anybody watching. It took me about thirty seconds to get the cuffs locked down over his bony wrists, and I squeezed them tight, the ratchet clicking through steel teeth. I shoved him onto the backseat, peeled out, and made a U-turn.

I drove around the Battery loop, then uptown on the West Side, and backed in against the Hudson near Christopher Street. The wind whipped whitecaps on the water and flapped the skirts of the hookers working traffic.

"Wash this fucking car, please," Bobo said, trying to sit up with his hands behind his back. "Look at the ants back here. Jesus Christ."

I reached back and pulled Bobo to a sitting position.

"I heard, I heard," he said. "What's a matter with your guy? He losing it, or what?"

"What did you hear?"

"I heard it was nothing. One in the leg, was all. Uncuff me, kid. They're cutting off my circulation."

"They shot a cop, Bobo."

"It was supposed to be a scare," he said. "That's what I think, I mean. If I knew anything about it. Which I don't. I'd say it was a scare. They hit him accidentally, that's my take on it."

I unlocked the cuffs. Bobo rubbed his wrists, then pulled out his wallet.

"Wash this thing, soon," he said, dropping a twenty-dollar bill on the seat next to me. "I heard your partner didn't show any respect. Acted like an asshole."

I threw the twenty back; he let it fall to the floor. "Since when do we have to show respect?" I asked.

"You know what I mean. Guys like us. Like me and you. We're street guys. You got to save face in the street. You know what I'm talking about."

"Oh, please, Bobo," I said.

"Hey, don't get me wrong. It's not my style, that shit. You want to straighten a cop out, there's other ways. Plenty of them."

Bobo looked off at the line of girls waving to passing cars. Some showed their breasts to the traffic to assure they were legitimate merchandise.

"I didn't know broads worked this block," he said.

"Enjoy it now. You know Ugo's going to kill you. Get you out of the way completely."

"He can have everything he wants," Bobo said. "It ain't like the old days, am I wrong? We were all gentlemen. Now you can't trust the cops, the politicians got no balls. In ten years we won't have nothing. The spiks own the coke, the niggers got the numbers. And the fucking chinks, mark my words, in five years the chinks will run all the rackets."

I could feel my knee stiffening, rubbing against the rip in my pants.

"I should pack it in, go to Boca Raton," he said. "Make the old lady happy. Tell me why I shouldn't go to Boca, sit in the sun."

"You owe us one, Bobo," I said. "It won't come back to you."

"In the open," he said.

We stood outside as the wind off the Hudson glued my coat around my legs. I could feel the crusting dried blood as I straightened my knees. We walked under the awning of a burned-out shipping warehouse, now an open-air trick pad for the West Side hustlers.

I jumped when Bobo slapped my sides, his hands under my jacket. He tossed me, the way cops had tossed him all his adult life. Tapping my chest, feeling for adhesive tape, wires, a microphone.

"Your fucking knee is bleeding," he said.

"No shit," I said.

He looked around one more time, then said, "I am not saying this, you understand?"

"It's between us."

"It can't be between us, I never said it. I have made inquiries. And all I know is who didn't kill your friend."

"He wasn't my friend."

"Whatever," he said. "On the day in question, Officer Mulgrew shows up in Fontana's. He wants fifty large to take a flyer. Throws his muscle around, says he has evidence he might give to the DA."

"Who told you this?"

"You want me to continue?" he said. "The person who took Mulgrew's request told him he didn't have that kind of cash on hand. They set up a meet for that night, Fourteen Peck."

"What time?"

"Nighttime." He shrugged.

"Time is important."

"It would be after the dinner hour. Maybe eight, maybe later."

"After numbers money is counted," I said. "Street money is in. What happened?"

"Nothing. Guy never showed."

"Who was he supposed to meet, Bongiovanni?"

Bobo nodded his head yes.

"Bongiovanni killed him," I said.

"I'm being honest with you, kid. Bongiovanni, that whole crew, are fucking head cases. If Bongiovanni should go away tomorrow, nobody's going to shed a tear. You get me? But I don't think he whacked your guy. Your guy showed, maybe he might have. But he didn't show."

The hooker in the leather skirt started walking toward us. "Going out, fellas?" she asked.

"No," I said quickly.

Bobo was smiling at her. She looked closely at me, then the car, but she kept coming toward us. "Cops get horny, baby," she said. "I taken care of plenty of cops."

Bobo laughed and began to cough.

"I can take care of that cough, Officer," the hooker

said. Bobo laughed as he lit his big cigar and coughed all the more.

"He's going to die," I said to her.

"I can grant his last wish," she said.

"Don't worry about me, kid," Bobo said, looking over his shoulder, winking at the hooker. "I'll get a cab downtown." Then he touched me on the shoulder and said quietly, "Your people killed him, kid. You got to face that. Happens in all families."

30

Bobo AND the hooker were still bargaining as I maneuvered the Buick into the uptown traffic. I should have gone back to One Police Plaza, reported to Eddie Shick, and taken my own car. But I was tired and confused, and my knee hurt like hell. I went home.

"I fell on it twice," I said.

I sat on the kitchen table reading messages while Leigh daubed my knee with peroxide. "Once would have been enough," she said.

My green clipboard was filled with notes of phone calls, mostly from cops and the wives of cops. Cops' wives and families suffer most at these times. Leigh kept busy; work was her balm. She doctored my knee, explained the messages, tinkered with dinner. I called Eddie Shick and told him the story while Leigh pretended not to listen.

"You better call her, too," Leigh said, pointing to the clipboard, meaning Katie. "If she hears you're hurt . . ."

The green plastic clipboard was a gift from Katie. It was covered with stickers: pencils, pens, books. I liked the fact that she thought of me like that, rather than in the world of guns. Children shouldn't have to fear for their parents or grandparents. On the bottom she had painted "To Pop-Pop. Love, Katie."

"I think you've cleaned it well enough," I said.

"Stinging too much?"

"Maybe for the average man, not me."

"You saw that woman again, didn't you?"

"What woman?"

"The one who wears that perfume. She must bathe in it, it's worse than last time."

"Immaculata," I said.

Gregory said we were bachelors of the night. Our wives, home in the suburbs, didn't know where we were, what kinds of women we were rubbing up against. I wondered how many other nights Leigh had smelled perfume on me.

"It's a perfume called Maja," she said. "Some of the girls at school wear it. Doesn't make the nuns too happy."

"You should have been the detective," I said.

"Women are born detectives," she said. "Who is Immaculata?"

"An old girlfriend of Jinx. She's been a big help."

"I'm sure she has. Things are going so very well." She stopped working on my knee and walked to the sink.

"The shooting was an accident, Leigh. Meant to scare us. They wouldn't shoot a cop."

"Oh! My mistake. Last time was a freak thing, this time it wasn't really a shooting. Just boys being boys. Playing a little rough, that's all."

She nodded her head, confirming some thought to herself. She kept her back to me and put the cap back on the peroxide, threw the cotton swabs in the trash.

"Let the air get to that for a while," she said. "It'll heal quicker."

"I have to see this case through, Leigh."

"I can't fix these pants," she said. "Just throw them away."

I got up from the table and put my arms around her. She pulled away, as if busy, so much to do. She turned around, her eyes wet.

"Remember that night I went to the movies with the kids?" she asked. "The car wouldn't start when we got out. You were home waiting. Do you remember that?"

"That was ten years ago," I said.

"I can remember how you acted, though. That was one night you had to worry. One night."

We spent the weekend moving gradually closer. It had been the history of our marriage to trust the healing process. When I woke up Monday morning, Leigh was in the shower. I knew it would be a normal Monday. She had the ability to forget about the past and to go on as if it had never happened.

Perhaps that quality had saved our marriage, because I tended to worry about yesterday. I walked across the hall to the computer and began typing in the events of the last few days, writing it like a story so I could get in the nuances I'd keep out of the official report. In the quiet of the house, after the shower stopped, the clack of computer keys sounded like a jackhammer.

Leigh stood in the doorway in a lime-colored towel, a matching one wrapped turban style around her hair. "I forgot to tell you what I found out," she said. "You were talking about passports, how you were surprised

Mrs. Mulgrew didn't have one. One of the teachers at school has an Irish passport. He says the Irish government will give them to Irish-Americans up to second generation. Part of some Irish government effort to get people to move back."

"That's good," I said. "That's very good."

"Worth a try."

"I love you," I said.

"I know," she said. "See if you can get some time off for spring break. We'll go south for a couple of days." She waved her hand at me and walked to the bedroom.

I'd taken Gregory's things home for safekeeping, a plastic bag containing his gun, shield, wallet, and his address book. I unwrapped the rubber bands and looked up passport info.

It was Washington's Birthday, and lots of federal offices were closed. I called five numbers, invoking the name of the Great Gregory, until I reached a woman, clearly disappointed it was me. Said she'd get right back.

Within twenty minutes the phone was ringing with more information than I wanted. Not only did Ellen Mulgrew have an Irish passport, but she'd been in Ireland often during the last few years. In fact, she'd flown home from Dublin a few days before our first meeting.

Then the woman said, "Isn't this interesting: March twenty-second, 1982, she flew Aer Lingus flight number nineteen, seat seventeen-A, from JFK to Shannon, and in seat seventeen-B there was a Liam Gregory." She asked me if he was related to Joe.

"Beats me," I said.

"Probably coincidence," she said.

This explained where Liam Gregory was spending

his time these days. It didn't explain why he was lying. At least now I knew why Ellen Mulgrew's recent statement was so remarkably similar to the statement she'd made ten years ago. She had a copy of the original.

I didn't hear Leigh leave the house.

31

SID KAYE'S new office was closed for Washington's Birthday, but Gregory had the home number of his boss. I called, and he told me Sid was on assignment at the Plaza Hotel, he'd notify him to expect me. When I drove up Sid was waiting out front, under the heated awning, checking his watch. He looked dapper, except for the porkpie hat.

"Make this snappy," he said. "I got a client inside."

"A client," I said. "You like this job, don't you, Sid?"

"Don't waste your time threatening me, kid. I been threatened by the best."

We stepped out of the way of the lunch and matinee crowd, letting them get to their cabs. Sid kept touching his rug; the heat blowing down screwed up the glue.

I said, "Last time we talked you said something about a fight between Liam and Jinx, over a woman. Was that woman Ellen Mulgrew?"

"Mulgrew's old lady, whatever her name is. Liam was boffing her for years. Fight happened at Chief Korski's racket at the Fort Hamilton Officers Club. They had some words on the staircase, next thing punches are flying. Jinx got a broken nose, big swollen honker.

Looked like Willie Pep after one of the Saddler fights. Strong fuck, Gregory."

"How soon after the fight did Jinx disappear?"

"Two years, maybe three. You thinking Liam whacked him?"

I was avoiding saying it for now. One step at a time.

"Don't strain yourself," Sid said. "It's impossible. If Jinx was whacked after the medal ceremony, Liam Gregory, that prick, didn't do it. And I can tell you why."

"Tell me why, Sid."

"That afternoon I was with my lawyer, in the Manhattan DA's office, making my deal. Lawyers are talking, I'm watching through the glass. All afternoon I'm there, and I can see Liam in the squad room. Guy never left his desk. We finish around five, and I'm driving uptown to Danny Boy's to meet Jinx. I'm on Bowery, and I spot that red-faced prick in his truck, behind me. First I thought it was a tail. Then he parks and walks in the joint ahead of me. Go figure, I said to myself."

"Jinx invited you, too?"

"We three. Me and Liam and Neddy bless-me-Father Flanagan."

"What was Flanagan doing there?"

"Beats the shit out of me. Trying to save Jinx's soul, something. Three of us sat there like new in-laws, talking about the weather."

Sid wiped a bead of sweat off his temple and waved to the doorman. The doorman hadn't stopped opening car doors since I arrived. Cabs and limousines pulled in, one after the other; overdressed people got in and out. I hadn't seen so much fur since *Dr. Zhivago*.

"That's Jimmy Kelleher, the doorman," Sid said.

"Used to be the warrant man in the Two Two. Says he's pulling down seventy-five grand calling cabs for assholes."

"When did Flanagan arrive at Danny Boy's?"

"He was already there when we walked in," Sid said. "You wouldn't have that look on your face if you knew Jinx. He never let the left hand know what the right was doing."

"Apparently he let the three of you know enough to meet him there."

"Yeah, that's why I figured he was already dead when he missed that meet."

"Why was that?" I said.

"Moola, kid," he said, rubbing the tips of his fingers together. *"Mucho dinero."*

"You had money for him?" I asked. Then it occurred to me that Sid Kaye, such a stand-up guy now, had given his partner up very easily ten years ago. Too easily. "Jinx knew that you were making a deal with the DA, didn't he?"

"Now you're getting it. Think about it. If Jinx had already taken off for parts unknown, I'd have nobody to give up, right? Nothing to bargain with. That's why it was fortunate that I signed my deal before he took off. Understand what I'm saying?"

"It was all arranged," I said. "You paid him to take the heat, knowing he was running. Then you made a deal to get away with only probation."

"You're a genius, Ryan, but let me correct you for the record. This is the story for the record, see? Jinx was a swell guy, right? That's the reason I was sitting in Danny Boy's with eighteen large in my pocket. Because I loved the prick, understand?"

"That was his price to let you make a deal with the DA?"

"We're talking hypothetics now," he said. "If Jinx had a price, hypothetically, his price would've been twenty-five. But this was a gift, remember? Eighteen was all the gift I could come up with."

"How late did you stay in Danny Boy's?"

"I left about seven, seven-thirty. Beer gives me the runs. I figured if he wanted my dough, he'd find me. They were still waiting."

A hansom cab wove between a Checker and a Peugeot with the sound of a nervous clop clop of hooves as the horse cantered to the curb and pissed powerfully, splattering the full-length mink of a blonde, who shouted "Fuck!" in clear, cultured tones. Jimmy Kelleher, the ex-cop doorman, looked back over his shoulder and gave us a "what assholes" smile.

Liam's truck was parked in the driveway. I rang the doorbell and waited. After three more rings I walked around to the backyard, following a banging sound. Liam was nailing the trellis along the deck. When the dog kept barking he realized I was there.

"Sorry, Anthony," he said, looking startled. "Didn't hear you. The hammering, I guess."

"Next year your son will have prize roses growing here."

"In a pig's eye," he said. "He doesn't throw the garbage out as long as he can walk around it."

He put down the hammer and shook my hand, covering it in his. The small brown mutt edged close to me, his tail wagging at my familiar smell. He'd come a long way since that night in Zipper's basement.

"Come, lad," Liam said. "Come inside."

The three of us walked up the steps and across a deck barely big enough for two webbed chairs and the milk crate that served as a drink table. The dog and I followed the old man through the kitchen and into Joe's bedroom. The afternoon sun was beginning its descent behind Staten Island.

"Here," he said. "Suit, shirt, tie, socks, underwear. Look at this. A shameful closet for a grown man."

"He's not a tidy guy," I said.

"I suppose he'll be on sick report."

"I suppose," I said.

I couldn't remember Joe ever being on sick report before. There was no question in my mind he'd ignore the doctors and come to work.

"He won't follow the damn rules," Liam said, waving his hand. "When he was in high school, I had to get down on my knees so the nuns at Bishop Lavin wouldn't expel him. It was a battle getting him to graduation."

"I heard you had quite a battle with Jinx at Fort Hamilton."

"Hardly a battle. Who told you?"

He led me into the kitchen. We sat at a gray Formica-covered dinette with chrome legs and four vinyl chairs. Liam clasped his hands together on the table, his skin rough and chapped. I noticed that someone had cut the white hairs he had growing from his ears last time I saw him.

"Sidney Kaye told you," he said. "The word of a convicted felon, Anthony?"

"That's not important. What's important is the fact you've been withholding important information."

"No, not important information. I held back some

things, true. This is a difficult situation. A man does not confess his indiscretions to his son."

"You call this an indiscretion?"

He took the black sponge ball from his sweater pocket and began squeezing. The dog lay at his feet, trying to sleep but shivering with every loud word. The dog's fur was beginning to grow back over the burns that had been raw, purple scars for so long.

"When Joe's mother died," Liam said, "I began drinking heavily. You probably know this, everybody does. I almost lost everything—this house, the job. Jinx and Ellen stuck by me, got me through it."

"What year are we talking about?"

"Sixty-eight, thereabouts," he said. "Jinx was running around in plainclothes then, doing his thing. Ellen and I became very close. Jinx got the wrong impression."

"You were having an affair with Ellen."

"Affair . . . If meeting for coffee and talking is having an affair, then we were. But Ellen Mulgrew is not a woman for an affair."

"She went to Ireland with you, Liam. To me that's a pretty close relationship."

In the quiet of the kitchen I could hear the buzzing of the electric clock on the wall and the occasional whimper of a dog with bad dreams.

He said, "We've been talking about what happened before Jinx disappeared. After he was gone, things were different."

"You told me you went to Ireland to look for Jinx."

"That wasn't a lie," he said. "I'd asked Ellen to marry me. But she wanted to find him first. Tell him face to face. That's the kind she is."

He rolled the sponge ball in circles on the table, pressing it under the palm of his hand. I had never thought Liam Gregory had a soft side. Maybe I hadn't looked close enough.

"You think I killed him, Anthony?"

"I didn't say that."

"Put me on the lie detector," he said, his pale blue eyes moist. "Go ahead. I'm a good suspect for you. I hated him enough, God knows. He beat her, treated her like garbage. Many's the night I swore him dead."

"Then why were you ready to give him so much money?"

"The money was a payoff. He threatened to take her with him if I didn't. I was ready to pay. And I'd do it again in a heartbeat."

I reached into my briefcase and pulled out the fishing picture. "Why didn't you tell me Sid Kaye and Neddy Flanagan were at Danny Boy's that night?"

"Men let men tell their own stories," he said.

I handed him the picture, stood up, and walked to the kitchen window. Patches of green grass were beginning to show above the mud.

"Was Jinx threatening Neddy Flanagan with that picture?" I asked.

Liam's face flushed deep red. He whistled softly. "Where did you get this?"

"Mulgrew's darkroom."

"Really?" he said. "You know everybody here?"

"I know Jinx, Sid Kaye, Bobo Rizzo."

He said, "This is Joel Cunningham, dead. Hank Ferguson, dead. Frank Coffey, went with the feds, had a stroke couple of years ago."

"You didn't mention Neddy," I said.

"I wouldn't have recognized him," he said. "God's truth."

"Why was he in Danny Boy's that night if not to pay off Jinx? Jinx was blackmailing him with this picture, wasn't he?"

"I don't know, lad. Sounds like the bastard. Rounding up everyone he could bleed. Did Sid Kaye have money?"

"Eighteen thousand," I said.

Liam smiled and shook his head. "Jinx Mulgrew was the king of the bastards," he said. "But this picture had to be an innocent mistake on Neddy's part. He was never a thief. No finer man in this department."

"Why is it, then," I said, "that you weren't surprised when he showed up that night in Danny Boy's?"

"I never said I wasn't surprised," he said. "But you'll have to ask him why he was there. Knowing him, I'm sure you'll get the truth."

"We're New York's finest, one big close family," I said. "We wouldn't lie to each other."

The third-floor desk nurse at Bronx Municipal was happy to see me. She told me to remind Mr. Gregory to watch his triglyceride count, then get him the hell out of there. I could hear the noise coming from the sunroom, Joe's voice booming.

"Use the whip," he yelled. "Use the whip, honey."

The Great Gregory and a dozen kids in pajamas had their backs to me when I walked into the sunroom. They were in a line, looking out the window that faced Pelham Parkway. Joe, in his plaid bathrobe, stood in the center of the kids with his face pressed against the glass. Everybody was yelling. A couple of dollars in quarters were stacked on a tray in front of a black kid in bed, both legs suspended in casts. He was pumping his arm in the air, screaming, "Go baby, go!"

I put down the suitcase and stood behind Gregory. Out on the grassy island in the center of Pelham Parkway a line of children on horses from a local riding academy ambled single file toward Eastchester Avenue.

"I'm in trouble again, pally," Gregory said. "I bet the lady in the green hat against the field."

The woman in the green hat bobbed along last, falling farther behind as she checked to make sure all her riders had cleared the intersection. Cars on both sides of Pelham Parkway sped by the slow-moving caravan.

Kids cheered as their horses reached Eastchester Road ahead of the woman in the green hat. Holding their pajama bottoms with one hand, they exchanged leaping high-fives as they snapped another easy quarter from the red-faced guy who knew how to pick a loser.

32

JOE GREGORY was quiet on the ride down from the hospital—silent after I told him about his father and Ellen Mulgrew. He stared out the car window at the curtainless windows of South Bronx apartments. I tried to talk about the case, because I had no personal advice for him. I had nothing wise to say about relationships and family. Work was all. But, unfortunately, the two were becoming entwined.

"Why didn't he tell us?" I said. "After all these years, it doesn't make sense."

Gregory said, "My old man was a cop; he don't talk straight about nothing. Besides, he was trying to keep what's-her-name under wraps."

"Her name is Ellen," I said. "Ellen. But I mean the meet in Danny Boy's. There was no reason for him not to mention it before. I think he's protecting Neddy Flanagan."

Gregory tapped his knuckles against the window, obviously nervous about my driving. The seat was pushed back to accommodate his outstretched, bandaged leg.

"So you thinking conspiracy?" he said. "They all did it. Like *Murder on the Orient Express*, or some shit."

"If it was conspiracy, they'd all have an alibi. As it is now, Sid hates your father, yet he gives him an alibi. They both love Neddy Flanagan, yet no one will vouch for where he was that afternoon. A conspiracy would be neater. Neddy is the wild card in this."

Gregory lit a cigarette from a cigarette and inhaled deeply. He'd been chain-smoking since we got in the car. "If Neddy did it," he said, "then what the hell is going on with the mob? Why kill Zipper? Why try to kill us?"

"I don't think those incidents have anything to do with Mulgrew's murder. They happened because we were pushing Bongiovanni, and he's a psycho, trying to show the mob how tough he is. Simple as that. I think Neddy Flanagan got himself assigned to this case so he could control us. I think that fishing picture, in his mind, taints his sacred career. And that gives him motive for murder."

"Motive, yes; balls, no," Joe Gregory said. "I don't see Neddy killing somebody because of a picture. Paying off, yeah. Whacking him, uh-uh."

"Maybe there's more in Neddy's closet than that picture," I said as the Buick rattled over the grating on the Triborough Bridge. "Let's find out."

"Finding out's our job. How, is the question."

"We float a nibble," I said. "We start a rumor that we found things stuffed in that daystick flask. Say we found Jinx's notes, a list of the pad: cops and payment amounts."

Gregory loved a good nibble. He'd once floated a story that a certain martini-drinking lieutenant had marched in the Halloween parade in Greenwich Village. He'd superimposed the lieutenant's face over a magazine shot of Divine in a strapless sequined ball gown. Then he'd worked his Xerox magic on a *Post* photo, placing this creature in the front row of six men, in formal drag, holding a banner. Copies were still on walls of a few precincts.

He squirmed on the seat, trying to get his leg comfortable. "Whatever you want," he said. "I don't know what the hell is going on anymore. But let's do it now, while I'm screwed up from sedatives and other shit. I can say I was out of my mind on drugs."

Brady's was packed when we walked in. Guys cleared a space at the bar; we still had some friends. Shanahan from Missing Persons clapped Joe on the back, saying he was lucky that the shot missed the brains in his ass. Patti O dropped some quarters in the jukebox and hit all the Sinatra numbers, turning up the volume on "New York, New York." We ordered Glenfiddich on the rocks. Always drink the best when other people are buying.

Gregory whispered in my ear, "The target is Brady."

Down at the end of the bar, Johnny Brady was sipping Maalox and swapping war stories with his buddies, the old money of the NYPD. These were heavyset guys with cigars, fedoras, and thirty years in the Detective Bureau. They're the storytellers, passing down the legends and myths of the NYPD in the oral tradition: on a stool, glass in hand, on department time.

"They'll all be drinking Maalox tomorrow," I said.

Brady's buddies had connections with the big brass, like Neddy Flanagan, going back to the bad old days. They were the untouchables, guys slick enough to wind up highly decorated and unindicted. Men without families, who would rather die on a bar stool in Bay Ridge than on a chaise longue in Coral Gables. Johnny Brady would run right to one of them, probably Eddie Shick.

"Everybody's glad you're okay," Brady said, his lips white from antacid. "Drink up, guys want to buy."

Bar owners say that the most beautiful words in the English language are "Buy my friend a drink," because it starts a vicious cycle of alcoholic obligation, where you can't go home until you buy back the guy who bought you, who must then buy you again, et cetera, et cetera. Some of my worst drunks have come from riding the buy-back carousel.

Brady was smiling as though his cheeks were pinned back. He pushed our pile of bills back to us. I still had some of my Georgie K money and the twenty Rizzo dropped on the Buick's floor, but we wouldn't be paying for a while.

"Those guinea bastards," Brady said as he backed up our drinks with two more Scotches. "Fifty-six years I been around wise guys, this is a first. Never heard of a bunch like this before. Dumping shit off the roof, shooting at cops. These are renegades, got to be taken off the street."

Eddie Shick was watching the fight on TV, but he worked his way down to us between rounds. He put an arm around Joe Gregory and told him how worried he was about his health, but he was too busy to get to the Bronx to see him. Gregory pointed at the screen with his single malt. The Leonard-Duran fight was on cable, Leonard dancing, tassels flying.

Gregory said, "Goddamn, Sugar Ray is something, ain't he, Eddie? Better than the original Sugar Ray."

Shick said, "Robinson would have kicked his ass."

"Bullshit," Gregory said.

Joe Gregory didn't know the first thing about boxing. Whenever a fight was on he watched the crowd, looking for mob guys, to see who was sitting ringside, on what date, next to whom. He once had Philly Sampel arrested on an outstanding warrant during the second round of the Ali-Norton fight in Yankee Stadium.

"Look at that footwork," Gregory said. "The guy's like a blur, a mirage."

Gregory stumbled back and threw some short jabs. He bounced off the group behind him, as if they were ring ropes, fell forward, and bear-hugged Shick.

"I'll bet you ten bucks Leonard stops the other guy, what's-his-name."

"Duran," Shick said, raising an imaginary glass and flicking it to his mouth. "You guys get an early start?"

"We had a few," I said.

"Make it twenty," Shick said.

The fighters moved around the ring—Duran flat-footed, talking, rubbing his nose with the thumb of his glove as if it itched from a line of coke.

"Let Ryan hold the dough," Shick said, handing me a wrinkled twenty. He slid out from under Gregory's arm, picked up his martini, and went back to drink with the palace guard.

I said, "This fight is a rerun, it's on tape. You just bet on the loser."

"That's the freaking point," Gregory said.

Gregory limped away to circulate. The front door was swinging open every few seconds. The word of a party spread faster than gossip. The dinner crowd from the telephone company arrived, a couple of tourists wan-

dered in. I thought about calling Leigh to tell her I might
be late, but then I thought we probably wouldn't be that
late.

Brady was at the far end of the bar with Eddie Shick,
who was firing one-liners as though it was the Improv.
Gregory worked his way down the bar as cops ducked
and covered their glass. Joe was pouring tomato juice
into any open beer glass: Gregory's Coney Island special.
Almost all of my old sport jacket sleeves were stained
red, a reminder from the bad old days. The smell of
alcohol was in the air.

Four, five, or six drinks later the bar crowd began to
thin out. I looked around for Gregory, I thought he'd
forgotten the nibble. Then I heard the high, strong voice
of Kate Smith belting the opening bars of "God Bless
America." I wandered into the dining room to watch
the chaos; I'd seen this act before.

People in the dining room stood over salads or entrées,
clutching napkins to their hearts. Gregory, acting like a
drunken cruise director, pulled reluctant patriots to their
feet. He limped over to a distinguished-looking man in
a gray-striped suit and half glasses, yanked him up by
the lapels. The cops at the bar were already standing,
everybody was on their feet. I joined Kate and my people,
singing our voices raw. God bless America.

After the applause died I wove my way to the men's
room. Eddie Shick was at the urinal, holding a stack of
three-by-five cards in his free hand. His joke file.

"Hey, you got to get Gregory out of here," he said.
"He's out of control. Brady's pissed."

"Must be the medication," I said.

Shick put his cards away, checked his teeth in the

mirror, and left. I stood over the urinal with my hand against the wall. Same old graffiti on the walls; Brady didn't bother to paint. If a clean men's room was the sign of a failing bar, Brady was doing very well. I wondered what was taking Gregory so long, then he blasted through the bathroom door with Johnny Brady right behind him. Brady wasn't smiling anymore.

"My dinner crowd, Joey," Brady said. "We can't scare my dinner crowd the fuck away."

I locked the bathroom door and stared at the mirror. When I was half-drunk I needed to stare into bar mirrors for a long time to make sure it was me.

Brady said, "Stay at the bar, Joey. That's all I ask. Lay off my dinner customers, please."

"Johnny boy, Johnny boy, Johnny boy," Gregory said. "Lighten up. Enjoy life. Especially you, Johnny boy. Be goddamn thankful you're not on the list."

"Joe," I said sternly.

"It's Johnny Brady. One of our own."

"Shut the fuck up, Joe," I said.

"What list?" Brady said.

"Joe, don't," I said. My hand was still on the locked bathroom door. I felt someone turning the knob, and I held tighter.

"Jinx, that asshole," Gregory whispered, a hoarse, drunken whisper. "Had notes, pictures, everything. Hidden in this phony daystick that was a flask. Lays out everything, names, ranks, amounts. Some big brass. One big, big, humongous surprise."

Gregory winked at Brady and blessed himself. I unlocked the door, grabbed Gregory, and slammed him against the partition. Then I swung him through the door, forcing him half out into the alcove. I pushed him through the crowd and past the bar as he banged off people protecting drinks with both hands.

Gregory was still working his fly when we fled Brady's, our nibble planted. Planted deeply, in the rich black soil of guilt.

33

For the next three nights we waited in the shadows of the Brooklyn Bridge and tailed Neddy Flanagan home. All three nights were a leisure cruise in the center lane. But Friday night, the fourth night, the tail was different from the moment Neddy's Chrysler reached the crest of the ramp. He made two hard rights and a left against the light, peeling tires up the ramp, up toward the FDR Drive. We lost him immediately.

"This is it," Gregory said. "Hold on to your ass."

Joe floored it, going up the hill. We checked the overpass but didn't see him in the traffic entering FDR Drive. On faith we picked the uptown lane, guessed right, and caught him in the backup of rush-hour traffic on the hill just past Bellevue. We sat back and relaxed; we didn't have to get close. Knowing we couldn't take that chance, Joe had altered Neddy's black Chrysler. While security in the headquarters underground garage were watching "Donahue" in their glass-enclosed booth, Gregory had drilled a pattern of holes through the red plastic taillights of Neddy's car. Amidst garage echoes, tires squealing on the ramp, and muted bursts of TV applause, you could barely hear the buzz of the drill. Neddy's taillights emitted a dozen slender white beams of light in a sea of solid red. The dotted X Joe had drilled in each taillight advertised Neddy like a Broadway marquee.

"Bearing right," I said as we passed the 125th Street exit. "Willis Avenue Bridge. Going to the Deegan."

Neddy fooled me and jerked a quick left over a painted safety grid to the Harlem River Drive. Joe bullied the Buick across two lanes of traffic and onto the Harlem, then edged a little closer in the intense tide of homebound suburbanites.

Because Gregory was still on limited duty, we'd spent the day doing paperwork in the office. He'd told Eddie Shick that he didn't remember anything after Kate Smith, blamed the medication. Shick called us lying bastards, and we took it with such good humor that he was positive we were lying. Liars were never angry.

"The scenic route," I said as we entered the Cross Bronx Expressway, the nearest thing to the Beirut Freeway, shells of bombed-out buildings on either side. Neddy was switching two lanes at a time, passing on both sides. I was getting dizzy from watching the taillights with binoculars, like looking through a kaleidoscope while riding a roller coaster. Gregory swerved around a refrigerator dumped in the center lane.

The Chrysler swung off the expressway at West Farms Road, squealed through the ramp turn, then went through the red lights at Tremont and Boston Road. We stopped at the light, then edged through the intersection, to watch him cruise slowly up Boston Road, checking his rear-view for a tail on the dark street.

Just above 180th Street he pulled to the curb and sat there in the darkness. Flanagan lived in the Bronx, but in an area of expensive homes on the water, on Shore Drive, ten miles and a thousand decencies away.

"A meet, guaranteed," Gregory said.

Gregory snapped off the Buick's lights and drove up the parallel street, Bryant Avenue. We cruised by moonlight to Bronx Park South, stopping just barely past the line of the corner building. Neddy was out of the car and standing on the curb as if waiting for a ride.

Joe turned off the Buick, and we rolled down the windows. The only sound was the whistle of cold wind across an empty lot.

"I had a cousin who lived on this block," I said.

"When?" Gregory said.

Thirty years ago, I thought. It was noisy, packed with kids.

"Maybe not this block," I said. It was so different, I thought I might have imagined it. I heard no slap of a jump rope, no baseball cards flapping on bike spokes, no Yankee game droning from a radio on the stoop, no Mel Allen saying, "How about that?" All I heard was wind and a scream, or maybe a cat shrieking in the darkness.

"Let's get closer," Gregory said.

"This is close enough," I said.

The sidewalks were empty, streetlights smashed. The curbs were littered with carcasses of stripped cars, stomped flat like dead roaches. Apartment houses were abandoned and condemned, but the sheet metal blocking the front doors was ripped aside. Inside, in the blackness, the new inhabitants were crack dealers and packs of wild dogs. Future demolition teams would find the skeletons of junkies and German shepherds.

Neddy looked relaxed. Hands in pockets, he bounced on the balls of his feet, glancing casually up and down the street. I heard the scream again, maybe an animal. On our left was the southernmost border of the pristine Bronx Zoo.

"Car's still running," I said, handing Gregory the binoculars. "Look at the exhaust."

Then Neddy took his hands out of his pockets, wheeled around, and walked quickly to the sixteen-foot-high fence. He stopped at a gate that appeared to be a zoo service entrance, a tall chain-link gate held together by long chain.

"He's got a key," Joe said.

Neddy pulled the chain through and swung the gate open. He went back to his car, drove through, then locked the fence behind him. The white X beam from his taillights disappeared into dense foliage.

"Security is on Fordham Road," I said. "We can get in there."

"Not enough time," Gregory said. "We'd need Tarzan to find him. We can climb this fence."

We left the Buick in the dark of Bryant Avenue and ran across the street. I told him he was nuts, we couldn't have climbed this fence twenty years ago.

A heavy-duty brass padlock held the fence together, but there was a little space if you extended the chain. I pulled the gate apart as far as it would go, then put my head through, feeling the squeeze of metal on both sides. Burglars said if you could get your head in, you were in.

My head felt as if it were swelling up, but I pushed through. My shoulders followed smoothly, then my hips, until my gun snagged. I reached around with my left hand, pulled the gun out of my waistband and the binoculars out of my pocket, held them at my side, and moved through.

"You got to be kidding," Gregory said. "A full-size man can't get through there."

He began to climb, struggling to lift that left leg, still heavily bandaged. But he couldn't even get a toehold with his clodhopper wing-tip brogues.

"Come on," I said, holding the gate apart. "Jam that melon through here."

"You mean mellow," he said.

Face first, Joe Gregory began pushing his head between the metal posts. He worked a leg, then a hip, grimacing as though trapped in a West Village S&M device.

"Couldn't be worse than childbirth," I said. "A woman could stand it. Push."

I tried to stretch every millimeter out of the length of chain. Gregory had worked his right leg and hips almost through, then told me to stand back. He grunted and jerked his head. I heard the scrape, the sound of sandpaper on a rusty pipe. Up on the post was a patch of skin and gray hair stuck to the metal, floating like gossamer in the dim glow of the streetlight.

"Welcome to the zoo," he said, showing me the blood on his fingers. "Got a handkerchief?"

I ran ahead of the limping Gregory, down the path where Neddy's car had disappeared. Within twenty yards the path became overhung with trees blotting out the moonlight, a tunnel of foliage black enough to hide the Headless Horseman. Joe's shoes slapped the blacktop unevenly, like the hooves of an injured Clydesdale.

When I cleared the trees I came out under a starless

sky. The moon was full. Around us four thousand animals bleated, bayed, honked, roared, and cried. Off to the right an el train headed uptown, above the Bronx streets, screeched around the Boston Road curve, shooting sparks into the night.

I ran up an incline and stopped at the crest. The Chrysler was parked below, at the foot of the hill, behind a truck. The truck could have been a city fleet vehicle, any old rattletrap used to haul elephant shit; but it wasn't. It was Liam Gregory's pickup.

Joe was coming up behind me, struggling like the drummer in "Yankee Doodle Dandy." I ran back down, holding my hands up in the traffic halt sign. A stream of blood was running down Joe's face.

"Wait there," I said. "He's right over the hill."

"Cut through the bushes," Gregory said, pointing.

A muddy path led to the edge of the Bronx River. Snakes entered my mind, their eyes watching from the trees or slipping through the muck. A trumpeting bleat came from off to our right.

"Joe, wait," I said as we pushed branches aside. "We have a problem."

"No," he said. "It's just the rhinos fucking."

I followed him along the edge of the muddy bank. Inky water bubbled over a truck tire resting in the center. We came to the edge of the trees, against a fence. A sign above us read "North American Range: Deer, Bison, and Buffalo."

We stood behind a weeping willow, looking down to the lights of the pedestrian path. The Chrysler and Liam's Ford pickup were both parked under a street lamp with a bare bulb. Both men leaned against the Chrysler.

Having to catch your breath is an excuse for silence. Exotic birds squawked and cooed, fluttering in the trees above. Off to the left rose a series of apartment houses. Small squares of light stacked five high winked on and off like the opening visual of the old "Late Show" on CBS; the "Syncopated Clock" was the music. Joe took the binoculars from me. I kept breathing deeply.

An ambulance sped up Bronx Park South, toward Fordham Hospital, the driver laying on the *woop-woop* siren. In the flash of red light I could see huge rounded shapes, moving toward us in the darkness. Something immense grunted and snorted behind the fence only inches behind me. I stepped away from the smell of sour matted fur and looked at Gregory, but he was too intent to notice anything. A patch of blood had dried on his forehead like a wine-stain birthmark. He handed me the binoculars without a word.

I could see the cloud of Liam's breath as he spoke. It looked like a serious conversation, not an argument or a plea. Neddy's white shirt looked like a clerical collar, sticking up under his black crew-neck sweater. His thin lips appeared blue in the cold light. Above their heads was a sign pole with a stack of arrows pointing in all directions: Jungle World, Lion Island, Reptile House, World of Darkness.

"Don't make a move," I whispered. "We won't gain anything by showing our hand now."

"Right," he said almost gratefully.

I knew this was a tough one for Joe: your father, what the hell did you do? I looked to Leigh when things got tough with our kids or our parents, so we avoided lasting damage. With me it was an absence of intuition, a lack of touch. I wanted to say, "Let's get out of here, get a drink, pretend it didn't happen." But I knew he couldn't walk away, even for family.

There were no perfect families, there was always a gulf that's difficult to cross. But there seemed to be an impossibly cold, blind chasm in families not guided by the strength of a woman.

We waited in the silence while they talked, and Neddy paced, waving his arms. The heavy fall of hooves and more animals came. The sickly-sweet smell of rotted fruit seemed to surround us. Both men got back into their cars and drove down the path, toward the gate. We waited until their taillights passed into the trees.

"Let's find security this time," I said. "They'll drive us to our car. Although I don't know how we're going to explain what we're doing in here in the first place."

"We're cops," Joe Gregory said. "We don't have to explain."

We walked along the fence toward the pedestrian path. I could feel the ground tremble, hear the bumping and snorting of the beasts walking with us. Escorting us to the door, like bouncers tossing out a pair of troublesome drunks.

"There has to be some reasonable explanation for this," I said. "We'll look into it, it'll be nothing."

At a fork in the footpath we went left, choosing the African Plain over the Himalayan Highland. We walked close together in the middle of the path, bumping shoulders, listening to growling on one side, the rustling of feathers on the other.

"It'll be nothing, Joe," I said. "You watch."

"They meet in the freaking zoo, you say it's nothing."

We were in the center of the park on a long narrow

path lit by old streetlights, endless dark fields behind high fences on both sides. We were out of sight of buildings, beyond the sound of traffic. At an arrow that said Astor Court, Sea Lion Pool, Security, we bore right. Red eyes glowed in the darkness.

"I'll take care of this one myself, pally," Joe Gregory said.

34

WE KEPT one shot glass in our house, in the corner of the top shelf in front of the big Pyrex casserole dish. I knew where to find it even half-drunk at four A.M.

"One more will make it just right," Leigh said, blinking, tying her robe around her waist.

"I'm not sleepy," I said. "Didn't want to wake you."

"Pour one for me while you're at it."

"Come on," I said. "I'm just having one."

"How many will that make? But who's counting when the Great Gregory returns? How long do we celebrate? A month, two?"

"I'm sorry," I said. "I didn't realize it was this late."

"You couldn't call, Anthony?"

"Sorry."

"Pour one for me, go ahead."

"Please, Leigh."

"I'll pour it myself, you're so damn concerned about my health? I can't believe you're driving home like this again. But then who's to stop you? Permission to drive drunk is a professional courtesy among cops, isn't it?"

"I'm not drunk," I said.

"Oh, no, not you. It's going to be just like before."

"No, it's not," I said. "Let's have coffee. I'll make coffee."

"Why do you do this, Anthony?" she said. "I don't understand. You're not like the rest of them. You're not like them at all."

I rinsed the shot glass and put it, dripping, back up on the third shelf next to the casserole, then bent down and pulled a coffee filter from the low cabinet, stood up, and cracked my head against the open door. I staggered back against the table.

"Sit down," Leigh said. Her warm hands pried my fingers off my head. She touched the spot, rubbing gently. I could feel each hair grating against my scalp.

"I'll make the coffee," she said. I sat there, just drunk enough to be unsure of how badly I was hurt.

"We were just talking about the case," I said, feeling the bump, feeling for blood. "I lost track of time."

She scooped the coffee evenly, measured the water, and poured. Working competently, as always, as if it weren't four in the morning.

"The case is getting complicated," I said. "Joe's supposed to be on light duty, but he's out there working. So what can I say? Sorry, my shift is up, time to go home?"

"He doesn't have a wife," she said, "a family."

"He's trying to end this case, Leigh. That's what you want."

"He'll find another case," she said.

"You don't understand."

"I understand perfectly," she said. "It's all he has. And he needs you."

I held my face in my hands, rubbing my eyes until they hurt. Leigh arranged things behind me, putting everything in order. These neat women, always cleaning up messes made by men. The click of glasses, cabinets closing.

"I had a phone call tonight," she said.

"A phone call, when?"

"About midnight."

"Jesus Christ, midnight? Who was it?"

"Some guy. I was half-asleep."

"What did he say, exactly?"

"I don't remember, exactly," she said. "Like, 'Tell Ryan watch out.' And he hung up. No name, no good-bye."

She walked over and looked at my head again, then opened the freezer and began putting ice cubes in a towel. "What's going on, Anthony?"

"I wish I knew. Maybe it was some cop who just found out about Gregory getting shot."

"Maybe," she said.

Our phone number was unlisted, but it was probably in dozens of NYPD file boxes. And unlisted numbers could be bought, for the right price. They had your phone number, they had your address.

"Let's get out of here," Leigh said. "Go to South Carolina for spring break. Katie would love to see you. You've got all kinds of time coming to you. Take some of it."

"Not until this case is over."

The ice felt like cement blocks falling on my head. I reached up, took the towel from her, held it myself.

"I'm going whether you are or not," she said.

"Just let me get through this case," I said, but there was no answer.

"I love you," I said. But she'd already gone upstairs.

"I love you," I said again.

I said those words easily, almost reflexively some-times, as if counting on the mere fact of my love to make everything right. I wanted things to be right. The problem was finding the balance: to be both a good husband and a stand-up cop.

The coffee bubbled inside the glass pot. In the quiet of the kitchen where we had talked through much joy and sadness, I began to plan my apology, logical even when drunk. The job, blame the job, always blame the job.

But it wasn't the job. Leigh and I had worked our way through decades of rough times. Together. We'd get through this. Leigh would see that. She always had.

35

MONDAY NIGHT, the last day of February, Gregory was back on full duty and talkative, glad-handing everybody. He told war stories while I took the hint from the stack of blank DD5s Shick dropped on my desk, and caught up on investigative reports. I waited for Joe to bring up the subject of his father, but he didn't. Around midnight we left the office and drove to the fish market.

"Where the hell is everybody?" Gregory said. Fourteen Peck Slip was locked up, the Paris Bar half-empty. "A convention, what? Got to be a reason."

We cruised past the Ravenite, then did the market streets several more times, listening to a late-night talk show. On quiet nights like this Gregory hung his transistor radio from the mirror. Between this, the citywide NYPD band, and OCCB on the walkie-talkie, all we needed was one more radio. The talk show host was taking calls about police conduct during a raid of an after-hours place on Christopher Street. We knew the team from Public Morals who handled the raid. It would be a hot topic in headquarters.

"You hungry?" Gregory said. "Let's grab a bite and take a ride to the Village, get a look at this joint."

Gregory loved to view the scene. We went to see plane crashes, bridge jumpers, everything. He wanted to smell the smoke, feel the flames, gaze at the body and blood. Why else have the front row seat?

We picked up a coffee and tea at the Market Diner, then Joe stopped at a deli meat wholesaler on Prince Street, an old friend of his. It was a place that worked through the night cooking and preparing meat for restaurants, supermarkets, and delis the next day. Gregory came out carrying a whole pastrami, away from his chest as if it were a wet baby.

The smell of hot spices filled the car as we drove to the Village. The transistor radio swung on the mirror.

"Talked to my old man," he said. "Got some things straightened out."

We parked opposite the after-hours place, which was in the basement of a bar called Rowdy's. Café curtains and hanging plants obscured part of our view, but Rowdy's was clean and well lighted.

Gregory said, "Neddy called my old man, wanted the meet at the zoo, mailed him a key."

"Seems like a lot of trouble to go to. The key, all the way to the Bronx."

We began the ritual of setting up. I rolled my window down and adjusted the side-view mirror so I could see who was walking up behind us. Joe opened the food, I took the lids off the cups and set them on the dash. Joe cut slices of pastrami with a penknife while I checked the binoculars and portable radio. I put the *New York Post* on the seat between us. We were like an old couple preparing for a night of TV. We had our favorite chairs and a snack; the city was our entertainment.

"Neddy's paranoid," Gregory said. "Bought the nibble

completely. He tells my old man we've been holding out information from Eddie Shick. Wanted to know if he knew what the story was. Said he heard a rumor about us having lists and evidence. All kinds of incriminating shit."

We talked while watching the bar. Rowdy's had a good crowd. Short-haired, slim men in jeans and sneakers, baseball jackets, watching something on TV or playing pool.

"Thing is," Gregory said, "he wasn't worried. Says if we got evidence, bring it forward. Wasn't even worried about the fishing picture."

"Bullshit," I said.

"Oh, he remembers it," Gregory said. "But listen to this. He admits Jinx was blackmailing him with the picture. Says he remembered the fishing trip, but didn't know Bobo Rizzo from Joe Shit the rag man; thought he was a cop. Still, he says he was scared shitless, ready to pay Jinx off that night. Avoid a problem. Had his money on him at Danny Boy's, like everybody else."

The pastrami was hot, greasy. We both leaned into the center of the car as we chewed to let the grease drip on the *Post*.

"Doesn't mean he didn't kill Jinx," I said.

"It's a stretch, though. Neddy's not a street guy. Makes sense he'd ante right up. Twenty-five freaking grand, he had."

Taxis were pulling up to Rowdy's every few minutes. Lone men got out and went into the bar.

"We can always check his bank records," Gregory said. "Probably on microfilm. Neddy says that's where he was that afternoon."

"What does Neddy think about us following him?" I said.

"My old man won't tell him that," Gregory said, then he shrugged. "Maybe he won't, I don't know. He did tell him about the fishing picture, didn't he?"

"I'll bet he believes Neddy's story, too?"

"Swears by the guy. We talked about Ellen, too. Told me the whole story."

"About asking her to marry him?" I said.

He looked at me and smiled, shaking his head. I wasn't sure whether he knew that part or not.

"It's his life," he said. "I don't see it, getting tied down at his age."

He pointed at Rowdy's with his coffee. "I got a theory about these guys," he said. "Look at the way they dress. Like teenagers. Like they're trying to relive the years when they were nineteen or twenty. When guys hung around together, no family responsibility. You play some basketball, then go for beers. Shoot pool, shoot the shit. Maybe go to a movie or the Knicks game. No pressure. No wife at home watching the clock, saying 'You spent too much, drank too much.' "

"But they're adults, Joe. With adult pressures worse than ours."

"I don't think so. Women complicate your life worse than anything."

"Should I go in and ask if Rowdy's softball team needs a first baseman?"

"No," he said. "You get that disease."

"Which one?" I said.

"Lou Gehrig's. Playing too much first base."

* * *

We gave the rest of the pastrami to a guy cleaning windshields on Bowery, then rode back down to the fish market. I sensed something was wrong as soon as we turned onto Peck Slip. After years of watching people, you develop a strong sense of the norm, a feel for the rhythm and flow of street life. You know immediately when the norm is violated: when someone is moving too quickly in a crowd or a scream is pain, not play; when a sharp pop is not a truck backfire. The pace was obviously wrong now, a thirty-three playing seventy-eight. We heard the warble of a siren.

"Paris Bar," I said.

As Gregory wove through traffic, I made notes on the yellow pad: descriptions, cars, plate numbers. I looked for men moving away from the Paris. Always watch those leaving the scene.

The Lincoln's door was open. Bobo Rizzo lay on the sidewalk under it, the courtesy lamp casting a diffuse light on his butchered face. The car was still running, I could feel the heat blasting from the Lincoln as I knelt over the body. A soft bong signaled the open door. Sinatra sang "Here's That Rainy Day."

Gregory identified himself to the uniformed cops and told them that Bobo was a capo in the Genovese family. More radio cars arrived behind me, doors slammed as flashing red lights were reflected in the Lincoln's black finish.

The inside door handle was covered with blood, but there was no broken glass. The car window was rolled down. He had probably been talking to someone he knew. Bobo had been shot while inside the car. He'd touched the side of his face and, with a bloody hand, opened the door of the Lincoln. They all doubted the miracle of their own death and stuck their hands in the fatal wound.

Several slugs had entered Bobo's head. One of the slugs had exited through his jaw and lay, like a bad dental filling, twelve inches from his mouth. Bobo's cigar had come to rest in a blood-filled crack of cobblestone. I picked up the small slug, wrapped it in a dollar bill, and put it in my pocket.

When I stood up Gregory was gone and the street was cluttered with abandoned radio cars. Doors were left open, motors running, turret lights turning, clicking two beats like heartbeats. Red-and-white light flashed off pale New York faces, ethnic faces with thick mustaches. I could hear the voice of a female dispatcher saying, "Repeat the location one-Adam" then, "An ambulance has been ordered."

I found Gregory in the Paris Bar.

"See anything?" he said to each man at the bar. "How about you, see anything?" But nothing was ever seen.

The Paris Bar was usually packed at this hour, with fishmongers wolfing prosciutto-and-cheese sandwiches or washing their eggs down with whiskey. Not this night. Tonight it was almost empty and smelled of bacon fat burning. A perpetual cloud of smoke lingered near a twenty-foot ceiling dotted with bullet holes from muskets or Uzis. I recognized most of the sullen men sitting on chrome stools held together with duct tape. They were not workingmen. I had photos of this family in my album, all with numbers under their chins.

We walked outside, and I felt the cold wind off the river. The body of Bobo Rizzo lay curled on the greasy pavement. A foursome of uniformed cops stood over the body, talking and laughing. Cops met, not at the water cooler, or in the cafeteria, but within a border of yellow tape, under streetlights, directly over blood. A fat detective from the 1st Precinct called to Gregory.

"You see this fucking fiasco?" he said.

"Missed by a minute," Gregory said.

I pulled the dollar bill with the bullet from my pocket and handed it to him. "I found this slug eight inches in front of his mouth, Dennis," I said. "I didn't want it to get stepped on, lost in the shuffle."

He banged his fat finger against my chest. "Don't you ever touch my crime scene again," he said.

"Let's get out of here," Gregory said. "Away from this asshole."

Two Crime Scene Unit cops, in baseball caps and blue chino jackets, were leaning over the Lincoln's front door. One held a four-battery flashlight while the other dusted the door handle with a small brush.

"Do the roof," Gregory said. "He might have put his hand on the roof, leaning in."

"Right, Chief," he said. "Whatever you say."

As news photographers circled the scene, Gregory bent over, close to Bobo's body, taking his front row look. I saw him pick the cigar off the ground. Bobo's pant leg was hiked up, showing a white old-man's calf above short black socks. A dark line was beginning to form along the bottom border of the leg. Blood settled to the bottom when the heart stopped pumping.

Foghorns sounded in the harbor as we walked up Peck Slip away from the river. Number 14 was locked, windows dark.

"Whatever we do," Gregory said, "we got to get in this freaking building. The answer is in this building."

36

FOR THE next few hours we drove around to the usual haunts, looking for any of the crew from 14 Peck Slip. A lot of people conveniently seemed to be elsewhere. Joe dropped me at One Police Plaza, then went uptown to the lab, to make sure the ballistics technicians checked the slugs taken out of Bobo against the ones from Zipper.

I sat in the office and worked up a report on the Rizzo shooting for Eddie Shick. Make him happy. He'd have something to show to the PC in the morning. A little before nine I called home, but Leigh had already left for work.

Gregory returned tired and frustrated. The bullets hadn't matched. I'd known they wouldn't; mob guys were smart enough not to help our investigation by using the same gun twice. Guns were cheap, lawyers were expensive. Both guns were probably rusting next to the clam shells at the bottom of Sheepshead Bay.

But Joe insisted that Ugo's crew was so cocky and arrogant, they'd keep their guns. He called the 1st Precinct, looking for Sylvia D'Angelo, hoping she'd know something that could get us a search warrant for 14 Peck Slip.

* * *

We caught up with Sylvia at lunchtime, outside the
Kam Bo Rice Shop on Bayard Street in Chinatown. The
three of us stepped under the cover of the Kam Bo tin
awning, facing down Elizabeth Street toward the 5th
Precinct station house. Above our heads, five-story tene-
ments jammed onto narrow streets and leaned into each
other, blocking most of the sky. It was raining, and
Chinatown was a sea of bobbing black umbrellas.

"Dennis is pissed," Sylvia said. "He says one of you
two put the cigar in Rizzo's mouth. I can guess who."

Dennis Banninger was the fat detective handling
Rizzo's case. The front page of the morning's *Daily
News* showed a picture of Bobo Rizzo lying in his own
blood, in front of the Lincoln, the side of his face black
and swollen. But his cigar was clamped in his teeth, as
though he were snoozing after a game of boccie in the
park. No one told the Great Gregory's partner not to
touch his crime scene.

"Dennis is a fat, lazy bastard," Gregory said. "He's
going to close that case without even looking. Might
have to miss a meal, investigating. I'm making some
calls trying to get you off the chart. Work full-time on
this."

"Don't do me any more favors, please, Gregory," she
said.

People pushed past us, leaving the restaurant: judges,
lawyers, court officers from Foley Square. I could smell
Sylvia's perfume, a subtle, spicy scent.

"What about a search warrant?" Joe said.

"What about evidence?" she said.

"We need to get inside Fourteen Peck," Gregory said.
"Guaranteed one of those guns is in there. Who do you

know in the DA's office with balls enough to issue a search warrant?"

"Curran owes me," she said. "But on what? The Great Gregory's hunch?"

A never-ending stream of people passed on broken sidewalks, on the most crowded streets in a crowded city.

"Why are you doing this for us, Gregory?" she said.

"Shooter's out of that club," Gregory said. "Same guys did Zipper, did Bobo, guaranteed. Maybe did Mulgrew, too."

"Bullshit," she said. "You're thinking if we get someone on these homicides, you can make a deal for Mulgrew's killer. Don't count on it."

"What about Murray Daniels?" Gregory said. "We get a search warrant, maybe we tie someone to that. Don't tell me you can't bend your freaking ethics to get that bastard."

"I thought that was in the works," she said, looking at me. I'd told her about Nicky Skooch's admission on the fed wire.

"Feds won't let us use it yet," I said. "They're not ready to blow their wire."

Raindrops tinkled off the metal awning above us.

"We need something of substance," she said. "A witness, something. How about OCCB informants? Anybody hear anything linking the club with either shooting?"

"What do you think, pally?" he said.

"I'm fresh out of CIs," I said, patting my empty pockets.

I was watching the streets, thinking about a raid of a Pell Street gambling den years ago. We'd arrested almost a hundred Chinese males playing fan-tan in a basement casino. We'd made several trips in the van, carting them to the 5th Precinct, until the station house was overflowing. On the last trip we'd had a full van but couldn't fit a couple of them in. Joe had told them they were free to go, waved good-bye. But instead of taking Gregory's dismissal, they had walked, by themselves, seven blocks into the station house and waited politely to be booked. True men of honor never took the easy way out.

Gregory reached his hand out from under the awning, then stepped out, looking up at the sky. "We can check with Eddie Shick," he said. "Get a list of cops who have registered informants in the market. See if anybody heard anything."

"Done that already," I said. "Only one registered was ours."

Gregory said, "We should be able to use some of that surveillance we did. The tapping, right? Stolen fish going into the club. We got pictures. Should be enough to get a warrant to search for stolen fish. Who knows, maybe stumble across the murder weapon."

"We need a complainant," I said. "One of the wholesalers has to say the fish is stolen. Otherwise it isn't."

The sound of static came over the portable radio, and Eddie Shick's voice saying, "Ten-one, forthwith." Joe took the radio out of his pocket and said, "Ten-four."

"Shick probably wants an update on Rizzo," he said. "PC probably asked him something you didn't have written down."

"Use the phone in the station house," Sylvia said.

We walked toward Elizabeth Street, past men in open white shirts stacking fish on a bin filled with crushed ice. The streets were lined with restaurants, curio shops, and bakeries. Wooden grocery bins held vegetables I couldn't name. I smelled raw fish and the odor of cabbages cooking in oil.

"I'll call from here," Gregory said, and stepped into a phone booth with a pagoda roof.

Sylvia waited until Joe was dropping coins, then said, "Look, Anthony. I'm not coming on to you, am I? Is that what you think?"

"No, not at all," I said. She had taken me completely by surprise. "I don't think that at all."

"Sometimes you seem uncomfortable around me. I don't want that. I don't chase married guys."

"I never thought you were coming on to me, Sylvia." I wasn't lying about that. I tried to remember what I'd said, what she'd said before. We'd talked a few late nights in Brady's, but just cop talk.

"Good," she said. "How is Leigh feeling, anyway?"

"Have you met Leigh?"

"No, just what Gregory told me. I just don't want you to be nervous around me. Nothing is going to happen that you don't want to happen."

We were standing at the top of a staircase leading down into a basement barber shop. I could see an old man sitting on a barber chair, smoking a nub of a cigarette, the flame close enough to burn his lips. Gregory walked over to us, laughing.

"Guess what?" he said.

"Chiquita Banana called," I said.

"Better than that," he said, tapping a cigarette against the back of his hand. "Vince Salvatore found our other barrel."

37

Within an hour Gregory and I were on the ferry crossing the East River to Governors Island. The Coast Guard had notified Vince Salvatore that a sealed white barrel had floated up on the north shore of the island. I shivered as we pushed off from the ferry slip, chilled from fatigue and too little sleep. The Statue of Liberty, mildewed green like an old penny, stood off to the right, the starboard side, according to Gregory. The ferry had the fresh-paint smell of military maintenance.

"We should have called Harbor to pick us up," Gregory said.

"Too much trouble. This is fine."

"It's not style, though," he said. "New York cops should travel in style."

Governors Island is off the southeast tip of Manhattan, with a view of the entire harbor. Looking up the East River, I could see the bridges filled with cars, trains, pedestrians. The Brooklyn and Manhattan bridges were visible, the Williamsburg just beyond the bend of the river. Underneath us, passengers crossed the water riding the IRT, IND, BMT, maybe the tubes or tunnels. People dozing or reading *The New York Times*, watching the skirt across the aisle, not thinking about being at the bottom of a river.

A Coast Guard officer with a slight lisp and southern accent met us at the ferry.

"I'll need identification," he said. Gregory and I flipped leather cases with the precision of a Rockette's kick.

The officer told us to follow him on a vacant macadam road, which had the empty feeling of every military installation in the world. We parked near a low wall and walked down a series of wide stone steps to the edge of a bulkhead. Water ran from the weed-covered barrel, which was rusted and scraped but basically intact. A young seaman hosed down the area around the barrel. Gregory told him to stop, not to wash anything away.

"We had a communiqué from NYPD, a Sergeant Salvatore, to look for a barrel with these markings," the officer said.

"This looks like the one," I said.

Bodies wash up here regularly. If they're determined to be floaters, the NYPD is called to claim the body and investigate. This case was unusual because we specifically requested a watch for this particular barrel.

The seaman began prying the lid off with a crowbar. I looked over to the Brooklyn side, across Buttermilk Channel. Tankers lined up in more ports than I thought we had. I'd never seen the Brooklyn waterfront from this angle. The streets of Brooklyn seemed to rise up the hill, up from the ships and the water. People actually arrived in Brooklyn by ship.

The lid flew off with a tinny clatter and rolled to the seawall. The kid had the first look; he jerked back quickly. The trick is to handle the smell. We've all seen worse sights in the movies, but we're unprepared for the smell. Breathe shallowly, keep swallowing, relax. The kid was gutsy, took a second, less tentative look.

"I think it's a blanket," he said.

Gregory kicked the barrel over. He and the seaman dumped it out on the clean deck. It wasn't a blanket, but a big brown-and-black blob of a Doberman pinscher.

"It's a dog," the officer said.

"It's Koch," I said.

It was the dog Zipper had walked, the watchdog for 14 Peck Slip. Too dumb to housebreak, so they'd killed it and dumped it in the river that night. Gregory squatted over the dog, poking it with his pen.

"He's been shot," Gregory said.

"For shitting in the club," I said.

"They executed him," Gregory said, looking close at the entrance hole. He turned the dog's head side to side, examining, poking with his pen.

"We can dispose of it," the officer said.

"No, we'll take it," Gregory said. "It's Koch."

He grabbed the NYPD gray-blue wool blanket from the trunk of the Buick. The blanket's tag read "Replace after covering DOAs." No mention of dogs.

"One thing we don't need is another dog," I said as I helped him push the wet mush of brown fur onto the blanket. It was still icy from the river.

"This ain't no ordinary dog," Joe said.

Joe checked the ground around the barrel as the officer shoved a clipboard at him. We signed for Koch, then carried him up the stone steps and laid him in the Buick trunk. We took the barrel, too.

I knew what he had in mind. On the ride uptown I didn't say it out loud, but before we turned into the driveway of the Manhattan Animal Hospital I'd made notes of the times and people involved in the chain of evidence. As if it were a homicide.

Gregory carried the thawing dog through the hospital door like a sick child. The blanket had soaked his shirt and suit jacket. An elevator opened and two men, one in hospital whites, led a horse off the elevator toward the parking lot. The elevator smelled cleaner than some I'd been in. The doctors here had saved a dog burned and traumatized by a violent death, which put them on Joe's approved hospital list. Digging out bullets should be easy.

I stood in the waiting room, looking out over the East River at a city that had its own beauty and variety. I wondered if I could really live in South Carolina, if I would become bored with sameness. Leigh said I would grow to understand the changes of the ocean, the beauty of the marshes, and be able to hear the sound of nature. For forty-three years my roots had grown here. I wondered if that was too long to survive a transplant.

I called Leigh from a pay phone, but no answer. We hadn't spoken last night or this morning. I sat on a Leatherette couch and began rewriting notes, putting the story in order. Joe came through the door, holding his palm out: a good bullet, small, but not a fragment.

"What do you think?" he asked.

"Small-caliber."

"Twenty-two, pally. I'll give you any odds this matches ones from Zipper."

While we waited for Ballistics to finish, Joe and I bought a coffee and tea and sat in the Police Academy gym. Recruits were doing calisthenics; about a quarter of the class was female. The instructor, on a makeshift stage, put them through a series of yogalike moves, many of which I'd never seen before. A long way from push-ups, sit-ups, and jumping jacks.

"What complications is this all leading to?" Gregory asked. "Where we going to hide all these women? What happens when they get pregnant? Look at the size of them. What happens when they got to wrestle a psycho?"

"They'll get the shit beat out of them, like we did. Then they'll be okay."

"Look at the tits on the one with the braid," he said.

I couldn't get over how young they looked. Compared with the academy, One Police Plaza was Sun City. I kept forgetting the whole world wasn't my age or older. It was frightening to think there were so many new people, so much younger.

On the way back to the lab I began to notice that the Police Academy was looking worn. The Twentieth Street Academy was not even built yet when Gregory and I attended Hubert Street. I remembered what I thought when I saw older cops hanging around. Hey, old-timer, get the hell out, you've had your chance.

Ballistics proved the Great Gregory right this time. The bullet taken from Koch matched the bullet from Zipper. We drove to Hogan Place to sell the story to a judge.

"Tell me again," the assistant DA said. Christina Curran, Fordham Law, 1979, on her father Captain Mike Curran's money. She said, "Call me Christina," as if she were one of us. But she hated everything about us. Christina had a round, pale Irish face, limp brown hair, pulled straight back in an attempt at elegance.

I told the story, using all the details to impress her with our thoroughness. How we watched Ugo Bongiovanni and his cohorts dump this particular barrel, in that river, at this exact time. I showed her records proving we'd notified harbor on December 11, 1982, describing this particular barrel. All we wanted was a search warrant to look for the .22 used to kill Zipper and Koch.

"Hold it," she said. "The divers found a barrel at that time, am I correct? The one with Jinx Mulgrew. I thought you had an informant who gave you Mulgrew."

"DOA," Gregory said. "In fact, he's the vic in this case. What happened was, when we were checking the spot he gave us, we saw these guys dump this other barrel. The white one, understand?"

"Okay," she said. "The victim happened to be your informant. You just happened to be there at this other time. You happened to watch these guys drop this white barrel. Two pair of forty-year-old eyes. Was it dark? What was the weather?"

"It just happened to be balmy," Gregory said.

"I can look it up," she said. "I know the lighting is poor. But you say you can positively identify this barrel, which washes up three months later on Governors Island."

"I swear under God, this to be true," Gregory said.

"I have no doubt about that," she said.

Lawyers are the one thing Gregory hates about law. Especially their superior "we're professionals" act and their clubbiness. Particularly when they go to lunch with mob defense lawyers, all laughs and snappy alma mater patter. If cops went to lunch with the alleged criminals they'd arrested, everybody would be indicted. Christina tapped her long fingernails on the desk.

"Our notes were dated and filed," I said. "The barrel and its connection to the location is described. The ballistics evidence is solid."

"We're talking about a dog here," Christina said.

"We're talking about a man, a dead man," I said.

"What's your problem?" Gregory said. "We're not asking for a warrant to break into a freaking private house here, kids screaming, women in nightgowns crying. 'Sixty Minutes' material. This is a warehouse, mob guys, stinking fish. Nobody lives there."

"It's what the judge thinks that counts," she said. "I'll be right back."

Joe and I didn't watch her walk. We were at the age where we only watched women who liked us. Irish girls are too stiff to roll their hips, he says. This one was trying to defeminize, but her bust was too heavy for man-style jackets. And the skirts did nothing to hide muscular, peasant stock legs and Mother of Eire hips.

"These people," Joe Gregory said. "They want a full confession before they risk a move. Well, look who finally got here."

Sylvia walked in and dropped the folder on the table. "Hear the rumor?" she said. "The department is getting you one of those kennel trucks, with the cages in back."

We ignored her; we'd been through it before. Joe and I looked through Sylvia's notes as Christina walked back into the room, heels clicking off the worn tile.

"Could I see your case folder, Sylvia?" she asked. We sat there while the lawyer read through it.

"You people," she said, sighing.

We figured she already had the go-ahead from her supervisor, but we let her play it out.

Finally she said, "Okay, now, Detective D'Angelo

will prepare the application. Date it March first. Gregory, your supporting affidavit should include whoever touched the animal. Who removed the bullets?"

"Dr. Oliver," Gregory said.

"What hospital?" she said.

"Manhattan Animal," Gregory said.

The lawyer shook her head. "How soon do you want to go?"

"Make it for night service," Joe Gregory said. "We'll go tonight. Tonight is right."

38

JUST BEFORE dawn I sat on the front seat of the Emergency Service truck, reading a copy of the search warrant with a flashlight. The print, speckled from a bad Xerox copy, blurred the *c*'s and *o*'s. Vince Salvatore, behind the wheel of the truck, played nervously with an automatic rifle. We were ten minutes away from hitting the door of 14 Peck Slip. Salvatore stuck the rifle in my face.

"Colt AR-15," he said. "Can't be more than six pounds. Feel it."

"Looks like a toy," I said, waving off the gun.

"They're all toys, Ryan," he said. "This ain't no job for a grown man."

Our strike team consisted of a dozen cops parked behind the rear entrance of One Police Plaza. We waited in two vans and two cars snaked around the circular brick driveway, exhaust smoke rising gray blue from four tailpipes in the cool night. Joe Gregory was point man, in the Buick with Eddie Shick, at the head of the coil. Vince and I were in the first Emergency Service van directly behind them, the others behind us.

"This gun is fucking butter," Salvatore said, aiming through the windshield. "Bad guys had these for years."

The Emergency Service radio frequency was more conversational, less covert, than the code-heavy air traffic I was used to on our OCCB band. Emergency Service cops had no need for deception. These cops were helping people, enjoying their work, requesting special wrenches, incubators, electricians. An elderly woman and a bichon frise were stuck in an elevator at Park and Seventy-second; a newborn was found in a maid's cleaning cart in the Hotel Pierre. Units identified themselves, accepted assignments, a blast of squelch, then radio silence.

"You putting in for a medal for this, Ryan," Vince said, "if it goes right? Maybe a promotion, huh? Bosses are happy, you look good. A hero."

An occasional cop appeared from the revolving headquarters door, buttoning a collar, pulling on gloves.

"We'll see," I said.

In these empty hours between the closing of bars and the start of commuting, the streets of a city were given over to the psychotic, the depressed, the guilty. Drunks have passed out, hookers gone home. Predawn New York streets were the stroll for the cops and the mad. In midtown, transvestites window-shopped on Fifth Avenue, admiring the silk teddies in Saks, the pumps in Gucci.

At this hour in all boroughs, the troubled paced the nighttime streets, heads down, arms swinging, immersed in private argument. Soaked with sweat, they pled their cases to themselves, reeking of that peculiarly sour, metallic odor of the mentally ill. We didn't stop them. They were wearing their demons down.

"Two minutes," Vince said. "That what you got, two minutes?"

The plan was simple, pure Gregory. Joe was going in first, before some lookout saw the crowd and locked the doors. I was supposed to wait a beat, then make sure the posse got to the right place. On the floor behind us was an assortment of ropes and small axes. Salvatore was examining them as if he anticipated scaling a castle wall.

"When you write this up," Salvatore said, "just remember how to spell my fucking name."

Gregory was out of the Buick, stretching, dressed in his pea coat and watch cap. He walked back and banged on the side of the van. I rolled the window down.

"You check the jeans D'Angelo is wearing?" Gregory asked. "Painted on. Great ass."

"One thing for sure," Salvatore said, "she ain't wearing a fucking crotch holster."

Gregory patted me on the chest, checking to make sure I hadn't forgotten my vest. "I'm telling them to follow you, pally," he said. "Give me time to get in the door, then roll. No lights or sirens, no slamming doors. We pull up like professionals."

I saluted, and he gave me the finger. He walked back, giving instructions to the rest of the crew. I could see everyone laughing from a Gregory line—everyone except Sylvia D'Angelo, who looked away from Joe, obviously angry. I caught her eyes in the side mirror.

I hadn't tried to call Leigh again. The longer you waited, the harder it was to call. Time and time again I'd said we needed an answering machine. I knew she was mad; I didn't blame her.

Gregory stepped back into the Buick and took off

immediately, never looked back. Our miniconvoy fell in behind. As we made the right turn past Brady's, I could see Billy mopping in the glare of a spotlight. Empty beer boxes were stacked at the curb.

We turned into Pearl Street, under the bridge, then one more block. The Buick made the left into Peck Slip. A delivery truck—fresh, hot bialys, bagels—passed us and went through the red light on Pearl Street.

I told Vince to drive to the edge of the post office building, just past the building line. Gregory was already out of the Buick, ten steps ahead of Shick, walking over the cobblestones to the front door, heavy arms swinging loose, big hands ready.

We watched from half a block away. Ten cops in four cars with an arsenal of toys, parked on the wrong side of the road between the post office and a new co-op that was once a piano factory. Gregory dragged his bad leg up the steps, swung the metal door open, and disappeared inside. That fast.

I grabbed the walkie-talkie to say "Go," but Vince was already squealing around the corner, fishtailing the topheavy van. We got out, slamming doors, banging equipment, running toward Eddie Shick, who was standing holding the front door.

"He went up, *arriba*," Shick said, pointing his thumb at a narrow metal staircase. "He said for somebody to check the warehouse downstairs."

To our right the floor of the warehouse was filled with stacked boxes, baskets filled with crushed ice. Flashlights scanned the floor, reflecting in puddles. I listened for noise, but the place was quiet. No shouting, no shooting, only the ring of dripping water. My voice echoed as I directed four cops to search the warehouse floor, secure the exits. Then I ran up the metal staircase to the second floor, Salvatore and his AR-15 at my back.

Joe Gregory was waiting at the top of the stairs, standing in front of a wooden door, his ear against the peeling layers of paint. He smiled and put a nicotine-stained finger to his lips. The boom of Rod Stewart's "Maggie May" came from behind the peeling door. Gregory lip-synched the song.

A half dozen cops lined the stairs behind me, breathing quietly. I pointed back down the hall to two rooms with closed doors and gave him a questioning shrug.

"*Nada,*" Gregory whispered. "Just offices."

"We ever going in?" I said, feeling as if I were spoiling his moment. A laugh came from behind the door; they didn't even know we were in the building.

Gregory yelled, "Police, open up!" a half second before he raised his good leg and kicked a spot three inches above the doorknob. The door slammed off the back wall and bounced back, but we were past it, yelling and pushing and grabbing people. Overpower them: be strong, be loud, be safe.

Four men around a wooden table stood up quickly, arms raised. Nicky Skooch, in a Harvard sweatshirt, dropped a deck of cards to the floor and placed his hands on his head in slow motion as Gregory's .38 printed a capital O on his cheek. The other three card players were familiar faces, bearded and insolent. Salvy rolled off the couch, holding a copy of *Hustler* in the air.

"We have a warrant," I said, waving it like a wand. Gregory patted my back and went past me.

"For what, some fucking bullshit?" Nicky asked, talking tough but licking his lips as though his mouth were dry.

"Where is he?" I said.

"Who?" Nicky said. "Nobody here."

Gregory went through the door next to the jukebox, through an orange neon glow. Rod Stewart was still accusing Maggie from the full-size Wurlitzer. I let Sylvia and her crew take over the card players, and I followed Gregory into a sparsely furnished room, lit only by a green shaded banker's lamp.

Ugo Bongiovanni was facedown on a table, naked, except for a towel draped across his ass. An Oriental woman in high white panties and bra stood frozen, with her hands held together, glistening oil.

Gregory flipped the light switch. Against the wall were two greasy couches the Salvation Army would refuse and a rolltop desk that held the lamp. Bongiovanni lifted up on his forearms.

"I'm sure you have a warrant," he said.

I laid the warrant on the table in front of Ugo, and started going through papers on the desk. Gregory held Ugo's pants, patting the pockets.

"I'll need to call my lawyer," Ugo said, but he didn't get up.

Vince Salvatore talked to the Oriental girl. She stood against the wall, her hands in prayer, fingers to her lips. A bead of dark oil ran down her forearm.

Shick appointed two cops to search the room and wrote their names on his clipboard. He was organizing, delegating responsibility as it said in the manual, so later he'd know exactly who to blame. The cops began pulling cushions off the couch. Ugo flipped a page of the warrant, unconcerned.

"Look at this, Anthony," Sylvia said, coming in behind me. She was holding a brown leather bomber jacket, more oil-stained than my old Ted Williams glove. It was Nicky Skooch's jacket. From the pocket she pulled a glassine bag half-filled with white powder.

"Quarter ounce, minimum," Gregory said. It had the slightly grainy look of cocaine, but we hadn't brought a test kit. And no cop was stupid enough to test drugs by tasting; it could be anything, LSD, rat poison.

"Get a plastic bag," Shick said. He switched on overhead lights. "I'll mark it."

"Read everybody their rights, Sylvia," I said.

"That's not my jacket," Ugo said, swinging up to a sitting position, holding the towel under his fleshy breasts. "I'm not even in close proximity."

"Close enough," Vince Salvatore said.

"You're Italian, right?" Ugo said, looking over at Vince. "You should be ashamed of yourself. Your father didn't raise you right."

"Don't you talk about my fucking father," Vince said.

"Look at these micks you're with," Ugo said. He pinched the flesh between his thumb and forefinger and held it up to Vince. "This is what's important paesano . . . skin. Not that bullshit badge you got. Remember that."

Salvatore said, "You remember this, scumbag," and he grabbed the side of the table, trying to dump the fat man to the floor. Ugo sprang, like the king of the jungle, and gracefully stalked away, his bare ass facing Salvatore as the empty table clattered to the floor behind him.

"Fuck him, Vince, he's trash," Gregory said, then winked at me. "Me and Vince'll search the back rooms."

Gregory put his arm around Vince and walked him out the door. Then a crash and the clatter of shattered plastic and the screech of a needle across vinyl grooves, ending Jerry Vale's "Inamorata."

"My lawyer will be pleased to hear about that," Ugo said. "That box is a classic."

"Should we let the chink whore go?" Eddie Shick said. "We don't need her, right, Anthony?"

He was even thinking like a boss now. Protect your ass, get rid of the witnesses.

The girl's clothes were folded neatly, stacked near the wall, black slippers together, white socks folded inside. I pointed to them and told her to get dressed. She looked Vietnamese or Cambodian, definitely young. I asked her where she came from. She bowed, handed me a card from her purse. Magic of the Orient, 323 Third Ave. Experience total relaxation as only we know how. By appointment only.

"Massage girl, Uki. Massage girl," she said, bowing. She pointed to the phone number on the card and made a dialing motion. I nodded, and she walked to the wall phone, bowing. On the wall next to the phone was a yellow decal that read "Call 955-BAIL, 24 hours a day."

Sweat was beginning to roll down my sides. I took off my jacket and tossed it on the couch. I didn't see how anyone could get used to wearing one of these vests. I could smell the shirt I was wearing, now on its second day. My shield dangled, banging against the vest as I walked. There wasn't much to search in the room. I walked back into the card room.

Sylvia D'Angelo said, "Salvy keeps looking out the window."

She was whispering with the raised eyebrow of Myrna

Loy at a Thin Man cocktail party. "He keeps looking at his car. New T-bird."

"We don't have a warrant for the car?" I said.

"But I love T-birds," she said, smiling. "Maybe he'll let me look inside."

I stood at the window, watching her animated conversation with Salvy as she negotiated the cobblestones in those tight black jeans. Uki, massage girl, got into the backseat of a private cab. The rising sun, coming through the grimy glass, felt good on my face. I thought about Leigh, what she was doing now, why I always put off calling her.

Eddie Shick's heels echoed in the hallway, clacking rapidly like an emergency telegraph in an old movie. He was walking his fast walk, as if booster rockets in his ass clicked in. His face was flushed, his breath whistling through his nose.

"Bingo," he said, pulling the trigger of an imaginary gun.

"You found it?" I said.

Salvatore was behind him, waving a plastic bag with a gun inside. But I could see it wasn't a .22.

"Found it up on a rafter in the back office," Vince said. "Some shit, right?"

The gun was a .38 Smith & Wesson, the blueing worn down to silver around the barrel and cylinder. I took the bag and held it to the window. Salvy was looking up at the window, pointing, laughing, while Sylvia D'Angelo rifled his glove compartment.

"I'm in the write-up now," Vince said.

The usual leeches had gathered in the street below. Salvy was reassuring them that everything was under control. The morning sun had come on like a bully over Brooklyn, scattering the night down narrow, black alleys.

I put my glasses on, but I knew what I was holding before I checked the serial number. It was Jinx Mulgrew's service revolver.

39

All Sylvia found in Salvy's T-bird were skin magazines and a cattle prod. But while checking the broken jukebox she saw an eighth of a kilo of cocaine wedged into a curved tubular panel. We arrested all six men in the club on possession, then went to the 1st Precinct to sort it out. The blood brotherhood began hemorrhaging long before mob lawyers arrived.

Leno Velardi, one of those at the card table with Nicky, was a Sicilian with a student visa and no prior record in this country. Velardi was the redhead we'd seen in the Chrysler with Nicky the day he'd dropped the pigeon coop. Sylvia matched his fingerprints with the bloody partial found in Zipper's house. When we told him he'd be booked for Zipper's murder, he gave up Nicky Skooch as the triggerman. Nicky toppled even easier than that.

After we'd finished the questioning, fatigue fell on me like a heavy curtain. I had my feet on Sylvia's desk, my head snapping back every time I dozed. Sylvia and two uniformed cops from the 1st Precinct were loading the prisoners in the wagon, going to Central Booking. Joe Gregory walked over to me, his face pale.

"They want me over in the PC's office, forthwith," he said.

"Why you?" I said.

"Senior man, I guess," he said, running his fingers through his hair. A nervous gesture, for Joe.

"Go," I said. "I'll grab a ride with the wagon."

"Meet you in Brady's later, maybe a victory brew?"

"No," I said. "I'm going to stop at Beekman to see Murray Daniels. Then I'm going home."

"No word from the old lady?"

"I remembered she was going to visit someone," I said.

While questioning Nicky, I suddenly remembered that Leigh had said she was going to go to South Carolina on spring break, whether I went or not. She'd never done anything like that before. But this time, I was sure, was different.

"Stop over Brady's," Gregory said. "Have one cold one. We need to talk."

"Just one," I said.

I wondered why Joe was nervous, because the case was a success. Even the feds were interested, offering everything they had on Nicky and Ugo in return for a piece of the action. Nicky knew he was facing life and offered to give up everyone in lower Manhattan, including Ugo Bongiovanni and the fish market operation. Bongiovanni told us to go fuck ourselves.

No one, however, admitted knowing anything about Jinx Mulgrew's gun or his murder. On the way over to the hospital my bullshit detector was buzzing like a hotel smoke alarm.

A good cop has a bullshit detector in the back of his head. It's a buzzer that rings annoyingly when it comes across a bogus story. It's a delicate instrument, but it never wears down, keeps buzzing and buzzing until you take care of it. Sometimes you can ignore it for years, but it's still back there buzzing.

Murray Daniels's skin had a gray look, cold as marble to the touch. Doctors kept saying they saw promising signs, but the promise of what? I began telling Murray about the case in a low voice, so the nurses wouldn't hear. Murray always wanted to know all the details. I told him all about how we nailed the bastards who put him there. But it didn't make me feel better. Pictures of Murray's wife and two girls were on the table.

I had waited for this moment, convincing myself that closing the case would resolve something. I was a fixer. I wanted to fix things, have the end result somehow justify my behavior. But nothing was ever really fixed, nothing resolved. And, quite simply, we were all responsible for the consequences of our acts.

"They said I'd find you here," Neddy Flanagan said.

I'd seen his reflection in the heart monitor, but I thought it was a priest.

"We have a problem, Anthony."

My first thoughts were of Leigh, and in that moment I swore to change, if God would give me one more chance. But Neddy said the name "Gregory," and I felt a wave of relief.

"Liam Gregory is being arrested," Neddy said. "He's confessed to the murder of Jinx Mulgrew."

Neddy put his arm on my shoulder. I could smell wintergreen and feel myself shaking. He said that Liam came into his office when he heard Mulgrew's gun was found in 14 Peck Slip.

"Joe planted the gun," I said. "I should have known."

"Listen to me," Neddy said. "Listen to me carefully. Joe Gregory didn't plant the gun. Liam confessed to putting it there years ago. Do you understand that?"

"No," I said. "Nor do I believe it."

"It's not your concern anymore," he said. "Today you'll be transferred into the chief of detectives office; a new squad being formed to investigate special homicides. It's a good assignment. You'll be promoted, your wife will be happy with the hours."

"What happens to Joe?" I said.

"He'll stay where he is," Neddy said. "And he's lucky enough at that."

I said, "What reason did Liam give for killing Jinx?"

"Money," Neddy said, raising his eyebrows, speaking between the lines.

"I don't believe that," I said. "Neither do you."

"Long ago," he said, "I gave up needing to believe everything."

Neddy touched Murray Daniels's hand. Laura Daniels had told me Neddy had arranged for this room, visited him many times. His touch was gentle as he mouthed a prayer. I watched Murray Daniels, expecting him to move when Neddy turned to leave the room.

"You know all you have to know, Anthony," he said. "We all admire your skill, but now is the time to stop questioning. The likes of Jinx Mulgrew has caused enough grief. It's over."

After he left I thought of one more question. I wanted to know how he knew my wife was unhappy.

"Here's to the guy who invented police work," Joe Gregory said, raising his glass in the bar mirror. "A freaking genius, guaranteed."

We were standing at the bar, side by side, facing the mirror, talking to each other's reflections in cloudy blue glass. Brady's crowd consisted of the early regulars: the guys who only drank until after rush-hour traffic thinned out. Patti O looked surprised when I ordered coffee.

"How's your dad holding up?" I said to Gregory.

"Rock of Gibraltar," he said. "Be out on bail in about an hour."

Sinatra was on the jukebox, singing "One for My Baby." I was exhausted, needed a shower, and hadn't spoken to my wife in more than two days.

"You want all the details, Ryan?" Gregory said. "All the dirty details?"

"Don't bother," I said.

"My old man . . . cool as ice . . . tells them he set the whole thing up to make it look like a mob hit. Pretty damn good job, I think."

"I don't want to know," I said.

"He says he found Jinx in a go-go joint on Tremont Avenue. Killed the bastard in the basement, our basement. Mixed the cement right there, loaded him in the truck, no problem."

"How long have you known?" I said.

"Get this: He drops the barrel, comes back with Mulgrew's car, takes the subway home. Next day he goes to work in the DA's office. Hot shit, ain't he?"

"How long have you known?" I said.

"You kidding me?" he said. "You know better than that. I found out today, like everybody else. But I knew something last week. After we tailed them to the zoo, remember? I tore the house apart. Looking for the goddamn notes you're always talking about. Found the gun."

"Don't say anything else, Joe," I said. "Please."

I looked up at the clock and told him I had to go. The clock above the bar in Brady's was about three inches to the right of the center point of the mahogany peak above the cash register. It had been moved to cover three bullet holes put there by an old hairbag who tried to shoot the clock out at midnight on his retirement date. I've never understood whether that tradition was celebration or an effort to stop time. They'd all missed high to the right.

"Gave up on account of you," Gregory said. "He says you'd never buy that story, finding the gun there. Says you're a great cop, pally. Can't hide nothing from you."

"Don't lay this on me, Joe."

"Not you, me. The guy did it to save my job. Wouldn't even let me help him now. I'm forty-eight years old and he's still looking out for me. I don't need this job. I could get another job, easy. Lots of good jobs I could get. Lots."

I said good-bye to Patti O, who was sitting down at the end of the bar reading *The Irish Echo*. I said good-bye to Johnny Brady while he bargained with a liquor salesman. I said good-bye to Gregory, who sang along with Sinatra. Nobody looked up.

When I pulled into my driveway, an altar boy, his hair still wet and lined with comb tracks, was coming down the street carrying his starched white surplice and long black cassock over his shoulder. His vestments blew behind him as he hurried to the Lenten novena at Sacred Heart. I got out of the car, and he crossed to the other side, looking back over his shoulder.

The green glow of the clock radio lit our bedroom. I threw my jacket across the chair and sat on the bed, reaching out for the curve of her hip, knowing that if she were there, her back would certainly be turned. But there was only her smell, Opium.

I picked up the note on the pillow, put it in my pocket. I didn't want to know just yet. I'd look around and figure it out slowly.

Her clothes were still in the closets, her dresser lined with her perfumes, brushes. A good sign. The computer room was empty but had been cleaned, the wastebaskets emptied. I held the banister, going back down through the quiet house. Wind blew through the trees.

I stood in the doorway of rooms that had the strangeness of a dream: the bedspreads, banners, posters of ball players, rock stars I couldn't name. Did I ever know their names? The taste of bile rose in my throat; I resented my weaknesses. I sat on the bed, listening to the wind. Then a tap-tap on the glass outside.

The sound came from the back of the house. I stood and pulled my gun out and walked toward the sound, backing along the wall toward the rear of the house. My shoulder caught a hanging picture, sent it swinging, crashing to the floor. The tapping stopped.

I crept to the back door, opened the dead bolt, and crouched below the window. The tapping started again. I slid the rug away and swung open the door, then stepped into the strong wind, my eyes tearing immediately. My gun punched out, I ran to one end of the house then to the other. Then I saw it.

My shirt smelled like smoke and sour sweat as I knelt to listen to the tapping of the exhaust vent of the new dryer. The dryer she never used. With every gust of wind the thin metal plate closed and opened, tap, tap. Like fingernails on glass.

I went inside and read the note, my hands still shaking. All it said was, "I love you. Leigh."

The picture I'd knocked off the wall was an old black-and-white Leigh had enlarged and framed. The kids and us in the backyard the first year we moved in this house. The trees were small, the kids wore knitted hats tied under their chins, diapers hung on the clothesline. Leigh and I were young, dark-haired. Anthony was a baby. Margaret looked like Katie does now. She was holding my hand.

The trees are huge now, the clothesline carries only wooden pins, strung out like birds on a wire. Anthony is no longer small, Margaret no longer holds my hand. The distance between us is more than can be measured on a map.

40

ON ST. Patrick's Day, the OCCB office was bustling with guys getting ready for the parade and the once yearly squeeze into uniforms. I was visiting from upstairs, closing loose ends on the Mulgrew case. The smell of Old Spice and shoe polish filled the room. Gregory beat dust out of his winter blouse, slapping it with a nightstick as if it were an old rug.

"New partner working out?" I said.

"Banninger, that fat bastard," Gregory said. "Got three ex-wives. And I can understand why."

In the two weeks since I'd been transferred to the chief of detectives office, things had changed. Gregory and I both had new partners. I'd been home for dinner every night, started working out and reading books again.

"Getting rid of the Buick, you know," he said. "Makes fat boy ill. Getting some six-cylinder Plymouth, might as well have cops painted all over it."

This was only the second time Joe and I had talked since his father's arrest. But I knew Liam was living in Manhattan with Ellen. Joe was spending more time in Brady's.

"You got white gloves?" Gregory said, his face damp red from rushing, the woolen uniform, and morning Scotch.

"Look in my locker," I said.

"I looked."

"Inside my hat," I said.

He pirouetted as though he were modeling a heavy-duty, navy blue woolen design, with a row of ribbons and medals on the chest. "How do I look?" he said.

"Pottsy lives," I said. "Why don't you take that old daystick flask. That stuff is still in the equipment room. I'm getting rid of it today."

"Only holds four ounces," he said. "Won't get me past Fiftieth Street."

St. Pat's was a holy day of obligation in headquarters. The place would be quiet once the parade detail and the marchers got out the door. I'd begun clasping our reports chronologically to the Mulgrew folder, my last duty in OCCB. The Manhattan DA had requested our case file in Liam's prosecution. I'd have to handle it; Joe couldn't be involved. He was sticking a shamrock pin above his medal board.

"Stop by St. Paul's later," he said. "Have just one. You can make an exception today."

"I'll think about it."

"Stop thinking. Be there."

The Emerald Society party after the parade is a madhouse of cops and retired cops. It wasn't a place I'd go now; I was just starting to feel good.

"Your father okay?" I said.

"Guy's amazing. Happier than I've ever seen him."

Gregory pulled his tan London Fog over the thick woolen sleeves of the uniform, then adjusted them back down to cover a hint of blue cuff. A tight fit, it strained the raincoat's seams.

"When does he go to trial?" I said.

"Pretrial conference is Monday," Joe said, yanking at the raincoat sleeve. "He keeps saying Don't worry, don't worry."

Joe was driving uptown, so he had to cover the uniform or else he'd never make the parade. Every citizen between here and midtown would be stopping him to report a fender-bender, threats from a crazy neighbor, or ultrasonic rays from Castro coming through the walls. Once you put on the uniform, everyone wanted to tell you his problems. They all saw you.

"You got a twenty to lend me?" Gregory asked. "Tomorrow's payday."

Being stared at is the first thing a cop must get used to. It's unnerving at first, the loss of anonymity. The day before your appointment you are Mr. Invisible, walking down the street. Then the first day in the blue uniform you feel the heat of eyes on you. You wonder if something is wrong, your pants ripped, fly open. But you are no longer a face in the crowd, and when the screams come, the gunshots, or the crash of broken glass, all eyes will lock on you. It's your move, Officer. And we're watching. I handed him two ten-dollar bills.

He was standing behind me. The rain had stopped, sun was getting stronger through the vertical blinds. Luck of the Irish, they'd say. I squinted up into the glare of light as he put up his raincoat collar. The bullshit detector was going buzz, buzz, in my head.

"Stop up later," he said. "Erin go braless." He shoved his hat in a plastic Job Lot bag and left. I felt the stunning nausea that accompanied bad news.

I stood at the window, watching Joe cross Pearl Street among dozens of men, all with the same black shoes and navy blue pants sticking out under myriad trench coats, windbreakers, mackinaws. The lucky Irish sun blasted out of the clouds a zillion candlepower bright. Like the flash from the muzzle of a gun.

Gregory disappeared behind the building line, swinging the plastic bag. I sat down and flipped through the reports, hunting through pictures, digging for the ones taken by Charlie Spinelli's wife. I was looking for a picture where nothing was unusual. We would have noticed if something was unusual.

The last picture of Jinx Mulgrew was taken by Donna Rose Spinelli after the medal ceremony, after lunch in front of Rolf's, in the drizzle of Third Avenue. I held it up under the desk lamp, under the magnifying glass. Charlie and Jinx, arm in arm in a drunken victory pose. Jinx Mulgrew was wearing a greenish-tinted raglan-sleeve raincoat, a dark stain in the shape of Florida down the front.

The office phones were ringing, going unanswered. Out-of-town cops calling, didn't know what day it was. I knew Jinx had driven to the Bronx that day in his own Impala. It was only natural he'd wear a coat to cover his uniform. And I knew where that coat was.

The equipment room would smell forever of mothballs. I locked the door behind me and pulled out the long box of clothes we had taken from Mulgrew's basement. I placed everything on the floor and pulled up one coat at a time until I reached the greenish raincoat with the stain. I compared it with the photo, looking closely through the magnifying glass. But I had no doubt this was the same coat.

The answer is always logical. Jinx Mulgrew stopped home after leaving Fontana's. He was on his way down from the Bronx, so to stop by his house on the way to change clothes, before going to Danny Boy's, was logical. Surely Ellen had hung the coat in the closet.

I went back to my old desk and pulled the notes on Mrs. Mulgrew's interview. She'd told us she never saw her husband after that morning. She'd said it twice.

My coffee was cold, bitter tasting. I needed to talk to Joe Gregory. I started to put my coat on, then sat back down. The marchers wouldn't reach St. Paul's for another few hours.

I pulled the files out again. I'd go through everything, all the files, all the interviews, until I found that I was wrong. In the quiet of a building that had abandoned me, the turning pages sounded like the slap of surf against the shore.

41

I DROVE up Twelfth Avenue, trying to avoid parade traffic and drunken pedestrians. The DJ on the radio introduced singer Dennis Day in a diddley-diddley Irish brogue. Everybody had a brogue today, eight million shticks in the naked city. I parked my Nova in the garage under Lincoln Center and walked down Columbus Avenue to St. Paul's. Green cardboard top hats blew in the gutters.

The day had turned bright and windy, a few puffy clouds raced across the bitter blue sky. A trio of half-drunk, uniformed cops walked toward me, banging into one another. Dangerous men, my wife would say. One of them, in a plaid tam-o'-shanter, was leaving the party, many drinks too late. I moved against the Fordham University fence, surrendering the sidewalk.

The party was in the hall underneath St. Paul's, the alcove littered with red plastic cups. Sergeant Marty O'Dowd, an Emerald Society official, and two other cops in civilian clothes were standing behind a table at the entrance, drinking beer. I waved to Marty and told him I had to talk to Joe Gregory for a minute. He grabbed me by the sleeve.

"It's about a case," I said. "I'll be out in five minutes."

Beer foam hung from his scruffy mustache. He gave me a slight push when he let go of my coat. "You believe this shit?" he asked, looking at his two protégés. "Got some balls, don't he?"

"Time me, asshole," I said. "Five minutes."

"Get it up, Ryan," O'Dowd said. "The tin's no good here. We all got one."

The two guys bounced on their toes, backing up their man. They thought O'Dowd was in the know, their ticket to the inner circle.

"You know what this shindig cost us, Ryan? Guys like you want to get in on the arm. No fucking way. Four bucks for members, ten for non. You ain't a member, show me Mister Hamilton."

I pulled a five and three ones out of my pocket and handed it to O'Dowd, then dumped a handful of change on the table. O'Dowd's novitiates chased down coins in puddles of beer.

"Coupla real dogs inside," O'Dowd said. "Your specialty."

The din began under the church steps, then leaped off the decibel meter inside. The noise level escalates with the flow of booze, because the loudest drunk keeps the floor.

Inside, the huge hall was a sea of navy blue and kelly green. Small huddles of portly figures floated like amoeba within the mass. At least a dozen celebrants bounced off me on my way to the line at the Guinness table. Gregory was not on line, and I couldn't pick him out in a room full of Joe Gregorys. The wooden floor was sticky with spilled beer.

Eddie Shick wrapped his arm around my neck in a

semiheadlock. Shick was in uniform, wearing a button that read "Kiss me, I'm Irish."

"Guineas out," he yelled, and began walking me back to the door.

"Where's Gregory?" I said, removing his arm, pushing him away. Being sober at a drinker's party is like watching someone else's nightmare.

"What?" Shick said. "Can't touch the big man from the chief of detectives office. Too good for us, you bastard?"

"Where's Gregory?" I asked again. He turned to look as if he could see him when I couldn't.

"He's dressed in blue," I said. Shick laughed and splattered beer on our shoes.

"Later, Eddie," I said. "I've got to find Gregory."

"You couldn't find a Jew in the Temple," he said.

I began searching right to left, pushing my way through fancy cops in headquarters uniforms and cops from precincts with threadbare uniforms, shiny white at the elbows and seat. Some guys wore green cummerbunds or tams; about a third puffed cigars. I worked my way back to the wall, through the entire crowd, knowing that I might have missed him in the blue logjam. Then I heard his voice.

"Geddovaheh, pally," he yelled. He was up near the stage with a group of nurses in blue capes.

"Best freaking partner in the world," he yelled. "My old partner," he yelled louder, pointing at me with sixteen ounces of porter. One of the nurses held her arms out to show she was handcuffed.

"I'm his prisoner," the nurse said.

I said, "We have to talk, Joe."

"He hasn't read me my rights," the nurse said.

"Where's your drink?" Gregory asked. "My old partner needs a drink."

He took a cup out of the hands of a tall, dark-haired nurse and handed it to me. Then he took it from me and gave it back to her.

"I'll get you a fresh one, without lipstick on it," he said, and began to walk away. I could see the redness in his face was not only from the windy walk up Fifth.

"No. We have to talk," I said. I held him and got in close to his ear. I told him about the picture of Jinx in the raincoat.

"That's not new," he said, yelling above the crowd. "I saw that before."

"Something's wrong," I said. "I think he was killed at home."

"What the hell you talking about?" he said, looking over his shoulder.

We were being shoved away from the stage, buffeted by bodies that couldn't be hurt. Amid cheers and skirt jokes, the Emerald Society Pipe Band filed past us, walking up the steps to the stage. I tried to hold my ground, and I showed him the picture of Jinx and Charlie Spinelli.

"That raincoat he's wearing here," I said, "he wasn't wearing it when we fished him out of the river."

"So?" he said.

His face was inches from mine, I could tell his mouth was dry, his tongue sticking. The handcuffed nurse pushed at him, trying to get his attention. The noise level rose as the pipe band began warming up, a cacophony of squeals, bleats, and blasts.

"In a goddamn minute," he told the nurse. "This is confidential."

The nurse held her hands up, showing the cuffs, as if that mattered. Joe turned his back to her. "What does it prove, pally?" he said.

"This raincoat here," I said, pointing to the picture. We were so close that I had to raise my hands over his belly. "I found that raincoat in the clothes we took from the Mulgrew house. Same one, no doubt about it. Ellen said he never came home. But he had to."

The roar and whine of a dozen bagpipes blasts you with the power of a freight train barreling past your face. We were about twenty feet from the stage, nose to nose, yet I couldn't hear what Gregory was saying. Then I realized that I was the only one with my back to the stage.

The moment turned sacred and deadly. The pipers' cheeks were stretched and swollen, and beads of sweat ran down their reddened faces. But the crowd had changed. Sweet, dumb, drunken smiles had turned to somber stares. Men with nice three-bedroom houses in the safety of Pearl River or Huntington stood under an IRA banner wearing grim faces of war. But the war was three thousand miles away, and it seemed to me that the farther away the bloodshed, the more hollow the bravery. It was easy to be tough when someone else's children were being blown up. I grabbed Gregory by the sleeve and pointed to the back alley.

We stepped outside, and I felt the cold wind against my back. My shirt was drenched with sweat from only a few minutes in the packed hall. The alley was crowded, so I walked to the far end, to the rectory side. Gregory was staring off, not looking at me.

"You and your hunches," he said.

"Hunches," I said. "How stewed are you?"

"Maybe Jinx drove downtown in uniform. He was a crazy bastard. He had nothing to lose, anyway."

"Oh, come on," I said. "How did his raincoat get home?"

Behind Gregory, a line of two dozen men in blue straight-armed the wall. The alley between the church and the rectory was known as the wailing wall. The church basement had only one men's room, and five hundred drunken cops will piss where they want to.

I said, "What's the problem here, Joe? Why can't we get the truth?"

"Jesus Christ, Ryan. Think I know?"

The squeal of bagpipes was muffled every time the back door swung closed. A river of piss ran past us, moving uptown toward Lincoln Center.

"Give me a day, okay?" he said. "Call you tomorrow, I swear."

I walked back up Columbus; the wind shrieked off the Hudson. At Sixty-Second Street a group of kids wearing Our Lady of Mercy jackets milled around the entrance to the parking garage, passing a gallon of Carlo Rossi red. A girl in soiled designer jeans sprawled across the sidewalk, puking into the gutter. Another girl, crying, sat on the curb, holding two purses in her lap. I wondered why the West Side always seemed windier than the East Side. I wondered why the world wasn't safe for families anymore.

42

LEIGH'S CAR was in the driveway, still dripping water, but the hose had been put away and pink rags were drying on the fence. I pulled in on an angle so my back end was off the road. She was in the backyard, taking clothes off the line, wearing my old army field jacket over a hooded gray sweatshirt with a pair of faded jeans and leather work boots.

"Half a day now on St. Pat's?" she said.

"They sent me home. I wasn't wearing enough green."

She folded a blue-flowered towel and laid it in the basket on top of other towels, took the clothespins out of her mouth, and put them in the pocket of the field jacket. The jacket, slightly older than our marriage, was faded now and sprinkled with dots of forgotten hues of paint; I had almost thrown it out, but she'd kept it for her backyard jacket. Leigh's eyes squinted as she watched my face. I kissed her and felt the cold of her cheeks. The PFC stripes on her right sleeve flapped in the wind.

"So what's going on?" she said. "You feeling okay?"

"Fine. Just thought I'd take a couple of hours off. Watch my wife work."

"What's wrong, really?" she asked, mouth full of clothespins again. I didn't see how she could stand the feel of wood in her mouth.

"Nothing," I said.

The air had that crisp, fresh smell of early spring. I walked around to the wooden clothesline poles we had put in the ground years ago. I had made a cross of two four-by-fours, screwed eye hooks into the top, and tied the ropes through. I pressed against the pole to see how far it had decayed this past winter.

"Might have to replace these," I said. "Feels like they're rotting."

"We'll get another year out of them."

She took a tissue from her pockets and wiped her nose. "What happened at work?" she said.

"Nothing. I've just been thinking. Where's Margaret's number?"

She put the tissue back in the jacket pocket, stood with her legs spread over the bushel basket, and looked at me. "In the address book near the phone. Why?"

"I thought I'd call her and have her make an appointment with the guy from that school."

She folded a big beach towel and put it into the basket. She had probably taken Katie to the beach during spring break. Her family checked the beach every day, a ritual. They rode down to look at the ocean, as if to make sure it was still there.

"What's going on, Anthony? Something happened at work."

"No. I just thought I'd try to set up another job. You need something to go to. You have to start early to get teaching jobs."

She walked to the other side of the line and began

taking in the sheets. I ducked under and took the other side, held it as she walked to me and folded.

"I thought you'd be pleased," I said.

She pointed to the clothespins in her mouth and shook her head. Suddenly she couldn't talk with them in there.

"Actually I thought you'd be very pleased," I said.

Grass was peeking up through the dark spring mud. The earth smelled of a fertile moistness.

"I thought that you decided to wait for your promotion to come through," she said finally. "I get the feeling something big happened at work today."

"God, you're suspicious."

"It just seems . . . sudden," she said. "Things seemed to be working out with this new job. You're home most nights; I'm not unhappy with this situation."

She pressed against me and put her arms around my neck. We were almost the same height when she wore those boots. "Now don't take this wrong," she said, "but a year or so down the road I don't want to get the feeling I forced you to leave a job you loved. I don't want you to be unhappy because of me."

I could smell the clean scent of her hair, feel the texture against my face. Kelly's tabby was crouching under his hedge, watching a robin.

"I wouldn't say that to you," I said.

We stood holding each other for a few minutes. I thought, Maybe this is how it should be, with time to stand in the wind and hold each other.

"You wouldn't have to say it," she said.

She put her hands on my face. They were red and chapped from the cold water and air.

"Let's do this, Anthony. Let's give this new job six months. If you still feel that way after six months, then retire. Whatever happened today, I don't want you running away. That never works."

I woke up five forty-five, thinking I heard the crying of a baby, then realized it was a cat. I went to the window and looked down at the street, just in case. Kelly was starting his VW.

The phone rang just as I fell asleep again. It was Joe Gregory.

"Let's meet away from the building," he said.

"Brady's," I said.

"No good. How about the dock about ten, ten-thirty?"

43

THE TUGBOAT *Lucy Moran* floated north in the mid-morning calm of the East River. It was almost eleven, and I hadn't heard another word from Gregory. I sat on the hood of my Nova, the warm sun against my back, and wondered what tugboat workers called themselves. Were they sailors, seamen, longshoremen, tugmen? What men called themselves was at the center of their very being. For most of my adult life I had gotten out of bed every morning and put my shield in my pocket, knowing that I would call myself Detective Ryan.

The Buick appeared out of the traffic on South Street and weaved between a scattering of parked cars. They'd come from downtown, probably the Brooklyn Battery Tunnel. Joe parked next to my Nova. Liam looked tired, his dark overcoat wrapped around him like a blanket on a sailor plucked from the sea.

We shook hands silently, then walked out on Pier 18. Seagulls fled from the edge of the dock.

"That nurse ever get the cuffs off?" I said.

"She told me she was an ex-nun," Joe said. "I threw her the goddamn key and ran like hell."

We followed Liam to the side of the dock near where

the barrel had been found. Time and weather had erased chalk marks, blown away cigarette butts. All signs of the crowd that weighed so heavily on the old structure three months ago were gone. I handed Liam the picture of Jinx in the raincoat.

"I don't have to see it," he said. "I believe you."

"You recording this, Ryan?" Joe said. "You wearing a wire?"

"Is that what you think?" I said.

Joe's face had the bruised and swollen look of sleeplessness. His neck was still red and chafed from the woolen choker collar of the uniform.

Liam said, "I have a favor to ask you, Anthony. I know I have no right to ask."

"Ask," I said.

"Forget about this damned raincoat," he said. "Let the case stay as it is. I'll plead guilty to killing Jinx, avoid a trial."

"I can't do that, Liam," I said.

The sounds around us were the everyday hum of steady traffic on the FDR, horns from the river, the echo of a jackhammer, the squeals of the gulls.

I asked, "How can I stand by and let you go to jail for a crime I know you didn't commit?"

"I damn well intended to kill him," Liam said. "I had everything: cement, the barrel. Even had a winch on the truck in case I couldn't lift it afterward. And I would have killed him, by God; don't doubt that for a second. She had every right, Anthony. The man beat and abused her. None of us know the half of it."

"She?" I looked at Joe, who shrugged.

"He wanted to tell you himself," Joe said.

The day was windy, whitecaps in the river. Liam

looked off at the waterfront and dock that hadn't changed since that night ten years ago. As if waiting for this scene to come back around.

"When Jinx didn't show up in Danny Boy's that night," Liam said, "I called the house. Ellen answered. Her voice was droning, like the nuns saying the rosary. Saying over and over that it wasn't right, that he should leave her like this."

"Not too late to get your lawyer here," Joe said. "Before you tell them everything."

I noticed I was now "them" to my ex-partner. The old man ignored him.

"I thought Jinx had told her he was leaving," Liam said, "that she was in shock. But when I got there I banged and banged. I had to get a crowbar from the truck and break the dead bolt."

Joe put his arm around his father, a picture I thought I'd never see. It always took tragedy to bring us closer.

"Jinx was upstairs in the bedroom," Liam said. "I carried him down to the basement. Worked all night. Dressed him in his uniform, poured my concrete. Never thought about that blasted raincoat."

"A good lawyer could make a case for Ellen," I said. "Show she was battered."

"Maybe he's right, Dad," Joe said. "I'm sure Roosevelt Hospital has records. They keep them forever, right, Anthony?"

A Circle Line cruise ship went by, tourists on the outside deck, in the warm sun of early spring.

"She's never even talked about it," Liam said. "Not once. As if it never happened. The strain of it, a trial, would kill her. Let me do this for her, Anthony."

"Maybe we can avoid a trial," I said. "Get away with probation."

"No," he said. "I know those headline-grabbing bastards in the DA's office. They'll prosecute her for murder, and me for conspiracy. Nope, nope."

Liam stared out at the old bridge, the sun flashing off the spiderweb cables.

"The guy was an asshole," Joe said. "Somebody should have whacked him long before she did."

"Does Neddy Flanagan know this, Liam?" I asked.

"No one helped me, Anthony," Liam said, "if that's what you're asking. It wasn't as hard as you think."

"Did Neddy help you to get Ellen's initial IAD interview?"

"I conducted that initial interview myself, as a favor to IAD. She wouldn't talk to anyone else. Everyone was sure Jinx had fled. The spouse interview was just procedure."

Liam took the spongeball from his pocket. "I'm not going to give you Neddy Flanagan," he said. "He's a far better man than you realize. A true friend. You'll find that out when you need him."

I could see the emotion in Joe Gregory's face, as if he wished he could embrace his father's pain. Then he looked at his watch, as if he had some schedule to keep.

"Let's go, Dad."

Liam stepped away from Joe, seeming to regain his composure, draw strength from somewhere. "Give us this weekend," he said, looking off, beyond me. "I have a court appearance Monday, nine A.M., part one-B. We'll let the lawyers discuss it then. It will give us time to build our strength."

"If that's what you want," I said.

"No question of it," he said.

When he hugged me I knew this would be the last time I'd see him. I could feel the rough stubble of his beard and, in the crisp spring air off the river, smell the mothballs from his coat. I knew what his choices were and couldn't be sure I wouldn't make the same ones. There were worse ways to spend your life than taking care of someone you love. But he was leaving me with a problem.

"They'll put a warrant out for you," I whispered. "You miss that court appearance Monday, they'll issue a bench warrant immediately. They'll find you, no matter where you go."

"I'll have to stay tough," he said. "Won't I?"

He smiled, his eyes watery, then turned and walked to the car. Joe kept looking back at his father until he was safely inside.

"You gotta do what you gotta do," Joe said. "It's okay, I understand. I want you to know you were a hell of partner, Anthony."

"Guaranteed," I said.

"Still getting out of the job?"

"Not today," I said.

"Stay out of the bars, you'll be okay," he said. "You could never hold your booze anyway."

He gave me his quick wave and walked to the car. The Buick merged into traffic, heading uptown to get Ellen. I had the raincoat draped over my shoulder like a lounge singer making a solo exit under a bare spotlight.

I looked down at the murky grayish water slapping off the bulkhead below, knowing well how easy it was to fall. But I knew I wouldn't. For once in my life I'd focus on the important things: I had new cases on my desk, and I had to be home for dinner. I had letters to write to children and bagels to buy: four plain, four poppy, four pumpernickel.

No simple answers, Murray Daniels would remind me. We all have difficult choices. You make the ones you can live with, forget what you must. You save what you can.

I rolled Jinx Mulgrew's stained raincoat into a ball and threw it as hard as I could. It spread out in the air like a great bird, landed flat, and began sinking slowly. It floated south with the current, gradually disappearing in the flow of the river.

Watch for

BRONX
ANGEL

**A New Warner Books Hardcover
by the same author**

Available at bookstores everywhere

1

In a freak April snowstorm they found the body of an off-duty cop on a Bronx back street, his throat slashed, his pants pulled down to his knees. He'd been dead for over two hours, and I was still crawling in three inches of wet snow on the Cross-Bronx Expressway.

"It's four A.M., New York," the radio DJ said, her voice a husky, intimate whisper. "And it's still coming down."

Police Officer Marc Ross had been discovered in his own car, an alleged prostitute seen fleeing the scene. The key word here was *prostitute*. The brass at One Police Plaza wanted the straight story, all the sordid details, undiluted by precinct loyalty. The NYPD does not bang the drum for all its slain comrades.

"The eighteenth snowstorm of the season," the DJ said. "Are we being punished by God?"

My Honda fishtailed as I swerved around a muffler in the middle of the exit ramp. I slid through the stop sign sideways and came to a halt in the middle of Tremont Avenue. Salsa music blared from a corner bar. Not a car in sight. I turned

3

the Honda around and made the right onto Boston Road. That's when I saw the crowd.

"Can't be," I said. Not just for a homicide. Not on a night like tonight.

The crowd, mostly women and children, carried flashlights and food they shared with each other. They were lined up single file, up the entire block, then around the corner and down into East 179th Street. I stopped at the corner of East 179th, a short dead end with a street drop ending at the Bronx River. The Bronx River flowed south out of the Bronx Zoo and eventually into the East River.

At the bottom of the hill I saw the flash of turret lights; NYPD cars filled the circle at the end of the cul-de-sac. The roadway was broken and slippery, the carcass of a dog stuffed in a pothole. Protective metal barriers separated the pavement from the grassy hill leading down to the river. Grainy shafts of lights rose from the riverhead below.

The Bronx saddened me. I'd been a rookie cop on the streets of this brawling borough, and my good memories outweighed the bad. These days, except for the occasional high-profile homicide, the only reason I returned was out of loyalty to the Yankees. But the Yankees, like many of the cops I'd worked with in the last thirty years, were in the warm Florida sunshine. And I was in the snow, in the burned-out Bronx, with nobody but myself to blame. Cops like me hang around too long, destined to revisit the past.

I parked behind Joe Gregory's new Thunderbird. Detective Joe Gregory, my partner off and on for two decades, had come all the way from Brooklyn and beat me to the scene. But the grim crowd I'd been following didn't stop at the murder scene. The line stretched along the riverbank, into the darkness, well past the last police car. To them, the cops searching a crime scene were only a curious sideshow, like jugglers working a theater line. Murder is not a blockbuster event in the Bronx.

The breath of two dozen cops puffed in the frigid air and

floated in the glare of floodlights. My brother officers worked quickly. Wet weather erases evidence.

"Detective Ryan, Chief of Detectives Office," I said, showing my shield to a tall, red-haired policewoman at the barriers.

"Hey, Mr. Ryan," she said. "How's it going?"

"Great," I said. "How about you?"

I had no idea who the hell she was. As I worked my way down the slippery bank, I figured I'd probably worked with her father somewhere; an extraordinary number of sons and daughters of cops were on the job. Her name tag said "Antonucci," which didn't ring a bell, but I'd worked with a lot of cops.

At the bottom of the hill, a dark gray BMW sat inside a border of yellow tape, the front end barely dipping into the icy river. All around the car the ground had been trampled. Fresh snow fell into a thousand footprints. Inside, slumped over on the passenger seat, was Police Officer Marc Ross, his jeans and white boxer shorts pulled down, his shirt dyed crimson. I shaded my eyes from the floodlights as I knelt to look at his butchered throat.

"Jesus Christ," I said.

"No, the Blessed Virgin, you heathen bastard," a gravelly voice said. My partner, the great Joe Gregory, stood with his suit pants rolled up, ice crystals on the cuffs. "You here for the homicide or the miracle?"

"What miracle?" I said.

"You didn't see the number of people?" he said.

"I saw the line."

"Down the whole goddamn street," he said. "See where the line ends? By the wall there. Look at the spot above all those flashlights. See her?"

"See who?"

"You can't see her? On the rocks? What kind of Catholic are you, you don't know the Mother of God?"

"Where?"

5

"Look where my finger's pointing," Gregory said. He moved next to me, his bulk blocking the lights.

The wall Gregory pointed to was fifty yards away. It looked like a stone retaining wall for the bridge over the Bronx River at East 180th Street. Water running down the stones had frozen into a mass of icicles forming one large striated figure, a mass of long vertical lines of ice like the folds of a cloak. The figure was lit by flashlights held by people who had climbed down to the river bed. Some knelt on the side of the hill, some knelt in the snow at the river's edge.

"Looks like Lourdes, don't it?" Gregory said.

"Looks like a big chunk of ice," I said.

Gregory blessed himself. "City says it ain't from the river; some underground pipes must've busted."

"How long has this been going on?" I said.

"Started last night, according to the Five One Precinct cops."

"Then we must have witnesses."

"We got more freaking witnesses than Carter got liver pills," Gregory said.

Up close I could smell gin on Gregory's breath, and his clothes reeked of smoke. I knew he was half drunk.

"Story is this," he said. "Oh two hundred hours, BMW stops up there. Driver, this dark-skinned woman, drives around the barriers onto the grass. Then she gets out, reaches in, releases the brake. Car rolls straight down here. Nobody saw the body till some kids started to strip the car." Gregory rocked back on his heels, then steadied himself as if on a balance beam only he could see. "Cop's name is Marc Ross. Uniform cop. Three years on the job. Works in the precinct combat car. Three-man car, supposed to make the drug problem go away."

"Married?"

"No, thank God. I wouldn't want to explain this one to a wife. Works steady six-to-twos. Off Sundays and Mondays."

"He was off tonight, then. What was he doing here?"

6

"Beats the shit out of me, pally. They say he's a musician. Moonlights in some band in Manhattan on Sunday nights. His trumpet is in the trunk."

"Maybe he met this woman there?"

"The squad thinks it's a hooker murder," he said. "I think they got another thing coming."

"Why would she drive him here and dump the car with all these witnesses?"

"They're saying she didn't know the church crowd was here. She drives in, sees the crowd. Surprise, surprise! She panics, dumps the car. Personally, I think that's a crock a shit."

"You're thinking she wanted it to look like a hooker rip-off."

"Actually, yeah," he said. "I'm betting it's a girlfriend, a barmaid, someone he knew. That's my take, but I'm in the minority."

A makeshift canvas covering had been constructed over the dark gray sedan. We stood out of the weather as the tech man, using curving strokes, dusted the roof with the fine, sooty black powder. If the car had been any darker, he would have needed a silver or white powder, for contrast. Every few strokes he'd step back to see if any powder had stuck to the grease left by a human hand. If a print was found, he would photograph it, then lift it with simple, transparent tape and place it on an index card.

"After she dumped the car," I said, "where did this mystery woman go?"

"Walked away. Up the hill, then toward Tremont."

"Just walked away?"

"Affirmative. Cool as ice."

"Description?"

"Dark-skinned Hispanic. Slender build. Five foot to five four. Black hair, styled big. Black coat, red dress, red shoes, white gloves."

"White gloves in this weather? Sounds like your date book."

7

"I don't know from gloves," he said. "But slender ain't my style. I still like 'em zaftig. Meat on the bone."

"So what do you think?" I said.

"Blow job that went very wrong," Gregory said. "Ended up a slice and dice."

"No possible way it could be a hooker robbery?"

"Guaranteed," he said. "The only thing missing, far as the squad can determine, is his gun. Holster's empty. But she left his watch. Not a Rolex, but not a cheapo. Two rings, wallet, credit cards, about seventy bucks in cash."

"Maybe she saw the crowd and panicked, forgot the money."

"Hookers don't forget the money, pally."

Officer Marc Ross had been cut very deeply, an artery, perhaps. Blood had pooled on the passenger seat beneath him and dyed the leather a dark red. But the driver's side was also brushed with blood. Wide red streaks slashed across the driver's seat door, steering wheel, and center console. Marc Ross had probably been slashed as he sat on the driver's seat, then moved to the passenger seat.

"Pretty strong woman," I said. "To pull him over the console."

"He ain't a big guy. Looks like he only goes about one fifty. Lot of women could handle one fifty, easy."

"Not dead weight," I said. "Not easily. Tell me this: If it was a girlfriend, why didn't she leave him where she killed him and run?"

"Because she iced him near where she lived. Maybe in the parking lot of a bar where she worked." Gregory pointed to the body with a crooked index finger, yellowed from nicotine. "Look at the wound," he said. "All that ripping and gouging. Classic overkill. My money says this is personal. We got an adrenaline factor working here."

"Who caught the case?" I asked.

"The Ivy League detective over there with the shit-eating grin." Gregory pointed to a young, balding guy smoking a

8

pipe. "Asshole rookie third-grader. Wouldn't make a pimple on a real cop's ass."

Sergeant Neville Drumm was talking Ivy League through the search. Sergeant Drumm had been the squad commander when I was in the precinct. His hair, now completely white, gave him the look of a kindly plantation butler in an old Civil War movie.

"Anyone talk to Ross's partner?" I said.

"Partners," Gregory said. "Three men, remember? POs Verdi and Guidice."

"Not Sonny Guidice?"

"One and the same," Gregory said. "He just arrived, some blonde on his arm."

I hadn't seen Sonny Guidice since I'd left the precinct twenty years earlier. Not that I gave a shit. He was in civilian clothes, standing in a circle of young uniformed cops, his arm around a woman. A very young, very blond woman, her eyebrows so white and thick, it looked like snow clinging to a ledge.

"Drumm says he'll interview Sonny and the other guy," Gregory said.

"Suits me."

Sonny Guidice had small black eyes, puffy cheeks, and pointy features that made him look like an overweight rodent. He'd arrived in the precinct from the academy shortly before I left. He shot and killed a seven-year-old boy, Martin Luther Hopkins, in the bedroom of apartment 4C of 1645 Bathgate Avenue, at five minutes after six on a warm evening, June 23, 1968. The grand jury declared it to be accidental. I was a witness.

"Where the hell were you tonight?" I whispered to Gregory.

"Auto Crime retirement racket out in Flushing. I told you I was going. I just got home, the chief calls. What'm I supposed to say: 'Sorry, Chief, I'm shit-faced'?"

I stepped back away from him. No need to whisper. The

precinct detectives were giving us a wide berth, pissed off because we were "downtown" invading their turf.

"I grabbed two coffees on the way," Gregory said. "What can I say? I ain't ready to do brain surgery, but I can sleep-walk through this scene."

"What makes you think the woman was Hispanic?" I said.

"Not me." He pointed up at the line. "That's what Ivy League tells me the people say. Personally, I don't think he could find a brother in Harlem. These cops today, I'm telling you, we're in deep shit."

"Looks like everything is under control to me."

I climbed back up the hill. Within a few minutes I found an interpreter: a friendly, bilingual woman dressed in an air force parka. We started working the line. It didn't take long to confirm the old truth that too many witnesses were worse than none. The kids knew all about the car, the model, year, and accessories. The women noticed her clothes and hair. They all thought the hair was a wig. The dress was red, the gloves were long and white, spotted with blood. She walked away carrying a black coat. But the more I asked, the more the range of age, complexion, height, and weight increased.

It was near dawn when the Crime Scene Unit finished and began lugging gear up the hill. Morgue attendants yanked the body out of the car. The smell of burning tires wafted from the junkyards of Hunts Point. Gregory scrambled up the slippery bank, burly and agile as a grizzly bear.

"For the sake of argument," I said, "let's say our killer chose this location purposely for the presence of the Blessed Virgin. Who are we after now?"

Gregory was breathing hard as we walked to our cars. Down the block, women were lighting rows of candles set in paper bags, creating a fiery path to the vision.

"A whore, an angel," he said. "It don't freaking matter, pally. Either way we're looking for a psycho."

2

The snow stopped and the sun came out when they tossed Marc Ross to the back of the morgue wagon. The body bag screeched across the metal floor and stopped against a former Bronx resident who'd OD'd while making Egg McMuffins in the borough's newest McDonald's. Joe Gregory exchanged notes and fuck-yous with Ivy League and the Five One Precinct squad while I sat in Sergeant Neville Drumm's car and talked old times.

I felt oddly comfortable, a peaceful sense of place . . . a place more familiar than I wanted to admit. I thought about quiet mornings when I was a foot cop working school crossings, the sun coming around the corner, warming my back as I joked with the kiddies, smiled at the mamas.

"Mallomars?" Drumm said, offering the open box of cookies. I waved them away. "Better take one now. They don't ship them to the stores in summer. Come July you'll be begging me for one."

Drumm bit into the cookie, then examined it, as if counting the layers.

11

"Sonny Guidice still looks the same," I said.

"He's still an asshole, if that's what you're hinting at. But he knows the streets. Works hard. He's got balls."

"What about Marc Ross?"

"Good kid. Liked to talk about music. Very thorough cop. Meticulous with reports."

I thought carefully about how to phrase the next question, trying to remember that I represented "downtown" and in the eyes of ghetto cops lacked the simpatico of the scummiest local street thug.

"You know what they're going to say downtown, Neville."

"Yeah," he said, seeming tired and distant. "They're betting he was trying to get a blow job on the muscle. Tells her he's a cop, says, 'I ain't paying you shit.' Hooker goes berserk, starts slashing."

"It's happened before," I said.

"Tell me about it."

"What do we tell downtown about it?"

"Tell them like it is," he said. "You think I'm going to cover this up? Uh-uh. Those days are long gone. Long gone. You've been away from the bag too long, Anthony. We don't protect nobody out here anymore. Cop screws up, it's his tough shit. Moral is, don't screw up."

Cops sense they're being watched. It comes from years of being in uniform, feeling eyes upon you. I'd been aware of a hulking, bearded man across the street. He was kneeling at the side of the hill, facing the Blessed Virgin. Wood scraps crackled and burned in a barrel behind him.

"You recognize that guy?" Drumm said. "With the rebel hat. Staring at us."

"The bum with the beard?"

"I think he remembers you."

The bearded man wore a long black raincoat, a Confederate Civil War cap. A large wooden cross hung around his neck. When I finally acknowledged him he raised his fist and smiled through stained teeth.

12

"That's Francis X. Hanlon," Drumm said.

Instantly I remembered. "The cop fighter."

Francis X. Hanlon was a name burned into the memory of every Bronx street cop. Cop fighter. I knew of only two or three persistent cop fighters in my career. Guys who'd get drunk in some local bar and wander the streets looking for a cop and a battle. I'd always thought cop fighters had to be desperately seeking punishment, because that was surely what they received. Francis X. was the most prolific and feared. Sometimes it would take a dozen cops to subdue him.

"He's wasted. Mind's gone," Drumm said. "Cops today don't know who he is. They call him the Padre."

Sergeant Drumm and I agreed to split the legwork. He'd do the Bronx, canvass the area around the scene; I'd check the Manhattan bar where Officer Marc Ross played trumpet on Sunday nights. I reassured him it was still his investigation, that "downtown" wasn't out to take over the case. I expected a sarcastic response, but he said nothing.

The morgue wagon left in a puff of blue-black smoke. Then we left in separate cars as the pilgrims shuffled slowly to the ice Madonna. A high in the upper forties was being predicted. I didn't want to stay around to see the temperature rise.

Gregory pointed his T-bird east toward the Throgs Neck Bridge, a circuitous route he claimed would save time. He was circling around to his house in Brooklyn, the house he'd inherited from his ex-cop father. He was going to clean up and grab a quick nap while I inched down the Major Deegan Expressway in the morning flow of commuter traffic into the East Side of Manhattan.

Our boss, Lieutenant Delia Flamer, had notified me to meet a Roderic Ahearn, who played sax in the PM Ramblers, Marc Ross's band. As I sat in traffic, three letters kept running through my mind: BMW. Nice car for a cop.

I swung off the highway and crossed the Macombs Dam

Bridge into the streets of Manhattan. Traffic always moved much faster on the Adam Clayton Powell Jr. Boulevard, even at the height of rush hour. Most New Yorkers avoided the route because it took you through the center of Harlem. Cops knew it, used it.

After thirty years I was an encyclopedia of cop knowledge, some of it useful, most of it destructive. I knew shortcuts like ACP Boulevard and that traffic lights worked on a ninety-second sequence: the avenues stayed green for fifty-four seconds, while the side street traffic had just thirty-six seconds to get across. But I also carried the memory of the day Sonny Guidice shot Martin Luther Hopkins. I knew the moment I saw the hole in the boy's chest he wouldn't live until the next green light.

Twenty-eight minutes after leaving the Bronx I parked in a taxi stand on Park Avenue and Fifty-second Street. I flipped the "official police business" plate onto the dash, made sure the doors were locked. The NYPD bureaucracy was hot on official parking plates. The laminated cards were being stolen from the windshields of unmarked police cars or borrowed and creatively photocopied.

The Park Avenue Plaza was impressive, two security guards in the lobby, bookends for an indoor waterfall. Roderic Ahearn's firm, Mohawk Associates, took up three floors: nineteen to twenty-one. I'd waited with the receptionist for less than three minutes when Ahearn jogged up an inner staircase.

"Lieutenant Ryan," he said.

"Detective Ryan," I corrected.

He was about six two, slender, late twenties. He wore suspenders over a white button-down shirt and a tie with huge hand-painted lilies and kept running his fingers through his moussed sandy hair. He motioned for me to follow him back downstairs.

Ahearn's office was on the corner, cut on an angle as if

they'd tried to make two corner offices out of one. His desk, centered to the rear of an Oriental rug, was a long glass table. On it, only a white legal pad, a black fountain pen, and a banker's lamp.

"Sit, please." Ahearn pointed to a studded leather armchair. "Marc's uncle called me this morning. This horrible thing really happened, didn't it?"

"I'm afraid so."

"You got here so quick. I'm still walking around in a daze. I keep thinking this isn't real." Ahearn's hair stuck up in back as he nervously mussed and finger combed. "I'm sorry," he said. "I'm not normally like this. But this isn't a normal day, is it?" He put his hand in the air in a stop gesture and took a deep breath. "You want to know about last night. Last night . . . last night we were at Millard's Red Garter, Fifty-first off Madison. We've had a standing engagement for four years. Sunday nights only."

"Marc play last night?" I said.

"Both sets."

"What time did he leave?"

"We finish at twelve-ten. Marc left maybe ten, fifteen minutes after the last number."

"Alone?"

"Far as I know."

On the walls, framed oils and watercolors, beach and marsh scenes that looked like the Hamptons. A vase of fresh-cut flowers stood on a low table. Ahearn took off his glasses and rubbed his eyes.

"How well did you know Marc?" I said.

"Since high school. Power Memorial. All the original band members went to Power. That's what the PM means."

"Tell me about the band."

"Nothing to tell, we were a one-gig band. Millard's Red Garter was it. Nobody was going to leave their day job for the music life. It's more of a night out. Make a few bucks, have a good time while we're doing it."

"Were you having a good time last night?"

"We all sucked down a few brews, had a few giggles. But we weren't wild men."

"What about wild women? Any women with you last night?"

"Dixieland groups aren't known for attracting groupies, Officer."

"I assume that's a no," I said. "How about between sets? Could Marc have met a woman on the way to the men's room? At the bar?"

"Anything's possible, but between sets we stayed in the back room. Watched the Rangers game."

"Perhaps one of the other band members saw something," I said.

I stood and walked to the window while Ahearn spoke to his secretary through an intercom. He gave her the names of the other band members, asked her to list addresses and phone numbers. Floor-to-ceiling windows looked southeast across Park Avenue, toward the squat round-domed beauty of St. Bartholomew's Church, a priceless gem dropped into an erector-set village.

"Are you saying a woman did this?" Ahearn said.

"No, I'm not. Did you all leave together?"

"Marc left first. But within a few minutes we were all out on the sidewalk. Snow was starting to come down. Marc wasn't there; apparently he'd already started walking home. Let me get back to this woman thing. We have a standing rule. Three of us are married. We didn't want it turning into stag night."

I sat back down on the studded leather chair. "You said he walked?"

"Always walked, there and back."

"You're sure he didn't bring his car?" I said.

"You kidding? Where the hell you going to park over there? It wasn't that bad a walk. Just to Sixty-second Street. Opposite Lincoln Center."

"We found him in his car last night."

"He didn't have his goddamn car."

"A 1989 BMW 325i, gray in color, license KAM-626, New York."

"Christ, my heart is pounding." Ahearn took a deep breath. "I can't swear that he didn't have the car with him. He usually kept it in a garage directly across the street from his building. But, Christ, I don't know. I can't even remember the last thing he said."

Ahearn put his hands to his face. I waited for him to look up, then walked him through the usual questions: What about enemies? Did he seem worried? Anything unusual happen last night or in the recent past? His head kept shaking: No. . . . No. . . . No. . . .

"Mr. Ahearn," I said, "we have a description of a woman seen walking away from his car: slender, young, possibly Hispanic. Dark skinned. Does that sound like anyone Marc would know?"

"I'm sure he knew all kinds. From his job. He dealt with those people all the time."

"Have you ever known Marc to be involved with a prostitute?"

"Whoa, please, Officer. Let's not drag his memory through the gutter quite yet."

"Is that a no?"

"Absolutely." He glared at me across the desk. "I don't understand what you're driving at."

"Would he have dated anyone who answers that description?"

"I don't think he'd let the color of someone's skin bother him, if that's what you mean."

"Have you known him to date black or Hispanic women?"

"No," he said quietly.

When his secretary came in with the list of band members, I stood up to leave.

17

"Nice office," I said, gesturing around the room. "For a sax player."

"I live to play, but I litigate to live."

I thought about asking further; I had a nagging question about money. Ross's BMW was expensive, but young people extend themselves financially for cars. His Columbus Avenue address was harder to explain: rent had to be into four figures, and the parking garage had to go for three hundred a month. Money created a trail that begged to be followed. But there was no rush. Money left deep tracks.